sprout

sprout

or

My salad days, when I was green in judgment.*

DALE PECK

BLOOMSBURY

LONDON BERLIN NEW YORK

*Um, that's a quote. Duh.

Bloomsbury Publishing, London, Berlin and New York

First published in Great Britain in 2009 by Bloomsbury Publishing Plc
36 Soho Square, London, W1D 3QY

First published in the USA in 2009 by Bloomsbury USA Children's Books
175 Fifth Avenue, New York, NY 10010

A CIP catalogue record of this book is available from the British Library

ISBN 978 0 7475 7762 1

FSC
Mixed Sources
Product group from well-managed
forests and other controlled sources
Cert no. SGS-COC-2061
www.fsc.org
© 1996 Forest Stewardship Council

The paper this book is printed on is certified independently in
accordance with the rules of the FSC. It is ancient-forest friendly.
The printer holds chain of custody.

Printed in Great Britain by Clays Ltd, St Ives plc

1 3 5 7 9 10 8 6 4 2

www.bloomsbury.com/childrens

This book can only be dedicated to
Lamoine Wiebe
in the hope that he'll always find his way back home.

Salt the earth with serpent's teeth . . .
                                —Ovid

sprout

This is the first part!

. . . (picnic, lightning) . . .

—Nabokov

I have a secret. And everyone knows it. But no one talks about it, at least not out in the open. That makes it a very modern secret, like knowing your favorite celebrity has some weird eccentricity or other, or professional athletes do it for the money, or politicians don't actually have your best interests at heart. I.e.:

Hollywood actors marry for love, not money, fame, or hiding the fact that one (or both) of them is gay. *Sure* they do.

Professional baseball players—and cyclists, sprinters, linebackers, oh, and bodybuilders too—never "knowingly" use steroids. *Uh huh*.

Wars are fought for the sake of freedom or democracy or self-defense, and not because it happens to make some people very, very rich.

Right.

And I was born with my green hair.

"Weird eccentricity" is redundant, by the way—an example of what my writing coach, Mrs. Miller, calls "the devaluation of meaning." *Eccentric* is no longer enough on its own; you have to add *weird* to get people to pay attention, even though weird doesn't actually change the meaning of eccentric. Just restates it.

Or prestates it, or whatever. Emphasizes it, in case you miss it the second time around.

Greenback dollar. Greenbacks *are* dollars, doofus.

Twelve midnight. Dude, midnight *always* happens at twelve. Ditto twelve noon.

Specific example. Prior history. Unconfirmed rumor. Redundant, redundant, redundant.

You might've noticed how I steered the conversation away from my secret, yet managed to allude to it with my digression on redundancies. I'm slick that way—you'd better watch me.

And oh yeah: green hair, along with which comes a (pretty unimaginative, if you ask me) nickname: Sprout. More on that later.

But first:

4

We must've made a wrong turn at Albuquerque

My dad and I moved here four years ago, when I was twelve. Long Island to Kansas. Fifteen hundred miles, most of it on I-70. We drove it in twenty-three hours, pausing only for food— McDonald's, Cracker Barrel, more McDonald's—and gas. There was no reason we didn't stop. It's not like there was anything waiting for us in Kansas. It was more like we were trying to get away—or he was trying to get away, and I was his hostage. I'm not even sure Kansas was our destination, or if it's just where my dad ran out of steam. Maybe it's just where he realized he couldn't run away from his memories.

A few days after sixth grade ended, he woke me up and told me to pack.

"How much should I pack?"

"Pack everything you need."

There was something edgy about his voice, out of control. I glanced at the clock. 6:53 A.M. I wondered if he'd started drinking already. I sat up, tried to slow things down.

"Well, how long are we gonna be gone?"

My dad looked around my bedroom. The only room I'd ever called my own. It took him maybe five seconds to take it all in—the posters, the dresser and bed, the clothes strewn on the floor—and then he turned back to me and said:

"Pretty much forever."

He rented the second-smallest-sized U-Haul and we packed our stuff in until it was full. Anything that didn't fit we left behind. Somehow all the things that didn't fit belonged to my mom: her clothes, her dressing table with the big circular mirror, every single dish in the kitchen. I took her picture though—the framed wedding portrait that had hung in the same spot for so long that the paneling had changed color beneath it. Or, I guess, stayed the same color while the rest of the walls faded. The picture had faded too, yellowed a bit. My mom's skin and dress both had an ivory, kind of sickly tone to them. But maybe that's just projection on my part: it's hard to look at the past and forget what you know about the future.

Her eyes stared out at me, bright, focused, fearless. They looked into the days ahead as though they were filled with nothing but health and happiness. I could almost understand why my dad ignored it with each trip to the U-Haul, but I took it anyway. Wrapped it in a sheet from my parents' bed, which my dad also didn't pack, and slipped it into the soft space between two sofa cushions. I took her jewelry box too, and her favorite book.

I'm not going to tell you the title, though, because that's mine alone.

During the drive my dad kept talking about how we needed "space."

"Distance."

"Fresh air."

"A fresh start."

"Country living, Daniel. That's what we need."

"Good country people."

I let him talk. I'd brought a dictionary into the cab of the U-Haul, and I thumbed through it at random. *Rhumb, foramen, collogue: the line followed by a ship sailing in a fixed direction; an opening, an orifice, a hole; to speak flatteringly or feign agreement.* Sometimes the words had some kind of association with what my dad was saying but usually they stood alone, bricks of meaning without any mortar to hold them together. Just like the words that came out of my dad's mouth.

"It'll be different, Daniel. You'll see. Everything's gonna change."

Even after we set up camp in the Trail's End Motel, we continued driving. Only this time, instead of following a single endless ribbon of highway, we crisscrossed Reno County. Hutchinson is the big town, with about 30,000 people, and over the course of a week it seemed we drove each and every one of its streets, west to east, north to south, even the alleys. Eight miles to the east was Buhler, the moon to Hutch's earth. The only thing that stood out was the school, not so much because of the way it looked (like, *bricks*) but because my dad said,

"I guess that's where you'll be going."

It wasn't until these words came out of his mouth that I realized he was doing more than getting the lay of the land. I suppose it should've sunk in sooner, but the whole trip was so unexplained I hadn't really pondered what it meant. What the consequences might be. But all of a sudden it was clear: that ochre brick building, rectangular yet amorphous, was going to be my new school. One of these dusty streets would bear my new address. Long Island, the ocean, my friends—my mom—were all just memories now.

7

In a way, it was almost as though all we'd done was move across the country, like half the kids I knew who'd lost one or the other parent after their families split up. The difference was, all those other parents showed up again, sometimes for a visit, sometimes to take you back—sometimes when you didn't even want them to.

But my mom was never coming back.

For whatever reason, living in town didn't suit him. Actually, the reason was pretty clear: too many people. For all his talk about friends and neighbors, good country folk and the salt of the earth, what my dad really wanted was to be alone. And so we ventured into the countryside, careened down two-lane highways or bumped and juddered over dirt roads, the trip made that much louder by a couple of boxes of dishes I'd tossed into the backseat right before we left Long Island. Their rattling had a dense, almost solid sound, as if the plates and cups and bowls had broken into tiny pieces and settled in a single mass on the bottom of the boxes, but I was too afraid to unfold the lids and check. I kept my eyes trained on the unpaved roads instead. They fascinated me. In Long Island, all the roads were, first of all, *streets*, and they were also, you know, *paved*. Dirt roads belonged to movies set in other countries, other centuries. Yet here they were, their washboard ridges shaking our suburban car to pieces, as if to punish us for disturbing a quiet pastoral afternoon.

The Arkansas River ran through the southern part of the county (that's pronounced *R*-Kansas by the way, as in: Sen. Sam Brownback, R-Kansas). We'd crossed other rivers that'd given their names to states, the Ohio, the Mississippi, the Missouri. By contrast, the Ark was small and shallow, rent with sandbars and fringed with stunted, scared-looking trees. The land around the river was almost entirely carved up into wheat farms. It was late June, remember. Harvest was almost over, and the stubbled fields were golden in the sun—them good ol' amber waves of grain—but still, I preferred the real waves we'd left behind. You know. *Water*.

The wheat didn't appeal to my dad either. He turned the car around, aimed for the northwestern corner of the county, where the land was drier, hillier. The unplowed pastures were mostly empty, or dotted with Herefords destined for grocery stores and chain steakhouses, although one of them, surreally, was filled with ostriches.

"Good meat ostriches," my dad said as we drove past the flock, or herd, or whatever you call a group of ostriches. The big gray birds regarded our car with level, malevolent gazes, but before I could ask him when he'd ever tasted ostrich I saw the sign:

GOOD MEAT

OSTRICHES

Only later would we learn that the dryness of this part of the county was an illusion—that the water table skulked a few feet below the surface, and bubbled up each swampy spring. But summers come fast to Kansas. By the time we got here the land was hard and brown, and pearly spikes of prickly pear cacti glinted amid tangles of withered grass. Where there *was* water, streams as thin as untied shoelaces, a line of ubiquitous cottonwoods huddled over the shallow trickle like pigeons converging on a dropped pretzel.

Of course, I didn't know they were called cottonwoods then. But when we drove over a tiny shaded bridge I could see their leaves, heart-shaped, shiny as plastic, and their bark, rough and jagged as granite (rough *and* jagged: I know, Mrs. Miller,

I know). Only later did I learn that if you separated the thick gray bark from the trunk that its underside turned out to be reddish brown and smooth as the inside of a walnut shell. That September we met a woman at the State Fair who sold paintings made on sheets of cottonwood bark. Nature scenes mostly. Little bitty trees painted on little bits of trees. I thought that was a little sad—I'll take the real thing over a painting of it any day—but my dad bought three. Hung them in the living room next to the front door, in the place where my mom's picture had been in our house on Long Island.

It was with money from the sale of our old house that he bought eleven and a half acres about eight miles north of Hutch. Our property wasn't as barren as some of the other plots in that part of the county. In fact it was covered in trees. *Covered*'s a bit misleading. It implies woods, forests, wilderness, whereas our catalpas grew in orderly if slightly tattered rows. They'd been planted orchard-style in the 1920s; according to Mrs. Miller, they were to have been used (what *is* that tense called? anterior conditional? future subjunctive? bass ackwards?) in the making of pickle barrels, but something, either the pickle maker or the pickle-barrel maker, went bust in the Great Depression. I think that's Mrs. Miller's idea of a joke—they were probly supposed to've been fenceposts—but no matter what the real story is, they were never cut down, but left to grow and flower and fall and seed themselves, until, at least to the glancing eye, they gave the illusion of nature. But if you peered through the underbrush (equal parts ragweed, marijuana—er, hemp— and itch ivy) you could still see the perfect lines stretching north, south, diagonally.

Mrs. Miller calls it "a composition of balanced tensions": the regularity of the planted trees juxtaposed against the chaos of their splayed limbs and vibrant, vibrating leaves (alliteration, *ahem*). I tended to think of the trees in a more metaphorical—mythological, ahem, ahem—kind of way. It was as if my neighbors on Long Island had been transformed by a Greek god into beings of bark and sap instead of flesh and blood. This cottonwood had a hollow trunk, just as the boy who'd lived down the block had a tubular prosthetic arm. That dead hackberry was laced by vines, just as the brown-haired girl who got on the bus after me had worn braces on both legs. A slanting but sturdy mulberry was the bent back of the old Italian woman who walked every day to the grocery store with her trolley, or dolly, or whatever you call those little cages on wheels that old people use to carry their stuff in. The old Italian lady's cart was red; the mulberry was covered in five-leaved creeper that turned crimson in the fall.

But the myths I thought of most, at least when I was in the forest, were the ones in which women get turned into trees. Not just women, but mothers. Mothers of sons usually. Adolescent boys who always find their way to the shelter of the maternal limbs. Deep within its trunk, the trapped spirit groans with the desire to communicate her love, but all her son hears is the creak of wood. The tree showers fruit on him, but all the son does is take a bite from the apple or orange and curl up for a nap, and sometimes—because life is like that—the son ends up cutting his mother down, and the woman who gave birth to him is turned into a table or a bed or maybe just logs for the fireplace, the maternal body warming its son in death just as it had in life.

I suppose that's where the story breaks down for me. Eventually I came to love our forest. Even on the coldest winter days I trekked through the trees for an hour or two after school, and during the summers I sometimes even spent the night there, curled up in a sleeping bag on the bug-infested remnant of the sofa that had sat in our living room on Long Island. But no creaking or cracking of tree limbs, no cawing or gnawing or patter of paws ever made me feel anything other than alone when I was there. During our first months here I pretended the constant creaking of the trunks was like our gossiping neighbors back on Long Island.

    I hear the mother's got

             The old man's been hitting the

                      Do you think the boy is

                              Wait, where'd they

If I was silent long enough, I thought the trees would forget I was there and reveal their secrets to me. But as time went on I realized they never would—not because I wasn't listening hard enough, but because they weren't actually saying anything. The only thing I heard was the echo of my own thoughts, obsessions, fears. The trees weren't trapped souls: they were just trees, and the most likely reason they'd been planted was to cover the barrenness of the prairie. To limit the vista, create places to hide. To shelter a lonely widower and his only son so they could nurture their grief while they hid from the world.

Or at least that's what it felt like. Because after my dad bought the trailer and moved as much of our stuff in as would fit and threw out the rest (the aforementioned sofa and my mom's easy chair, the antique writing desk my grandmother had given her as a wedding present and a half dozen other pieces of furniture, not to mention boxes and boxes of books, clothes, knickknacks, and plain old junk) he never left. I mean, sure, he went to town to buy groceries and stuff (by which I mean booze) but he made no effort to get a job or meet people, just lived off the proceeds of the sale of our Long Island house.

"Life's cheap out here, Daniel. With a little budgeting, I can get by till you go off to college."

"And then?"

My dad reached for whatever he was drinking that day.

"There don't always have to be a then." He poured, drank, swallowed, grimaced. Left his hand on the bottleneck. "Hell, there ain't really a now, so why should there be a then?"

And he poured, drank, swallowed, and grimaced again.

You might recognize my dad's words as a tautology. Circular reasoning. The unsubstantiated assertion that there won't be a *then* is based on the equally groundless claim that there isn't a *now*, when, clearly, there is, whether or not my dad chooses to sober up and face it. Mrs. Miller taught me you can get away with these kinds of logical fallacies when you put them in dialogue, which transforms them from rhetorical errors to idiomatic expressiveness.

I.e., poetic license.

I.e., lies.

There were a lot of lies in our life, and if I end up telling a few, it's only because I'm repeating what I heard.

What *else* would I do with my summer vacation?

Mrs. Miller drills me on grammatical issues like tautologies and redundancies and the like because I am my school's representative for the statewide essay contest held each year in Topeka between the fall and spring semesters. (Man, *that* was a boring sentence. Glad I finally got it out of the way.) Buhler High is small even by Kansas standards—not quite five hundred kids in all four grades—but Mrs. Miller's had four winners and three runners-up in fifteen years of teaching, which pretty much makes her the Bob Knight of the Kansas essay-writing circuit. Even to be selected as our school's representative is an honor, since I'm only a junior, and there's a $2,500 scholarship at stake, as well as a traveling silver cup that gets displayed in the cabinet along with the handful of dusty trophies that commemorate various football and basketball and tennis and track victories that took place in the distant past. In Mrs. Miller's "considered opinion," I could be the first person to win the cup two years in a row. All the other teachers in the state, she added proudly, hate her.

In fact she didn't have to look that far. All the teachers at Buhler hate her too. But that's getting ahead of the story.

· · ·

It played out like this:

Shortly before the end of sophomore year, a tall, thin (well, thinnish) teacher with not particularly natural-looking blonde hair approached me in the hall. Wispy bangs had been tortured with repeated applications of curling iron and hairspray in clear violation of the Geneva Convention; a pair of oversized square-framed glasses rode so low on the bridge of her nose that I had to resist the urge to push them up; her pleated khaki pants had been ironed so viciously that the creases had turned white. She carried a couple of pieces of paper in her right hand, which she used to fan her face in the un—air conditioned hall. Something—ketchup maybe, raspberry jelly?—stained the corner of the top page. The stain winked at me as though it had some kind of Rorschach significance, but the teacher was fanning the pages so rapidly I couldn't get a good look at it, or them.

"You are"—she stopped fanning long enough to push the glasses up her nose—"Sprout Bradford?"

I thought it was a little pretentious to say "You are Sprout Bradford?" instead of "Are you Sprout Bradford?" so I said, "I *are* Sprout Bradford!" in my best half-hick, half-retard voice.

Behind her square frames, the teacher's eyes rolled. They were gray and large and . . . and *skeptical.* No one had ever looked at me skeptically before. I'd never earned anything more than garden-variety doubt. It made me feel grownup. A little scared, but grownup.

The gray eyes floated to the top of my head.

"Well. At least I understand one thing now."

I scratched my scalp. The dye job was fresh, so my fingertips came away green, and I wiped them on my pants. Like most of my clothes, they already had a liberal smattering of green:

stains, smears, and smudges; flecks, flakes, and drops (one of which turned out to be a pea, and which I flicked off as discreetly as I could).

"Look, uh, Miss—"

"Mrs."

Like *that* helped. "Look, Mrs.—"

"Miller."

I must've pulled some kind of face, because she smiled, kind of grim, but kind of proud too.

"You're not the only one with a reputation."

I resisted the urge to scratch my head again. "Um, yeah. Right. Well, look, Mrs. Miller, I gotta catch my bus. So if I'm not getting detention . . . ?"

Mrs. Miller's detentions were famous: thousand-word essays on the history of wheat; dramatic monologues on the Homestead Act of 1846; or just copying the complete definition of the verb *to be* from the dictionary—by hand, in crayon, using a different color for each letter.

Mrs. Miller turned the paper towards me. She held it by the corners, using just her fingertips, as though it were a slightly offensive photograph still wet from its chemical bath.

"Did you write this?"

By now you can tell Mrs. Miller liked the superfluous gesture (just as I'm kind of fond of anachronisms, what with the paper dictionary and non-digital photography and words like "fond"). It was pretty clear I'd written the paper—um, duh, she'd looked down and seen my *name* on it—but I'd written it for Mrs. Lentman's sophomore English class, which made me wonder how Mrs. Miller, who as far as I knew only taught seniors, got a hold of it. The paper was called and I suddenly remembered: the red stain was strawberry compote, which, when spread liberally on toaster waffles, ranks seventh on my dad's list of favorite hangover cures. Fortunately I like it too, so it works out all around.

The sound of Mrs. Miller's tapping foot brought me back. We were standing on carpet, so she must've been wearing really hard-soled shoes. I looked up at her.

"Did it suck so much the teachers are passing it around?"

"On the contrary," she said (except she pronounced it *au contraire*). "Unlike most people your age, your irreverence has a considered, mature quality to it." *Matoor*, she said, in that pseudo-classy soap-opera-y kind of way. But at the same time she leaned in close to me, and a gap opened between two buttons of her blouse. The lace on her bra matched her collar, except it was pale purple. Lavender, I guess you'd say, although that makes it sound a little, um, sexy? Just thinking that made my face turn about the same purple as her bra, and, what with my spiky green hair, I must've looked like an over-cooked stem of asparagus (which, btw: *gross*).

When Mrs. Miller gave me the paper back, I saw that Mrs. Lentman had given me a B+. She took off a half step for the strawberry compote, and another half step for a couple of green fingerprints on page three, but the last deduction was for "unconventional interpretation."

"Lesson one, Sprout," Mrs. Miller said to me with a twinkle in her gray eyes, "know your audience. *The Catcher in the*

Rye is Sharon's favorite book. You bash it, she bashes you. Strictly between us," she added in a stage-whisper (except it came out *entre nous*), "I always thought Holden Caulfield was a *simp* myself."

Because Mrs. Lentman had been "criminally tardy" in bringing my "linguistic prowess" to her attention, Mrs. Miller suggested the two of us meet during the summer to get a head start—the contest was only seven months away, after all. First I was like: state essay contest? and then, when she explained what it was, I was like, state *essay* contest? Because the truth is I'd never thought about writing as anything besides something you did for school. It wasn't like my secret dream, I mean. I didn't have any dreams beyond getting the hell out of Dodge, which makes me about as unique as a playlist on the average cheerleader's ipod. And I didn't actually need the scholarship because my dad had set aside some of the money from the sale of our house on Long Island for my college tuition. And then, well, the idea of meeting once a week over the summer with an English teacher who wore sexy underwear beneath prim blouses didn't exactly *thrill* me. I mean, I'd just turned sixteen. I'd graduated from my learner's to an unrestricted license, and had worked out a deal with my dad to have the car on Saturdays. ("Dad, I won't get a tattoo of a teardrop on my cheek if you let me have the car on Saturdays." "Sounds like a deal, son.") I was thinking pool parties, ultimate frisbee, the new video arcade in the mall. But the truth is I didn't have anyone to invite me to pool parties or ultimate frisbee (which is for losers anyway) and, being jobless, I didn't have any money for the arcade. But there'd been that wink. And, you know, the idea I was *good* at something. You show me a teenager who doesn't like to be flattered and I'll show you a teenager who's got a steady source of sex. Since it seemed pretty clear Mrs. Miller wasn't going to let me catch my bus till I gave her an answer, I told her it'd be up to my dad.

Mrs. Miller looked at my hair one more time.

"You mean, Mr. Sprout?"

Something about the way she said it told me she was a little curious about Mr. Sprout.

She was punctual, I'll give her that. She showed up at my house at 11 A.M. the first Monday after school let out. I heard her pulling up the driveway and went out to meet her in an attempt to head off the whole Mrs.-Miller-meet-Mr.-Sprout scene, but my dad, who has been known to say "Is that you, Sprout?" when I walk past him in the living room in the morning (as though anyone else might be in our house at 8 A.M.) decided that today he was taking a paternal interest in my welfare, and followed me outside.

"This is my dad," I said to Mrs. Miller. "He's drunk."

"I *am* drunk," my dad raised his glass, guilty as charged. "Nice to meet you," he said, and went back inside.

I got in the passenger's seat and waited. Mrs. Miller was staring slack-jawed at my house. You might think she was staring at the invisible figure of my dad, but I was pretty sure she was just staring at the house. Most people stare at my house when they see it for the first time.

She stared at it.

After a minute or two she closed her mouth with an audible click. Then:

"Is that . . . kudzu?"

"Kudzu, grapevine, Virginia creeper, morning glories, bindweed, and ivy, both English and itch. Oh, and my dad planted sweet peas this year, but they haven't come up yet." I had the list down pat.

Mrs. Miller managed to tear her eyes from the trailer, looked around the yard.

"And the—?"

I nodded my head yes, she was seeing correctly. "Stumps."

A nervous smile flickered over Mrs. Miller's mouth.

"Stumps."

She turned and looked at me. There was so much hairspray on her tortured bangs that when the tips tapped against the lenses of her glasses they actually clicked.

"*Stumps*?"

The house first:

The day after we moved here my dad left me to arrange the furniture however I wanted while he returned the U-Haul. After the taxi brought him home, he didn't come inside to see what I'd done. I was particularly proud of the pair of dining room chairs I'd balanced on two coffee tables and draped with an old sheet to make a tent, blinkily lit from within by a couple of strings of Christmas lights; since we didn't have a dining room anymore (or, for that matter, a dining room table), it seemed as good a place as any for them. Instead he just walked around our trailer, taking liberal sips from the long-necked bottle of hooch he'd brought back from town. I followed him from window to window, wondering what he was doing. After about the tenth revolution he suddenly stopped, turned, headed into the forest. He had the air of a man setting out on a long journey. Part of me wondered if I'd ever see him again. A larger part wondered what was for dinner. Not that we had anything to eat off of. My ears hadn't deceived me: every single dish I'd packed in the backseat of the Taurus had smashed to pieces.

He was back an hour later, covered in dirt, his arms full of plants. Not just any plants: vines, which draped over his shoulders and tangled in his legs and trailed behind him for dozens of feet. It made me think of when you take your first bite of cup-a-noodles and you get a big glob of ramen plus like a foot more spiraling off your spoon. Or maybe hunger made me think that. At any rate, magnify that image by fifty (and paint it green) and you sort of know what my dad looked like.

I.e., he looked like the Wild Man of the Forest.

I.e., he looked crazy.

Suddenly I was a little less hungry.

Since we didn't have a shovel (we'd had a shovel, on Long Island, two in fact, but neither made it into the U-Haul: yup, Christmas lights but no shovel, that's my dad) he used a stick to dig a shallow trench around the trailer, into which he planted the vines he'd taken from the forest. It was only the next morning when he was more or less covered by a rash that we realized some of the vines must've been itch ivy. The rash went away but the vines didn't. Now, four years later, our trailer is covered in a shimmering green cocoon more than a foot thick. The only opening in the foliage is for the front door—although copious amounts of itch ivy still make getting into and out of our house a bit of a risky undertaking. At least in spring and summer anyway. Come winter, the leafless brown strands look like a fisherman's net tangled around a beached whale. People tend to have two reactions when they see it, one of which is "Cool!" and the other of which is:

"*Weird*."

Well, most people say "weird."

In fact, only one person ever said "cool."

Mrs. Miller's eyes floated to the top of my head, as if wondering what kind of man would encase his house in bright green vines and let his son walk around with bright green hair. She shook her head—*click click* went her bangs against her glasses—a little amused, a little perplexed, a little scared.

"Your *father*," she said carefully, "is very, very weird."

And now the stumps:

One time my dad and I were driving on the western side of the county. I forget why. Sometimes my dad liked to drive. Sometimes my dad liked to take me with him when he drove. Sometimes I didn't manage to sneak into the forest before he found me. This must've been one of those times. So:

We drove past a cottonwood that'd fallen over. The big bristly ball of roots was open and exposed, a dense, knotted tangle like a virus magnified a million times. It had been out of the ground long enough that the dirt had washed off and the bark had fallen away and the sinewy wood had gone almost white. My dad slowed the Taurus as he looked at it, then just stopped and stared. Finally, he said,

"Son, that is an amazing sight."

"*Tolutation*," I said. "*The action of ambling or trotting.*"

From the corner of my eye I saw my dad glance at the dictionary, but he didn't say anything. Just pulled the car off the road before we got rear-ended. We must've sat there for like a half hour while I made my way into the U's, until finally a woman came out of the house with a cordless phone in her hands, which she waved threateningly.

"What's she gonna do," my dad said, "throw it at us?"

"I think she's gonna call the cops."

"Oh right." My dad pulled back onto the road. He looked both ways first, though. He might be crazy, but he's a considered kind of crazy. Careful.

A week later the stump was in our back yard. My dad cut the trunk off about two feet above the rootmass, which was a good six feet in diameter, and brought it home on the back of a rattling flatbed trailer he'd gotten who knew where. With the help of a couple of buddies (drunks can *always* find a couple of buddies), he balanced the stump upside down on the grass, so that the roots reached up into the air. On the one hand, it looked a little like an enormous dead cauliflower, or the head of a giant troll doll. On the other, you could stare at it for a *really* long time. Not just at it, but into it. Even in broad daylight there was something about the shadows created by all those tangled roots that made you think the stump contained limitless hidden spaces. It was a paradox. Something that was normally hidden beneath the earth had been exposed, yet in the process new mysteries were created. I had to admit, it was kind of impressive.

It was also really ugly.

It also started multiplying.

The stumps became my dad's hobby. He combed three counties looking for them. Would go up to strangers' houses and ask if he could haul away the tree that had fallen in their field or front yard. At some point he got the idea of cutting up the non-stump part of the tree and selling it for firewood, which proved surprisingly lucrative. So you could never say his hobby was indulgent, or took time away from his job.

On first glance, the stumps look like leafless trees, dead or merely dormant depending on your outlook on life. But when you get closer you see the difference. Roots don't grow the same way branches do. Branches tend to be straight or gently curved, easing their way through open air towards a sunlight that's all around them. Roots have to push though solid earth. To say they inch their way is an overstatement. They millimeter their way, micron their way even, searching blindly for water or nutrients or patches of ground strong enough to hold up the huge mass growing invisibly above them, the evidence of their labors in their gnarled, stunted shape (and yeah, I know I switched from old-style to metric in the middle of that metaphor, but "fraction-of-an-inch" makes an even more awkward verb than "millimeter"). It's sort of like the difference between the Eloi and the Morlocks in *The Time Machine*: the surface dwellers pretty and tall and slim and careless, the underworld beings hunched and ugly and doing all the work. Of course, in *TTM* it turns out the Morlocks are also eating the Eloi. Sometimes I wondered if my dad's stumps had a similar fate planned for us.

By the time Mrs. Miller came over, there were thirty-six of them. Six rows of six, evenly spaced over the whole acre and a half of our clearing. My dad had even taken pictures, got some kid from the JuCo to make him a website. He paid him in booze.

Check it out: www.thestumpman.com.

Make sure you type *the*stumpman, or you're going to end up seeing something you *really* don't want to. Trust me on that one.

It turned out Mrs. Miller was a nervous (read: incompetent, or maybe just dangerous) driver. Our driveway is a good quarter mile long, but it's still pretty much just a couple of straight lines connected at one end (that's called an L, by the way, which maybe I should've just said). Despite this, she somehow managed to back onto the lawn and get stuck between two stumps. She slammed on the brakes to avoid hitting one, shifted gears so hard they ground. This was impressive, since she drove an automatic. The first thing she said was:

"Your father should *not* be buying alcohol for minors."

The second thing she said was:

"That is a *great* subject for an essay."

I looked around the clearing. Sometimes I thought my dad was a genius. There was something so extreme and obsessive about his strange, bristling grid and the weird green thicket of our house in the center of it. But I was also afraid that liking these things might mean I was like my dad—that I would end up like him, alone and drunk and devoting all my time to building a monument that communicated nothing besides its maker's lack of connection to the normal world.

"Listen to me," Mrs. Miller said now, trying to maneuver her car out of its trap. "It's like they say on *American Idol*. It's all about song choice. Or, in your case, subject choice."

"You watch *American Idol*?"

Mrs. Miller did something with the gear shift, and the car made a sound like a cow being stuck with an electric prod. I'm not sure if it had something to do with driving, or if she was just using the car to communicate her impatience.

"Most kids your age either write earnest essays about how they're trying to understand 'this crazy world' "—she said this like, Al-Qaeda Al-Schmaeda, what's the big deal—"or else about how they want to 'fulfill themselves.' No offense, but no one really cares what a teenager thinks about Islamic extremism. I mean, we want you to devote a due measure of consideration to these kinds of blah blah blah [yes, she actually said the blah blah blahs] but we don't exactly want you writing policy papers for the State Department. A solid, concrete essay about a personal experience will stick in the judges' minds far better than some earnest tract that begins 'The problem of terrorism is a complex one.' Getting out of your clearing is complex, tell me something I *don't* know."

"Um, Lawnboy."

"Do what?"

"Lawnboy. Like the lawnmowers. That's what I wanted my nickname to be. After I started dying my hair."

Mrs. Miller's eyebrows knitted in confusion. "Lawnboy."

"You said to tell you something you didn't know. I figured you probly didn't know that."

Mrs. Miller opened her mouth. Closed it. Didn't say anything until we were safely on the highway. Then:

"Is that a dictionary?"

I shrugged. "I don't exactly have a computer anymore."

Mrs. Miller turned and looked at me for so long that the car began to edge off the asphalt. She sighed, and jerked the wheel to the left.

"You're not going to make this easy, are you?"

Now I gotta cut loose . . .

So about seven pages ago, when I was talking about how I had no one to invite me to pool parties and ultimate frisbee, I think I might've given the impression that I'm an outcast or a geek or something (too geeky for ultimate frisbee even, which is like *super* geek).[1] Anyway, I hope you don't think I'm one of those troubled teens with a subscription to *Guns & Ammo* who walks around in a black trenchcoat with death metal blasting out of his headphones, just waiting to go all Columbine and stuff. I don't even *have* a walkman,[2] let alone an ipod,[3] let alone any death metal. No trenchcoat, no *Guns & Ammo*, and (more to the point) no guns. No BB gun or air rifle or bow and arrow (although we

---

[1] For the record, I *am* aware "frisbee" should be capitalized—and ultimate frisbee, for that matter. Ditto cup-a-noodles, peppermint pattie, tabasco, internet, sharpie, vaseline, magic marker, post-it, etc., etc. In fact, most of them should be written with a ™ and ® too. What can I say? Sometimes that shift key just seems so far away . . .

[2] See note above.

[3] Ditto; if there's anything worse than a word with a totally useless capital letter at the beginning of it, it's a word with a totally useless capital letter somewhere in the middle. And now, having pretty much run this whole footnote gimmick into the ground, I'll stop. Your eyes can return to the top of the page with my promise that they won't have to wander back down here again, except to look for page numbers.

do have this old set of lawn darts, which why my father didn't pack the shovel but did pack lawn darts—and Christmas lights, and something that I'm pretty sure is the top half of one of those screw-together pool cues—is beyond me).

Anyway.

While I freely cop to being something of a loner, I'm not a dropout or a hater or anything. I mean, I'm junior captain of the cross-country team (although I suppose that's the ultimate loner extracurricular activity, unless maybe it's essay writing) and I *do* have a few friends, and one good friend, Ruthie Wilcox, who's probly p.o.'d it took me twenty-eight pages to namecheck her (sorry, Ruthie). When you add that to the fact that the nearest kid my age lives 5.8 miles from my house (why yes, I *did* measure it) and I only get the car one day a week, I think I have a pretty good excuse for spending a lot of time by myself.

The truth is, Buhler's both hermetic (he said, stuffing his dictionary behind his back) and (glancing over his shoulder) pretty monolithic too. In Long Island, groups tended to form along the Old Big Lines—girls and guys, whites and blacks, Jews and gentiles, south shore and north shore. Buhler, by contrast, is completely white, completely Mennonite, and (to keep with the rhyme scheme) com*plete*ly uptight. Of course there are the usual cliques—jocks, cheerleaders, geeks—plus a couple of local staples, my favorite being the Fuffas (from FFA, or Future Farmers of America), who all chew tobacco and wear belt buckles bearing the logo of their favorite make of truck. But all of these are pretty relaxed. I mean, nobody's ever *shot* someone over whether the Chevy Silverado is a better ve-*hic*le than the Ford F-150. The one hard and fast division, though, is between locals and outsiders. People We Know and People We

Don't. Although in the second case "people" should really be "person."

I.e., Daniel Bradford.

I.e., me.

I mean, look. Everyone knows it's rough being the new kid. But I was the new kid in a school where all the other students had known each other since, like, *birth*. In a crate of bright red apples, I was a hairy kiwi of indeterminate but slightly *blech* color. To make matters worse, I had a funny accent. I freely admit this. When, every year on Christmas, I call my Aunt Sophie (dad's side, in case you're wondering) and she gives me one of her "Was Santer Claws nice to youse guys this ye-ah?" I think, *Man*, you talk funny.

But Buhler. New kid. Me. The age-old immigrant saga, from Vito Corleone in *The Godfather* to Kevin Bacon in *Footloose*. Only this time it's twelve-year-old Daniel "Not-Yet-Known-as-Sprout" Bradford in:

"LOVE AMONG THE WHEAT SHEARS"

(A little heads up: there's no love in the next couple of pages, or wheat shears for that matter, but Mrs. Miller says "a good title is half the battle.")

Curtain rises on a typical elementary school classroom in a typically Bauhaus-inspired elementary school. Along one wall, a line of shallow awning windows is cranked open as far as they'll go, which is to say about six inches, as if to remind students There Is No Escape. To make the setting more realistic, I suggest the theater pipe goodly amounts of wheat chaff through the windows, just to the brink of

Man-I've-really-GOT-to-sneeze level. The theater should also be heated to approximately one thousand degrees, filled liberally with flies (and a couple of yellowjackets), and twenty-seven students wearing identical Children of the Corn *overalls and straw hats. A bell rings, announcing the start of class.*

<u>SEVENTH-GRADE TEACHER:</u> Class, we have a new student joining us this year.

CLASS giggles.

<u>SEVENTH-GRADE TEACHER:</u> (*squinting around the room in mock-confusion, as though she might not realize who the new kid is, or maybe just needs glasses*) Daniel Bradford, are you here?

<u>DANIEL BRADFORD, a.k.a. THE ONE KID NOT WEARING OVERALLS AND A STRAW HAT, a.k.a. ME:</u> Um, yeah?

CLASS giggles louder.

<u>SEVENTH-GRADE TEACHER:</u> (*whose name was MISS TUNIE, by the way, and who would later turn out to be okay, but who was pretty much THE ENEMY at that particular moment*) Do you prefer Dan, or Danny?

<u>ME:</u> Daniel.

<u>SEVENTH-GRADE TEACHER, a.k.a. MISS TUNIE, a.k.a. THE ENEMY WHO NEEDS TO GET A HEARING</u>

<u>AID AS WELL AS GLASSES:</u> Okay. Well, welcome to our school, Danny, and to Kansas. I understand you traveled quite a distance to get here.

<u>ME:</u> I'm from Long Island.

<u>IAN ABERNATHY:</u> *(spitting out the stalk of wheat he's been chewing on)* Long Guyland? Is that right next to Short Gayland?

CLASS giggles become CLASS guffaws.

<u>ME:</u> *(intellectually distancing my fragile psyche from Ian's lameoid joke by reminding myself that hazing is an unavoidable but finite adolescent ritual, and also staring at my desk, where the word "crap" had been carved about an inch deep into the wood, and seemed to sum up how I felt)* It's in New York.

<u>IAN:</u> *(slapping his forehead so hard his straw hat is knocked to the floor)* Noo Yauk? Noooooo Yaaaaaaaauuuuuuuuk?

<u>MISS TUNIE:</u> Thank you for your generous offer, Ian. Yes, you *can* prepare an essay on the State of New York for next Monday. I'm sure we would all appreciate learning about where our new classmate comes from.

CLASS, fickle in its loyalty, redirects its guffaws at IAN ABERNATHY.

<u>IAN:</u> *(blushing so hard the smattering of freckles on his cheeks disappears like lily pads subsumed by algae in a dead pond)* Miss Tunie!

<u>MISS TUNIE, a.k.a. THE TEACHER WHO MEANS WELL BUT DOESN'T REALIZE HOW MUCH TROUBLE SHE'S CAUSING:</u> You'd rather have it ready tomorrow? Why, thank you, Ian. I'm impressed with your zeal. (*continuing in a louder voice when IAN, who will later demonstrate his love of lost causes by playing for Buhler High's football and basketball teams, opens his mouth to protest*) Why, yes, I *do* think an hour after school in the library would help you finish your paper. Is there anything else you'd like to volunteer for, Ian? Or anyone else for that matter?

IAN is silent. As is CLASS, save for one snort from a tall, angular GIRL sitting in the desk one row over from mine, and scratching a word into her desk with a pencil. A hint: it's a synonym for the word that had been carved into mine.

<u>MISS TUNIE:</u> Well, Dan, I believe you were telling us why you moved here?

<u>ME:</u> (*wishing MISS TUNIE, who got props for taking down Ian, had forgotten about me in the excitement*) My dad said he heard about a job.

<u>MISS TUNIE:</u> (*smiling naively, like well-meaning elementary school teachers everywhere*) And what does he do?

<u>ME:</u> Nothing. He didn't get the job.

CLASS is silent. Dead silent. The sound of the tall GIRL's pencil scratching into the wood is the only thing that can be heard.

MISS TUNIE: (*oh so naive*) A–ha. (*which, to be fair, might've been uh-huh, although that's not much better*) And what does your mother do?

ME: (*mumbling*) Mpmf–mpmf–mpmf.

GIRL scratching well-known but unprintable four-letter word into her desk suddenly lifts her pencil—No. 1, I later learned, which has a harder lead than No. 2, and cuts into laminated wood better. From the corner of my eye, I notice that one of the straps of her overalls is undone, exposing a faded T-shirt from Hole's 1994 Live Through This *tour, which occurred when the GIRL was approximately one*

MISS TUNIE: (*really, really unwilling to let well enough alone*) Pardon me, Dan? I didn't catch that.

ME: (*e-nun-ci-a-ting*) She. Is. Dead.

MISS TUNIE: (*smile hardening like Play-Doh left out of the can*) Oh. Well. Welcome to our school, Dan. Daniel. (*fiddling with papers*) I see that your English and composition skills are exceptionally high. Perhaps you can, um, write about . . . Well. Would everyone please open their copy of *The Outsiders* to the last page? What do we make of Ponyboy's assertion that quote It-was-too-vast-a-problem-to-be-just-a-personal-thing unquote? What do we think Hinton is trying to communicate . . .

Lights dim until the entire class is shrouded in darkness, save for a lone spot on the new kid. Another bell rings. Class exits, their

shadowy forms more heard than seen as they squeeze through the
closely packed desks. But the boy known for one more week as
Daniel Bradford remains in his seat as the last spotlight fades, until
eventually he too disappears in a darkness punctuated not by noises
from the stage, but from the audience. Seatsprings creak beneath
squirming bottoms as they wait for the house lights to come up; the
electric hum of the EXIT sign at the back of the theater calls them
back to the real world. At long last, rubber-soled chair legs squeak
over freshly waxed linoleum. There's a crash, hollow metal being
tripped over by not-so-hollow flesh as, invisibly but not inaudibly,
the new kid heads for his next class.
One down. Five more to go.
And nine more months of the school year.
And six more years of school.

<u>ME:</u> Shoot me now.

CURTAIN

So.

That was the first time I'd ever mentioned my mom's death
out loud, and afterwards everything was pretty much a blur. I
drifted through my classes, did the whole sitting-by-myself
thing at lunchtime, which took all of about five minutes to
(not) eat, then wandered outside. The playground was a big
dusty square of asphalt next to an even bigger dustier field of,
well, dust. Something had been planted on the field that I
think was supposed to be grass, but it was so brown and dry
it looked more like stale chocolate frosting. I wandered the
perimeter like a prisoner checking for holes in the fence, but

in fact there was no fence. Buhler Elementary was located more or less in the middle of nowhere, which meant there was nowhere for potential threats to hide, and nowhere for fleeing students to run. On the eastern edge of the playground I found a couple of stumps from trees that had been cut down, or maybe just died. This was before my dad started his collection (and besides, their roots were still in the ground where they belonged), so I didn't think too much about them. Just sat down and prepared to wait out the twenty-three minutes until my next class.

The sky was big and empty and not quite blue because of all the dust in the air, and after a while a combination of gravity and boredom caused my eyes to fall to the horizon, which looked like it was about a hundred miles away, and then to the two-lane highway that ran past the school, on which a rattle-trap truck or car passed every four or five years or so, and then finally to my shoes. My dad had taken me to the mall to shop for school clothes the day before. Unlike my mom, he hadn't vetoed any of my choices. The coolest thing I'd bought by far was a pair of Vans. The classic red checkerboard print reminded me of a brick wall, which had inspired me to bomb it with a purple sharpie I'd picked up at the Hobby Hut. I was trying to come up with a good answer for what *other* word might begin with F-U-C, but, since I didn't have my dictionary handy, it was harder than it might seem. Suddenly I heard a throat clear.

"Well well well. If it isn't Long Gayland."

I looked up to see—duh—Ian Abernathy. You'd think the whole dead mother thing would've given me the pity vote, but Ian Abernathy was not exactly what you would call sensitive. Since an essay to him was what a hike up Mt. Everest would be to a blindfolded paraplegic with acrophobia and asthma, he wanted revenge. His eyes glowered out from beneath his straw hat, and his football-throwing arms were bursting from his over-alls. Okay, so maybe his overalls were actually a pair of Diesel jeans and an A&F T-shirt, and his straw hat was a baseball cap (Yankees, in fact, which isn't ironic as much as it's a coincidence, although I was pretty sure that wasn't going to help me).

I must've made some kind of funny expression because Ian's eyes blinked rapidly, and in a slightly unsteady voice he said, "Um, nice kicks."

I looked at my shoes, then back up at Ian. Before I could decide what to say to this true but, let's face it, pretty unexpected statement, I saw a second figure in the field behind him. Because of the height I thought it was a teacher at first, or maybe one of Ian's friends come to join in the fun. Then I realized it was the girl who'd sat next to me in first period. She strode rapidly across the dust, as tall and thin as a periscope poking from the waves. She was even more angular standing than sitting, the cardboard flatness of her body heightened by the super-severe eighties wedge that cut across one of her eyes like a slice of pizza taped to her face. This isn't to say she was awkward or anything. On the contrary. Her body seemed as taut and strong as the wires that hold up a suspension bridge. And her face . . . man, how do I describe her face? Her face seemed to rise above the usual set of seventh-grade adjectives: PrettyUglyCoolWeirdEtc. Instead you thought of grownup words like "haughty" or "composed" or "striking." It was a face that seemed to come with its own frame; no matter what angle you looked at it from, it seemed more like a picture than flesh and blood. In tenth grade I saw a painting called *Liberty Leading the People* and I thought, *That's* it, but that day I just thought the girl approaching me looked like a pop star in front of an invisible troupe of backup dancers. You could almost hear the internal soundtrack—my guess, based on the T-shirt, was Hole's "Rock Star":

Well I went to school in Olympia, and everyone's the same . . .

"Ahem. I *said*, 'Nice *kicks*,' newbie."

I looked back at Ian. He had an interesting face too. Well, maybe not interesting as much as handsome—a little bit like Josh Hartnett in *The Virgin Suicides* (hey, just because I'm a teenager doesn't mean I can't like old movies), although he was thicker than JH, more muscly.

I lifted both feet up (I wasn't levitating, I was sitting on a stump, remember?) and stared at the graffiti on my shoes. "Fucate," I said. "Painted, or disguised with paint."

"*Hey*, Ian."

Liberty Leading the People had arrived.

Ian jumped, turned.

"Ruth Wilcox," he said, the way some people say "George Bush" and other people say "Osama bin Laden" and Matt Groening says "Walt Disney." He pretended to look for something in his pockets. "Too bad I don't have a letter that needs opening. I could use your nose."

I kind of doubt Ian Abernathy had or has any idea what a letter opener is, unless maybe he thinks it's an email application or something. Ruthie's nose, however, was most people's go-to place for an insult. It was just so, well, in your face. Or, in this case, in Ian's: Ruthie stood so close to him that the tip of her very long, very sharp-looking proboscis practically touched his forehead.

"Fuchsia," I said. "A purplish-red color." Neither of them noticed.

"Beat it, Abernathy."

"You beat it, Wilcox."

"Fucoid. A seaweed."

I could've been talking to the wind for all the attention either of them paid to me. Not that I was surprised. This wasn't about me. It was a turf war. Crips versus Bloods, schoolyard-style.

Ruth Wilcox walked around Ian Abernathy like a drill sergeant checking out a sorry-looking recruit.

"Let's face it, Ian. We're not kids anymore. Now that I've got these"—she grabbed her chest, which, if anything, was flatter than mine—"it's no longer okay for you to throw down with me. Which means I can beat the tar out of you, but if you lay a finger on me the whole school will come down on you like a ton of bricks for hitting a girl. So either I kick your butt until you crawl off in shame, or you just crawl off in shame. What's it gonna be?"

I'm not sure if it was the basic truth of what Ruth Wilcox said that drove Ian Abernathy away, or just the sheer number of words. His mouth opened and closed several times, and so did his fists, and then he turned to me. "This ain't over, newbie," he said, and marched across the playground.

Neither of us said anything while Ian walked away, the sound of dead grass crunching beneath his sneaks gradually drowned out by the distant screams of first- and second-graders playing tetherball and four-square and game boy. Why *do* little kids scream like they're dying when they're supposedly having fun?

"I *said*, is that a *dic*tionary?"

I glanced up at Ruth Wilcox, who was staring at me as

impatiently as Ian Abernathy had a moment before. I found myself wondering if she'd chased him off so she could beat me up herself.

I glanced at the ground on either side of the stump. "Huh?"

"Home room, *duh*. Did you actually bring your own *dictionary* to class?"

I shrugged. "You know, budget cuts and all. I wasn't sure what sort of resources a rural school would have."

She rolled her one visible eye. I'm guessing the eye under the wedge of hair rolled as well, but I couldn't say for sure. Ruth Wilcox struck you as the kind of girl who could learn to roll one eye at a time.

"Miss Tunie said you were good at English and composition."

"Yeah, I don't really know what she meant by—"

She held up her hand, not so much "stop" as "Stop! In the Name of Love" (although, given Ruth Wilcox's love of all things eighties, it would've been more like *Stop Making Sense* by the Talking Heads). She reached into her purse, pulled out a sparkly silver notebook and something that was, depending on your point of view, a long pink pencil with a troll doll on the eraser end, or a troll doll that just happened to have a pencil hanging from its butt. She held them out until, not knowing what else to do, I took them. Then:

"Describe me," Ruth Wilcox said.

"Um—"

"Don't *think*. Do."

I stared at her for a long time, but she showed no sign of going away. I looked at my watch. Nineteen minutes till recess ended. I looked at the troll doll, its googly eyes and tangled polyester thatch of green hair, then back up at the strange girl standing in front of me. Her skin-tight acid-washed jeans were tucked into a pair of beige Uggs, her oldies concert tee worn underneath an outer garment that was less a tanktop than a couple of strips of fabric holding up a little square of cloth. Her face could've been a clear glass pitcher filled with milk, with that impossibly long sharp nose sticking out of it like a spout. A striped bluejay's feather dangled from her left ear, and her right eyelid was painted some kind of bronzy red. The words "etaoin shrdlu" (which aren't Gaelic as I thought at first, but rather the twelve most frequently used letters of the English language) were painted across her fingernails. Since she only had five fingers on each hand, this was perhaps the most impressive part of the whole ensemble.

After a long time I sighed and wrote three words. I wrote in all caps, put periods between them, underlined the last one, and then I handed the notebook back.

Ruth Wilcox stared at what I'd written. In profile her face was so thin it seemed two-dimensional, as if it'd come out of a photocopier. I couldn't stop looking at it.

She nodded and closed the book.

"What's that all over your fingers?"

"Huh?"

"Fin-gers." She waggled the *etaoin* digits at me. "Yours are fil-thy."

I looked down at my fingertips, saw that they were covered with black and purple stains.

"Um, rubber cement and pokeberry juice."

She nodded like this was a satisfactory explanation, then tapped the closed notebook.

"I like it. It's like the opening monologue before the curtain goes up, when the audience is still leafing through their programs and trying to decide whether they'll wear their coats or stuff them under their seats or maybe just sneak out at intermission. It's tantalizing. It could go in any direction." She looked down that incredibly long, sharp nose at me. "I believe we were destined to meet, Daniel Bradford. Together you and I are going to ditch this loser town and rule the world." And, turning on her heel, she walked away.

I stared after her in disbelief, the troll doll pencil still dangling from my hand. All I'd written was:

YOU. ARE. WEIRD.

"Sucks about your mom," Ruth Wilcox tossed over her shoulder, and I looked down at my dirty fingers and burst into tears.

The margarita was the only virgin in the house

"**C**all me Janet."

Mrs. Miller opened an amber door and beckoned me into a tawny living room. Beige dining room to the left; ochre hallway to the right; dun-colored patio through a pair of sliding-glass panels. Beyond that, a yard full of dry grass yellowing beneath the merciless Kansas sun.

On the wall next to the door, where some people hang framed squares of needlepoint that say "God Bless This Home" and other people hang pictures of their children or parents or dead wives, Mrs. Miller had hung a brass plate reading:

GOD BLESS SYNONYMS,
METAPHORS, AND EUPHEMISMS TOO!

"God Bless Synonyms, Metaphors, and Euphemisms too!" is a pretty weird sentence all by itself, but it's even weirder when it's stamped into solid brass and fastened to one of those heraldic wooden plaques that usually have a moose's head or a stuffed pheasant mounted on them, and is the first thing you see when you walk in someone's front door to boot. Now Mrs. Miller ran a hand through her blonde hair and said:

"Would you like a 'drink'?"

She used her fingers to make the quotation marks, which kind of threw me. No teacher had ever offered me a "drink" before, or even a drink for that matter. I wondered if "drink" was a synonym for something—or, God forbid, a euphemism.

"Okay . . . ?"

"Okay what?"

"Okay . . . Janet?"

" 'At's my boy."

"I got married when I was twenty-one," she called through the kitchen window, her voice barely audible over a roaring blender. "Divorced at twenty-three, but that's a whole 'nother story. Somehow during the past decade and a half I never got around to taking my name back. I tried doing the whole 'Ms.' thing, but I couldn't even get my head-in-a-bucket colleagues to say it, let alone the students. *Kansas*," she added, as if that explained everything.

I glanced up from my dictionary (*thermotype: a picture obtained by wetting an object with hydrochloric acid, then taking an impression, then heating it*) when the sliding-glass door slid open. Mrs. Miller was hunched over a tray containing a couple of glasses with cactus-shaped stems and a pitcher filled with icy yellow liquid sloshing over the top.

Oh, and a bottle of tequila.

"Anyhoo," she set the tray on a table, and a little more liquid sloshed out of the pitcher, making me wonder if she wasn't a bit sloshed herself. "Since, technically speaking, I'm not your teacher during the summer, I thought we'd stick with first names. Okay, Daniel?"

I put the dictionary on the floor. Sometimes definitions

don't help much. (For example: do you have any idea what a thermotype is based on what I just told you? I don't, and I'm sure not about to splash acid on my face to see if it takes a picture.) Mrs. Miller's "I'm not your teacher" left me similarly unenlightened, and all I could do was stare at the bottle of tequila. I mean, even my dad doesn't drink tequila at 11:30 on a Monday morning. He drinks whiskey, but that, to borrow a phrase from Mrs. M., is a whole 'nother story.

"Uh, it's Sprout."

"Sprout." Mrs. Miller glanced at my hair, then followed my eyes to the bottle. "Yes, Sprout, it's true. Teachers are human too, surprise, surprise. Relax, the pitcher's virgin." She poured some in a glass and pushed it towards me. "I'll doctor mine separately."

If you're a virgin-margarita virgin, it tastes a little like a lime rickey. If you're a lime-rickey virgin, it tastes a little like a limeade with something dissolved in it—a peppermint pattie, maybe, or a Ricola, or several bags of mint tea. Since margaritas aren't supposed to have any mint in them, this was especially weird, or maybe just gross. Luckily I wasn't thirsty.

"Wojadubikowski."

I looked at Mrs. Miller, again wondering if she'd had a nip in the kitchen, or maybe an epileptic fit. Her hand was steady enough as she dosed her drink.

I held up my glass. "Delicious!" When in doubt, hide behind a compliment.

Mrs. Miller laughed. "My maiden name. Woy-a-du-bi-kuv-skee."

"Oh! Woya, Woya—wha?"

"Don't bother. I couldn't say it myself till I was six. There are *some* benefits to Miller." She poked a bendy straw into her drink and took a sip, made a face, half grimace, half smile, and again I wondered if she were having a fit. But:

"Ooh!" was all she said. "*Ow*. Brain-freeze."

"So," her wet voice going all teacherly: "The essay contest is timed. One hour, which means you can write six, maybe eight good pages. The topic is selected randomly, but always falls within certain parameters. 'If you were president, what would you do?' 'If you had a million dollars, how would you spend it?' 'If you could invent one thing, what would it be?'"

Oh.

Right.

Essay contest.

I'd almost forgotten about it, what with the novelty of a teacher picking me up at my house and serving me frozen margaritas, virgin or otherwise.

I have to admit, though, in the two weeks since Mrs. Miller had put the idea in my head, it had grown on me. The truth is, I *do* enjoy playing around with words (if you're still reading, you might've noticed that). And I was also beginning to think maybe I had something to say. Like, you know: I'm a creep, I'm a loser, I smell like Teen Spirit but I'm beautiful, no matter what they say, and I'm bringing sexy back, yeah! Does that make me crazy? Probably. But now it seemed Mrs. M. was telling me I couldn't write what I wanted. That I had to discuss a topic someone else picked out. This was starting to sound less like an extracurricular activity, more like, well, *school*.

I glanced down at the dictionary, resisted the urge to start leafing through in search of words to hide behind.

"So, uh, if the topic's chosen at random, how can I practice for it?"

Mrs. Miller did a combination sip-and-nod, which almost sent her straw up her nose.

"A couple things. The first is: ignore the topic. Anything they'll ask is basically a version of 'So what do you want to be when you grow up?' or 'What formative experience made you realize that the U.S. of A. is the best country on earth?' You prepare a stock answer to that question and then adapt it to whatever they actually put in front of you."

I nodded, being careful of my straw. "Kind of like when a reporter asks the president about the state of health care in America, and he says, 'Health care is goin' great—and so is the war on terror!' and then rambles on about that for five minutes."

"Please, Daniel—"

"*Sprout.*"

"Sprout. Please. This is a red state. No politics. Although it never hurts to throw in a little God."

"A little God?"

Mrs. Miller held up an imaginary Grammy ('though how I knew it was a Grammy is anyone's guess). "First of all I'd like to thank *Almighty God* for this award," she said in the worst fake black accent I've ever heard, then laughed *way* too long at her own joke. When she'd regained her composure, she said, "God always goes over well, but any strong conviction will do in a pinch." Another sip. "We can also do time trials."

"Time trials? Like wind sprints? Or board races?"

Mrs. Miller ignored me. Glanced at her watch. Then:

"You have five minutes to describe the sunset from the point of view of a man who's just lost his wife to cancer. Don't mention cancer, the wife, or death. Ready . . . set . . . *go!*"

I stared at Mrs. Miller, trying to figure out what she did or didn't know about me. I mean, *really*.

"Four minutes and fifty seconds. Forty-nine. Forty-eight. Forty-ni—I mean, forty-seven."

She couldn't have looked less like Ruthie, with her pleated navy blue pants pulled up to her bellybutton, her long-sleeved buttondown shirt tucked into the tightly belted waistband. Yet something about her reminded me of my best friend when we first met. Giving me orders. Telling me what to write. (Ruthie was spending the summer in England with her dad, by the way, which is another reason why I'd consented to meet with Mrs. Miller.)

"Thirty-two, thirty-one, thirty . . ."

Well, what can I say? I like it when women tell me what to do. I reached for my dictionary.

"Daniel Bradford, if you *dare* start an essay with 'Webster's Dictionary defines . . . '"

"Re*lax*," I set my notebook on the dictionary's front cover. "I just need something to write on." I grabbed my pencil. As with Ruthie, I wrote three words, then handed the page to Mrs. Miller.

"You've got four minutes left."

"I'm done."

Mrs. Miller pursed her lips—not a flattering expression when you've left half your frosty lipstick on a bendy straw. In a slow voice she read:

" 'It is dark.' "

She looked up at me. Opened her mouth. Closed it. Opened her mouth again, but this time to take a drink. Then:

"It is dark."

She didn't look at the page, but at the horizon, where the sun wasn't even close to setting. "It . . . is . . . dark." She shook her head and handed the notebook back to me. "You know what? You're too damn clever for your own good."

I bent forwards, shook my green locks in her face.

"I'm too damn clever for my own good what?"

Mrs. Miller tried and failed to keep from smirking.

"You're too damn clever for your own good, *Sprout*."

" 'At's my girl."

"Tragedy, adversity, triumph, and a little humor."

During the next three months, these were Mrs. Miller's buzzwords (although sometimes they were "keywords," and other times they were "talking points," and occasionally they were just slurred, but I didn't quiz her about the distinction). I.e.:

Tragedy: dead mom. Duh.

Adversity: drunk dad; poverty. Again: duh.

Triumph: in Mrs. Miller's terms, "articulation, education, and matriculation," to which I was like "Huh?" But then, when I figured out she meant winning the contest, graduating high school, and going to college, I was like, Oh. *Duh*.

A little humor: lest we forget, I have green hair, and everyone calls me Sprout.

"I mean, don't take this the wrong way," Mrs. Miller told me sometime in early July. "These are serious issues, I don't want you to ex*ploit* them or anything. But, you know, everything happens for a reason."

"I don't think my mom died so I could write about it."

Mrs. Miller looked at me for a long time, then picked up my glass and headed inside.

"This is why teenagers should be kept away from alcolol," she said, and hiccupped.

For the record: I wasn't drunk. I wasn't even tipsy. In fact, I hadn't had anything to "drink" at all. A few weeks into our lessons, Mrs. Miller developed the habit of "remembering" she'd left something in the kitchen after she came out to the patio with the pitcher of virgin margaritas (or virgin daiquiris, or virgin mojitos, which, if you've never had one, *DON'T!*). I guess she liked to think of herself as a cool teacher or a with-it kind of grownup or whatever; the trip back to the kitchen was to allow me to doctor my own drink while allowing her to maintain plausible deniability. But I liked tequila (or rum if it was mojitos, or vodka if it was bloody marys, or cachaça if it was caipirinhas, or Pisco if it was Pisco sours) even less than the various virgin versions, so all I did was pour a jigger of whatever kind of alcohol was on offer onto the grass beside the patio. Over the course of the summer a dead spot spread there, which provided as good an illustration of the deleterious effects of drinking as anything else (this is your brain; this is your brain on cocktails). At any rate, when she came back outside with the straws or napkins or tabasco (for bloody marys) or whatever she'd pretended to forget, she would always wink at me, and I would always wink back, trying to make it look as intoxicated as possible. It didn't cost me anything, and it made her feel like she was down with the kids.

"And ready . . . set . . . *go!*"

The school banned my graffiti'd Vans on
Tuesday; on Wednesday, Ruthie drove me to the

mall to buy a new pair of shoes; on Thursday she
wrote "FU" in tiny letters on the heel of my right shoe,
and "CK" on the heel of her left, so that when we
stood next to each other it read "FU

"And . . . stop. Stop stop stop stop stop stop *stop*."

"Huh? It can't've been five minutes."

"It's been fifteen seconds."

"Then—"

"C'mon, Sprout." Mrs. Miller tapped the last word on the page. The last partial word. "You know you can't write that."

"Can't write . . . ?"

"*Profanity*, Sprout."

"I'm sorry, I don't understand. Could you tell me more about this 'profanity'?"

Mrs. Miller nodded at my dictionary. "I assume you don't need a definition. Perhaps you'd prefer an example?"

"That would be *so* helpful, thank you very much."

Without missing a beat, Mrs. Miller rattled off a stream of obscenities so fully and completely unexpected that I fell off my chair. Mothers were defiled, and their male and female children, as well as any and all offspring who just happened to've been born out of wedlock. As for the sacred union that produced these innocent babes, the pertinent bodily appendages were catalogued by a list of nicknames so profoundly scurrilous that a grizzled marine, conceived in a brothel and dying of a disease he contracted in one, would've wished he'd been born as smooth as a Ken doll. The act itself was invoked with such a variety of incestuous, scatological, bestial, and just plain *bizarre* variations that that same marine would've given up on the Ken doll fantasy, and wished instead that all life had been confined to the single-cell stage, forever free of the taint of mitosis, let alone procreation.

Somewhere during the course of all this I noticed that I'd snapped my pencil in half, and now I used the two ends to gouge out my brain.

"Guhhhhh guhhhhh guhhhhh guhhhhh guhhhhh," I said, by which I meant: "You have shattered whatever tattered remnants of pedagogical propriety I still possessed, and my tender young mind has broken beneath the strain." Nervously, I climbed back into my chair, the two halves of my pencil sticking out of my ears like an arrow that had shot clean through my head.

Mrs. Miller allowed herself a small, self-congratulatory smile. "So look. I could tell you that profanity's just not going to fly at the contest, but you already know that. You broke the rules on purpose, to see what I would do."

I sort of grin-grimaced, which had the unintended effect of causing my ears to rise, which in turn had the unintended effect of driving the two halves of my broken pencil a little deeper into my auditory canals, which in turn, well, *hurt*. I took them out gingerly, inspected them for wax, or blood.

"It's easy to shock people, Sprout, as I just demonstrated. But you have to realize that it doesn't always stop with the initial jolt. Sometimes the tiniest stunt can alienate people forever, which in turn causes them to lose sympathy for you, and what you're trying to say."

"You're saying keep it clean."

"I'm saying remember lesson one. Know your audience."

I thought back to the B+ Mrs. Lentman had given me on my *Catcher in the Rye* paper. I'd raised my grade to an A+ by writing my final paper on *To Kill a Mockingbird*, which, I piously informed Mrs. Lentman, had taught me, "along with countless generations of readers," that racism is, you know, wrong. Really, really *wrong*.

"You're saying dumb it down."

"I'm saying *know your audience*. Remember that when you sit down to write your essay in that gymnasium-turned-testing hall on Jan. 4, you're writing *about* yourself. Not *to* yourself, or to your peers, but to an audience that will be composed almost exclusively of white, middle-aged, middle-class educators with an equally conservative educational profile. The three R's. Family values. Intelligent design. You have to find a way to make *this* audience understand who you are, not some imaginary group of people you might wish was reading your words. Save that for the locker room, or your Facebook page."

"I don't have a computer," I said. "And teenagers curse. It's just something we do."

"You think we don't know that, Sprout? We all know the words. And we all know everyone says them. The people we tell not to say them, and the people who tell the people not to say them. But if using them is going to cause you to lose the contest, you have to think of a creative way to let people know what's being said without actually writing them down."

"What, like when a spammer puts a space in the middle of a word so the spam filter doesn't recognize it, or an asterisk or something? F-star-C-K?"

"I said *creative*. And I thought you didn't have a computer."

"Duh. I use the ones at school. And how do I know where to draw the line? Like, is 'butt' cool?"

Mrs. Miller rolled her eyes. " 'Butt' is cool."

"Ha ha, you said butt is cool. What about 'ass'? Is 'ass' cool?"

Mrs. Miller glared at me through her glasses. "Think about

it this way: if you've ever seen the word in a book you checked out from the Buhler High School library, it's okay. And if you haven't, then, well, there's a reason why."

"Buhler bans books?"

"All high schools ban books. Buhler just happens not to be ashamed of it. And Buhler's pretty much a bellwether for the state Board of Ed."

"Bellwether?"

"Look it up."

(I did. You should too.)

"What about sh—"

"Sprout!" Mrs. Miller's voice squeaked. She tapped her watch. "We'll set the clock at four minutes. Now go."

I held up my broken pencil. "I was going to say, what about *showing* me where you keep the pencils."

Mrs. Miller pulled a pen from her cleavage and handed it to me. It was shockingly warm.

"Here," she said, "use my ballpoint." She put the slightest extra emphasis on the first syllable, and whatever mental circuits hadn't been fried by her stream of profanity fizzled out for good.

When she was seven years old, Ruth Wilcox saw Cate Blanchett in Elizabeth. Even before her parents shut the TV off she'd decided she was going to be a queen or a movie star. Regardless of which role she eventually chose, she realized she needed to be at least a foot taller than her mom—and four inches taller than her dad—so she immediately set her mind to growing. The photographic evidence was on display the first time I went to her house. At eight,

Ruthie could rest her chin on top of a yardstick; at ten, she already came up to her mom's eyebrows; at twelve, her mom stood eye to eye (well, eye to nipple I guess) with the very visible ribs of her daughter's chest—which, despite her height, remained as flat as the Kansas

"No no *no*," Mrs. Miller cut in again. "Exposition. Background. Don't start with a character sketch. And for God's sake, *please*. No *nipples*. I'll give you three minutes. Now go!"

"Maybe if you'd stop inter—"

"Two minutes fifty-five seconds. Go, Sprout. Go!"

My pen quivered above the page, just as it had when Ruthie first commanded me to write. How were you supposed to compose something meaningful when someone was standing over you, stopping you every time you got started? Telling you what to write about, but not what to actually *write*. But that reminded me:

"I will be your muse," Ruthie said to me, standing on one of the stumps at the edge of the playground with her arms in a Statue of Liberty pose. "Nancy Spungeon to your Sid Vicious, Patti Smith to your Robert Mapplethorpe, Courtney Love to your Kurt Cobain."

At first I was like, my muse? And then, after she explained to me who everyone was, I was like, my muse?

"I'm a little worried here. All those guys are dead."

"Death," Ruthie didn't bat an eye, "is a crucial component of fame. Marilyn Monroe, James Dean, Eva Peron, River Phoenix, Tupac and Biggie. Heath Ledger. Anybody worth their salt is planning for death from the moment they're born. Otherwise what's the point?"

"How much is salt worth?"

"I mean, everyone knows Princess Di, but who was that guy in the car with her? No one remembers."

"Dodi Al Fayed. And isn't salt, like, cheap?"

"I'm thinking pills," Ruthie pirouetted on the stump. "On the eve of my fortieth birthday. Or maybe I'll become a terrorist. Patty Hearst was so glam in the SLA. She wasn't smart enough to get shot though, and what is she now? Just another heiress with bad plastic surgery and a tall gate around her house, dreaming of the days when life used to be fun. Like, yuck."

"Di's boyfriend was named Dodi Al Fayed."

"Yeah? And who read his biography?"

"And . . . time. Pen down, Sprout."

Mrs. Miller looked over what I'd written.

"Getting there, getting there. You've certainly got good material in your friend. Although I wonder if I need to report her to Mr. Philpot."

The Phil-bot was the school counselor.

"Mrs. M.!"

"Just kidding, S.," she said, her laugh fluttering behind her own joke like a Confederate flag on the antenna of a muddy

55

pickup truck. "But seriously. I'm wondering where *you* are in all this. You kind of disappear, you know."

I nodded. I did know.

"Ruthie's like that."

Mrs. Miller's nod echoed mine, although, like her laugh, it went on too long. Then, out of left field:

"Have *you* ever talked to Mr. Philpot?"

Cue smile going hard and sharp as a pizza cutter, eyes blinking faster than a gat, fingers clutching at my dictionary cover. (That'd be me, by the way, not Mrs. M.) I had the sudden urge to drop my glass on the patio, but I fought it off.

"Have *you* ever talked to the Phil-bot?" That was me, too. Duh.

"The—? Oh." Mrs. Miller couldn't quite suppress her smile. "I know he can be a bit stiff."

"He wears bowties."

"Effective counseling doesn't require that he be 'down with the kids,' as you say."

"If I ever employed such a doof-butt phrase, I was doing so ironically. And the Phil-bot's bowties have smiley faces on them."

"In *fact*"—apparently Mrs. Miller was feeling persistent today—"it's often better when you don't think of your counselor as a peer, so you don't feel he's judging you in the same way kids your age might."

"He has a poster in his office that says 'Mental Health Is Mental Wealth.'"

Mrs. Miller closed her mouth. Then: "He does?" (She opened it again to say that. Duh.)

"Where the E's should be there are old-timey gold pieces instead."

"*Really?*" Mrs. Miller grabbed the empty pitcher and stood up, wobbling slightly. "I didn't realize it was as bad as all *that.*"

As she walked away, it occurred to me that mentioning the poster was a mistake, since it gave away the fact that I'd actually been to see the Phil-bot. I guess now's as good a time as any to tell that particular story. So:

In ninth grade my dad got picked up for drunk-driving. (Wait, don't act so shocked, you're making me self-conscious.) It being his first offense, the only thing that happened was his license was suspended for three months, which lead to the hil*ar*ious spectacle of him buying a dilapidated 10-speed and riding it fifteen miles to and from the liquor store (the hilarious part was more the riding than the buying). "Son," he said at the end of the first month, "I am the healthiest goddamn drunk in Reno County." The day he got his license back he drove the car over the bicycle, but that's another story. No, wait. That *is* the story.

So. Kansas being Kansas, the school found out about his arrest the day after it happened (it might've had something to do with the announcement that ran in the "Crime Blotter" section of the newspaper). In the middle of last period there was the familiar squeak of intercom feedback followed by a distracted-sounding man's voice, as if the speaker weren't facing the microphone but talking to someone in the administrative office.

"Is it on? It is? Oh." Suddenly shouting: "ATTENTION, STUDENTS AND TEACH—what?" The voice turning away again. "I don't have to shout? Sorry." In an almost whispery voice: "Attention, students and teachers. Would David, pardon me, Daniel—what?" Turning away once more. "He goes by Sprout? Oh, is *he* the boy with the green—oh, right. Sorry."

Back to the microphone. "Would Daniel"—dramatic pause—
" 'Sprout' "—audible quotation marks—"Bradford"—confused
pause, as the speaker tried to remember what he'd been going
to say after all those pauses—"would, um, Mr. Bradford please
report to my office? Thank you." There was a click and then, a
moment later, another feedbacky squeal as the intercom came
back on. "Oh, sorry, this is Mr. Philpot. The counselor." *Click*.

There were *ooh*s and *aah*s as I made my way out of Señor
Gutierrez's class, and just before I reached the door Ian Abernathy said, "Well, either he's pregnant, or this is about his dad's
glug glug glug glug glug."

"*¡Señor Abernathy! ¡Preséntese a la oficina del director para la
detención! ¡Immediatamente!*"

"*¡Mi placer!*" Ian said, following hard on my heels. "*¿Esta
cerca de la oficina del consejero, si?*"

Did I mention that Ian's mom was from Chile? Ian's mom
was from Chile.

"*¡Muy bueno, Señor Abernathy!*" Señor Gutierrez's voice followed us into the hall, "*¡Muy bueno!*"

The Phil-bot didn't ask why it took me twenty minutes to
get to his office, or why my hair was sticking out in seventy-nine
different directions like maybe someone had been giving me an
Indian burn, or why my T-shirt had long stretchy marks on it
like maybe I'd tried to run away from someone who'd been
holding on to it with one clenched fist. All he did was sit down
beneath a poster that showed a big sunny glass of OJ with the
caption "Orange juice glad you came to see me!" (the "Mental
Health Is Mental Wealth" poster was on the wall behind me).

"May I call you Sprout?"

I blinked. Let me rephrase that. I *felt* myself blink. Have you
ever noticed how once you feel yourself blink you can't stop

feeling yourself blink and everything gets all strobed out like a light is going on and off in front of your face? I think I counted about a hundred blinks before the Phil-bot finally said:

"Ahem, Sprout?"

I shook my head, smiled brightly.

"That's me!"

This made him gasp, which I thought was a bit of an extreme reaction. "Excuse me a moment," he said, but instead of walking away like you usually do when you say "Excuse me," all he did was open a drawer, pull out a pad with the word FLOMAX® written on it, and pick up a VAGISIL® ballpoint pen. He clicked the pen, which was already open (thus closing it), started to write something on the pad, stopped to actually click the VAGISIL® pen open, then wrote "Daniel Bradford (*Sprout*)" on the top of the pad and clicked the pen closed. When he looked up at me, he seemed surprised I was still in the room. Tell you the truth, so was I.

"I'm sorry, where were we?"

I blinked.

The Phil-bot spent about forty-five minutes asking me if my dad's "recent apprehension" (which made it sound as if he'd been frightened, not arrested) made me feel

confused?

scared?

sad?

ashamed?

angry?

suicidal?

homicidal?

like having a drink?

isolated and alone? (about which: redundant)

exposed and vulnerable? (about which: ditto)

etc., etc. These questions had to be answered on a scale of 1 to 10, where 1 is "reaction not present" and 10 is "reaction felt most intensely," which scale I asked the Phil-bot to repeat at the end of every single question, only to respond 5.5 each time, because there is no middle number on a 1-to-10 scale, which is just, you know, *stupid*.

"Okay then," the Phil-bot said when he'd completed his suicidality checklist. He tore the top sheet off the pad, which had nothing written on it besides my name, and put it in an empty manila folder, which also had my name on it, although in this case it had been typed onto a label and stuck to the folder's tab, which made it seem more official. He handed me a bumper sticker that said "MY SON IS ON THE HONOR ROLL," which is kind of ironic if you think about it, since the whole reason I'd been called into his office was because my dad had gotten a DUI and lost his license.

"If you ever need to talk . . ."

"I need to talk every day," I said, which put a bright, eager smile in the middle of the Phil-bot's pudgy face. "Just like anyone else who wants to, you know, *say something*."

The Phil-bot's jowls fell so far he looked like a basset hound in a bowtie. I almost felt sorry for him, but I told myself that's how they get you. As he pulled open his door, he glanced at his watch and said, "I'm afraid I've kept you past your bus. Do you have a way to get home?"

And there was Ian Abernathy, flirting with Mrs. Helicopter, the 125-year-old front secretary whose real name was Heliocopulate or something like that, but who had long since given up on getting anyone to say it right.

"Don't worry," Ian flashed Mrs. Helicopter his best James

Dean, then turned to the Phil-bot. "My mom's coming to pick me up. We'd be *honored* to drive Sprout

"Sprout? What are you writing?"

I looked up to see Mrs. M. in the doorway with a fresh pitcher of margaritas, and I flipped the page quickly. I pantomimed jogging in place, like a runner stopped at a red light.

"Nothing," I said. "Just keeping my muscles warm."

Mrs. Miller's time trials often involved leaving something out, like that exercise with the sunset she'd had me do the first day, where I couldn't mention why the husband was sad. "Less is more," she said. "Necessity is the mother of invention." One week I wasn't allowed to use any form of the verb *to be*, which was bad enough, but the next week I wasn't allowed to use the letter *e*. Let me tell you, I came pretty close to having a drink that day. Then sometimes I had to focus on some specific thing or another. Mrs. Miller was big on all five senses, but especially smells. I knew something was up that day, because she was wearing an especially strong perfume. My dad only wears cologne when he's trying to cover up the fact that he's drunk, so I assumed that was the case here, until she said, "Describe everything you smell in this car." Just to make her blush, all I wrote was: "Did you eat onions for lunch?"

And then other times she just let me freestyle. She'd press the button on her stopwatch (did I mention she had a stopwatch? she had a stopwatch) and off I'd go:

> At twelve, Ruthie was too young for a license,
> but that didn't stop her from driving wherever she
> wanted to go. With a little lipstick, she looked at

least sixteen. With a lot of lipstick—which is what she usually wore, along with a lot of eyeliner and enough eye shadow to keep Revlon's quarterly profits in the black—she looked like my mother, or maybe just the <u>Demoiselles d'Avignon</u>.

She drove her mom's hand-me-down BMW. The silver convertible emerged from the leafy tunnel of our driveway like a minnow jumping from a pond— Carey Pond, let's say, in Carey Park, on the southern edge of Hutchinson, which is where she took me to smoke cigarettes ("nature's natural appetite suppressant," she told me, which, as far as redundancies go, verges on <u>brilliant</u>).

"See, this is what I don't get." She stood on a fallen elm trunk admiring her reflection in the scummy water, took a drag and held the smoke in her mouth (she hadn't figured out how to inhale yet), then blew it out with a long sigh, peeking to see if I could tell she was faking. "This is what I don't get," she said again. "On the one hand, you have this incredible singer with this like in<u>cred</u>ible voice and this look no one has ever seen before, a junk-store carnival nymph whose first record sells fifteen million copies and produces four number ones. And on the other hand you have this grade-B bimbo with a voice like a parrot dying from throat cancer, who thinks wearing fishnet on your chest instead of your legs is somehow radical fashion, and whose first album, let's face it, pretty much disappears thanks to the fact that one: it was basically gay disco, which, I mean, nothing against gays or disco but gay plus disco equals, you know, <u>yuck</u>, and two: the videos featured routines that were half spastic imitations of modern dance and half crotch-grabbing. And so whatever, <u>this</u> is what I don't get: what I don't get is, why is it that the first girl's career ends up tanking and the second girl goes on to become the biggest-selling female recording artist in history, picking up a fake English accent, a Kabbalah addiction, and a Malawian orphan along the way? I mean, I don't get that. Do you?"

"Your cigarette went out." (Well, what would <u>you</u> have said?)

"<u>Madonna</u>," Ruth Wilcox said. "<u>Duh</u>. And Cyndi <u>Lauper</u>. I thought you were from New <u>York City</u>."

"I'm from Long Island, which, culturally speaking, is about as far from New York City as Malawi. And your cigarette really <u>did</u> go out."

"Oh <u>crap</u>," Ruthie said, except she didn't say "crap" but the more common, albeit unprintable (in this context) synonym that she'd been carving into her desk the day I first saw her. (She'd carved the "crap" into my desk too, the year before. "Crap, darn, fudge. They're all so sixth-grade. Son of a biscuit-eater. What self-respecting preteen can say <u>that</u> with a straight face?") Now, after a couple of failed attempts to light her cigarette (which is very hard to do if you won't inhale), she threw it into the pond. I thought she'd finally accepted the fact that cigarette smoking is pretty much the grossest thing ever, but instead she nodded toward something behind me. I turned and saw a twentysomething guy walking down the looping path that bounds Carey Park and staring at us with that proprietary look of accusation that adults love to brandish at anyone under the age of eighteen. As soon as he was gone, Ruthie said,

"We'd better go. Just in case."

"In case what? He throws a phone at us?"

"Huh?"

"Nothing. In case . . . ?"

"My mom gets back from pilates at four. I better drive you home."

And so ended the first of Ruthie's unfathomable soliloquies, veered into and away from with all the predictability of a rabid skunk trying to cross a highway (I saw it once: trust me, the ending ain't pretty). Here's another:

"I'm named for a character in a book. I tried to read it but it was boring. It was turned into a movie and I tried to watch that, but it was boring too. So I figure maybe I should change my name. What do you think of Desireh?"

And another:

"I'm not anorexic. Anorexics have a distorted body image. I know I'm too thin. You have to be too thin if you want to make it in L.A. Besides, I eat eight hundred calories a day, which is considered a lot for people in places like Malawi. What if I called myself something British, like Fenella, or Hermione?"

And:

"You know how when some people get a piece of

bubble wrap in their hands they have to twist it till it pops? Yeah, I'm not one of those people. I have better things to do with my time. Ruby? But if I called myself Ruby I'd have to dye my hair red, and then, well, Ruby and Sprout, that'd be too much."

But my favorite had to be this one:

"Why is it that the closest word in English that rhymes with anarchy is menarche?"

"Monarchy—"

"Menarche." When I just stared at her blankly, she said, "You walk around clutching a dictionary to your stomach like a cheerleader trying to cover up the gift the captain of the football team gave her, look it up. Oh hell. Why don't I just give in and call myself Britney?"

Meanwhile, school:

On Long Island, I'd been anonymous. Just one of 2,567 students, not at the top of the heap, not at the bottom. Just a brown-haired piece of the middle. Take me out and nothing would collapse. No one would notice.

But in Kansas, I was marked out. The new kid. The stranger. The boy with the weird accent. The boy with the weird dad, and no mom. From the moment Madison Pagels tripped me as I walked down the aisle of the school bus at 7:07 A.M. to the moment Madison's best friend Chelsea Monroe tripped me as I walked up the aisle at 3:56 P.M., and all the spitballs, hair-pulling, snickers, catcalls, "Kick me" notes, and fist-fights in between, the school day pretty much seemed to revolve around me. After one rock-solid week of this, I decided that if there had to be a target on my head, I'd paint it there myself.

When Ruthie honked in the driveway ("Daniel, your friend's mom is here!") I found my dad planting some vines to fill in a patchy spot in the back of the house, and asked him for some cash.

"How much do you need?"

"How about a hundred?"

"How 'bout twenty?"

"How 'bout fifty?"

"How 'bout twenty?"

"How 'bout twenty-five?"

"How 'bout twenty?"

"Really, I just need ten."

"Well, here's twenty. If you go by Wal-Mart, buy a couple of plates. You seem to've broken them all."

"Gosh, thanks, Dad. That's more than I asked for. You're the best."

A few days earlier, my dad had shown up on the lawn of some house in Hutch in the middle of the night and interrogated it for six hours—Why did you kill my wife? Why did you destroy my life? Why are you the cause of so much strife?—which made more sense when Ruthie drove me by the house and I saw that it was a one-story ranch made out of pale brown bricks topped by asphalt shingles. Our house on Long Island had been made of pale brown bricks. Its asphalt-shingled single story had barely made an impression against the sky. As I looked at its Kansas doppelganger, I vowed that I would be more than a

66

single story. I would sprout a second story, a third if I wanted, a fourth. I would grow like a beanstalk or a skyscraper. Like the Tower of Babel, I would tell my stories all the way to heaven.

I looked over at the colored streaks in Ruthie's hair.

"Where'd you get your dye?"

"Duh. This is Hutch. Wal-Mart."

"Let's go there. I need to buy some plates."

On Monday, when I walked down the aisle of the bus, I was greeted by silence, followed by titters. Then more silence. Then more titters. And then a shockingly long wave of silence, so complete that only the squeaking springs of the bus could be heard, and then scattered snorts that could've been backfires.

And then silence.

Blessed, blessed silence.

Of course, not everything goes according to plan. What I mean is, when I walked into Wal-Mart, I meant to buy red dye. Aggressive, but also clownlike. The color of anger, but also love. But my hand, or my unconscious, betrayed me. Who knows? Maybe it was just my dad's vines.

What I mean is, I reached for the red bottle, but I grabbed the green instead.

I put my pen down. I was pretty sure Mrs. Miller should've told me to stop about an hour ago, and I looked up to find her dozing in her chair. I took the margarita glasses and pitcher in the kitchen and washed them, filched a coffee cup from the cabinet and dropped it in the cargo pocket of my shorts, then woke her. I drove her car back to my house while she sat in the passenger seat and read over what I'd written, yawning occasionally, although I hoped this had more to do with the alcohol than my story. When she finished she looked up blearily at my head. Nodded one of those A-ha! nods; then:

"And 'Sprout'?"

From the corner of my eye I saw her curl the index fingers of her hands towards each other, like one earthworm popping up out of the ground and saying "Hi!" to another. "How you doin'? I'm an earthworm! Are you an earthworm too? Great!" If I'd felt confident enough in my driving skills to look away from the road, I probly would've realized she was just making quotation marks like she had at the beginning of summer ("Would you like a 'drink'?") but what can I tell you? I'm an even worse driver than Mrs. Miller.

"Sprout?" she said again. "Still there?"

I shook myself. "Ian."

"Abernathy?"

" 'Der, hey, Sprout!' "

Mrs. M. was silent for a long time. So long that I thought maybe she'd fallen asleep again.

"That's it?" she said finally. " 'Der, hey, Sprout'?"

"Like I said, I wanted Lawnboy." I shrugged. "You were only married to Mr. Miller for a year. Sometimes you don't know what's going to stick."

Mrs. Miller laughed quietly. "You should write that one down." She tapped the notebook in her lap. "You should write it all down," as if maybe the words in her hand weren't writing. "This is good stuff, Daniel. It's all good. Now all we have to do is whittle it down to six pages."

"You said eight—"

"Eight *tops*. And we'll have a winner on our hands."

"Yeah, about that."

My voice must have sounded tense, because Mrs. Miller turned in her seat. I suppose this is a good time to mention that it was the end of summer, and she'd already voiced worries about what was going to happen when school started the week after next. ("That Mrs. *Whittaker*. She could undo everything we've worked on with a single one of her compare-'n'-contrast essays.")

"Ye–es?" She broke the word in half like a pencil snapping between nervous fingers. Her eyes bored into the side of my head, as if she wanted to read my thoughts before I spoke them. I kept my own eyes on the road, but her stare was so hot it was like sitting too close to an open fire.

"I'm thinking I don't want to write about moving from Long Island. My mom, my dad, all that. New school, new friends blah blah blah blah." I tried to keep my voice light, but it squeaked on the last blah. Note to self: next time stop at three blahs.

"Look, Daniel—"

"It's Sprout, Mrs. Miller. Really. *Sprout*."

"I'm sorry, Spro—"

"And if I *do* do this thing," I said, talking over her, "I want to write about being gay."

There was a long silence, and then I giggled.

"I said do-do."

Rural gay boy, party of one

Betcha didn't see that coming, did ya? Neither did Mrs. Miller, and she actually knows me. Anyway, you know this much: being gay isn't my secret.

Bet you forgot about the secret too, didn't you?

Don't worry. I won't.

"You're . . . ?" Mrs. Miller didn't seem to know any hand gestures that would indicate homosexuality. I could've shown her a few, but I didn't think it would help the situation, and besides, I had my hands glued to the wheel in the approved 10-2 position.

"Gay."

"Gay?" She repeated the word as if she'd never said it before, and who knows, maybe she hadn't. She rubbed her head as if maybe the word had given her a headache, rather than the mojitoritas (she'd kind of combined two different recipes that day).

"Yup," I said. "Gay. Gay gay *gay*."

My voice squeaked on the fourth *gay*.

A year earlier, when my dad found a couple of gay sites in the cache of Internet Explorer, he threw my dictionary into our PC. I think he thought I'd learned how to be gay from the web, although the truth is I'd only looked at those kinds of sites after I was pretty sure about myself, and then only once or twice, or maybe three or four times (hey, I had to be sure). The fact is, they kind of weirded me out. The old guys were so muscly they looked more like statues than people, whereas the kids around my age were showing off their bodies with leering expressions that made me want to put on padded coveralls and zip myself into a sleeping bag. The only problem was, once I was in the sleeping bag, all I could think about was their bodies.

After my dad broke the computer—and knocked back a couple of shots—he went for a walk in the woods, leaving me to pry the dictionary out of the broken monitor and vacuum up the glass. The cover had half ripped away from the pages but it was otherwise okay. Score one for paper in the ongoing battle between books and computers.

Computer. One who computes.

What can I say, it was an old dictionary.

By the time he came back I was learning the definition of a nice set of p-words. *Produce, profane, profess.* It wasn't as exciting as the web, but you make do with what you have.

My dad wavered in the doorway like a tree in a heavy wind, an image reinforced by a couple of vines he'd dug up and curled around his upper body like a beauty queen's sash. Unfortunately for him, the vines were itch ivy—he never could remember what they looked like—which meant he was going to suffer more than I was.

"I should have seen it coming. Absent mother, poor role model for a father. I apologize, son. I should have found another maternal figure for you."

"I thought it was supposed to be too *much* mothering that made you gay."

71

My dad's eyes crossed as he tried to figure this out, and I thought he was going to fall down. The leaves shimmered as he shook, and he scratched at his neck. Finally he blinked hard, twice, and said,

"Whatever. Toss me a beer, would you?"

I looked at the dictionary, the TV, back at him. "That's it? A beer?"

"Oh, okay, two."

"Dad."

He didn't meet my eyes. "Hey. You're a fag. I'm a drunk. Nobody's perfect." The leaves shook as he scratched the first red speck of an itch-ivy rash. "That was mean. You're gay. I'm an alcoholic. Now toss me a beer so I can go get these in the ground."

I aimed for my dad's head, but you know drunks: they can't jerk the wheel of their car to avoid hitting a four-year-old running into the street, but they *never* drop a cold one.

Just before he went outside, my dad said, "Just promise me you won't tell anyone. I don't want to have to identify my son at the morgue."

"Does anyone else know . . . ?" Again Mrs. Miller's voice trailed off.

"That I'm gay?"

"That you're gay," she repeated, or, I dunno, echoed, since she didn't really repeat what I said. Paraphrased.

I wasn't forcing Mrs. Miller to say it just to be mean, by the way. The more you say something, the less strange it seems. The first time Mrs. Miller said the word "gay," it sounded like she was describing, I dunno, a new species of elephant, with six legs and pink and green polka dots, which for some reason was window shopping on Main Street. By the second or third time she could've been describing something much less weird, a deer with only one antler growing out the side of its head, say, or a high school writing coach who likes to get a little toasted while conducting time trials with her best-and-brightest.

"Sprout? You're kind of drifting over the center line."

I nudged the wheel to the right.

"Ruthie knows. And my dad."

"Ruthie." Mrs. Miller nodded. "Your dad. Mr. Sprout." She forced a laugh. "And, um . . . ?" There was that ellipsis again, the vague hand gesture.

"Ye-es?"

"Well, uh. I mean, have you, you know? Acted on your, um, *feelings*?"

Think about that for a minute. Do you honestly believe Mrs. M. would ever ask, oh, let's say Ian Abernathy, if he was having sex? *So, Ian, I hear you've joined the ranks of card-carrying het-erosexuals. Gotten any action yet?* Yeah, me neither. So, in keeping with my "Ask a stupid question" philosophy, all I did was look over and run a hand through my dark green hair.

"Ruthie's the actress, Mrs. M."

"Eyes front, Sprout." Mrs. Miller summoned the kind of instant authority that only someone who's been administering pop quizzes for the past fifteen years can muster. "Both hands on the wheel." I turned back to the road and waited for her to say something else, but all she did was repeat my name. "Sprout," she said. Only this time it came out the way she'd said *gay*. Like the word had lost all meaning. "Sprout Sprout *Sprout*." She looked down at the pages in her hand, then pushed them away as if they, too, had lost meaning. Lost worth. After a moment, though, she took one of those deep calming breaths and twisted in her seat to face me.

"Look, Sprout, I know where you're coming from. You see your friends dating and engaging in extracurricular activities my colleagues and I pretend we don't know about, and you want some of that for yourself."

My mind flashed on Stacy McTaverty and Troy Bellows. Troy's locker was close to mine, so I was treated several times a day to the sight of his tongue probing Stacy's mouth, apparently in search of a lost piece of gum or, I dunno, her tonsils, while his hands squeezed her breasts so tightly you'd've thought it was a football he was about to throw down a field. I didn't want anything *like* that.

"Love is a special experience," Mrs. Miller continued, "and everyone deserves their shot at it."

I knew Mrs. Miller didn't think that what was going on between Troy and Stacy had anything to do with love, but all I said was, "Are we talking about coming out at school, or writing about it?"

Long, frustrated sigh; vague hand gesture. Then: "I just don't want you to get sidetracked, Sprout. Kids who come out in school have a hard time. They get singled out. Their whole life becomes about being gay. By keeping your private life to yourself you can focus on your future. Your grades, getting into a good college, building a career. And this contest is part of that. I would hate to see you overlooked because some of the more conservative judges were incapable of seeing past your choice of subject matter to your talent." And then, as if I'd protested, she threw in, "This is Kansas, Sprout. *Kansas*."

Well. Even I knew what she meant that time.

Kansas: the first state to officially mandate the teaching of Intelligent Design—i.e., Creationism—i.e., my God made the world, not yours.

Kansas: the home of Rev. Fred Phelps, the founder of God-HatesFags.com and the guy who crashed Matthew Shepherd's funeral with signs proclaiming that he got what was coming to him.

Kansas: a pioneer of Defense of Marriage legislation. I.e., Straights Only. I.e., gays can design the wedding dress, photograph the ceremony, and cater the reception, but they can't actually get hitched themselves. Kansas didn't just pass a law to this effect: it amended the state *constitution*. Kansas was also the very first state to write a law making homosexual activity illegal, although that law was struck down by the Supreme Court in 2003.

Oh, and Kansas: the first—and, to this day, the only—state in the country to make it illegal for two kids to have sex with each other. Yup, straight or gay, if they catch you having sex in Kansas before you turn sixteen, you're going to jail.

Kansas.

This isn't to say homophobia was, like, *rampant* at my school, or anything like that. I was less worried about roaming bands of gay bashers than some testosterone-charged football player feeling guilty about his fascination with, I dunno, Mario Lopez—not the bubbly Mario Lopez of *Saved by the Bell*, or the can't-keep-his-hands-off-her-butt Mario Lopez of *Dancing with the Stars*, but the bubble-butted Mario Lopez of the Greg Louganis biopic. ("Gee, Mom, I don't know *how* this could've ended up on our Netflix queue. I must've clicked the wrong thing.") And it wasn't like coming out was going to help me find a boyfriend. Even though statistics say there should be fifty budding homosexuals enrolled at BHS, half of whom are male, they don't say *who* those other twenty-four boys are, let alone when they're going to work their issues out (statistics do say that only 34% of Kansas high school students are proficient in math, however, so I'm not holding my breath). And, you know, I wasn't even sure what *boyfriend* meant, at least not in this context. I tried looking it up in my dictionary, but it wasn't a lot of help. *A girl's or a woman's preferred male companion.* That seemed to mean I could *be* a boyfriend, but I couldn't *have* one.

Then again, it was an old dictionary, and this is the age of the internet, right? I mean, it wasn't exactly hard for me to realize what all those fantasies of Ewan McGregor were about (that would be the skinny jeans-wearing Ewan McGregor of *Trainspotting* and not the—ick!—bearded, bathrobe-wearing Ewan McGregor of the *Star Wars* movies, let alone the cheeseball-in-spandex Ewan McGregor of lameoid action flicks like *The Island* and *Stormbreaker*). All of which is another way of saying that coming out to myself wasn't all that different to staying in the closet. I was still alone. Still living in my dad's freakshow house and still going to my boondocks school. In a way, I was just like Mrs. Miller. I had a name for myself, for what I was. I just had no idea what it meant.

By the time we pulled into my driveway, Mrs. Miller was so agitated that she hopped out of the car and marched straight for the door. Well, actually she marched straight for the house, but then she had to walk around it three times before she could actually find the door in the middle of all the vines. But she managed to make it look very intentional.

She raised her hand to knock. Before she could the door swept open, and there was my dad.

Mr. Sprout.

Apparently he'd seen Mrs. M. walking around the house, and used the time to pour her a drink, because he was holding one in each hand. Either that or he was two-fisting it that day, which was an equally plausible explanation (although it didn't explain how he managed to turn the doorknob).

"Iced tea?"

"Long Island?"

I flashbacked (flashed back?) to the first day of seventh grade ("Long Guyland?") but I learned later that Mrs. Miller was referring to the drink and not my dad.

"But of course," he said.

"No thanks, I'll pass." Mrs. Miller whirled suddenly. She pointed at her car, only to discover it was empty. A look of confusion clouded her not-quite-sober face.

I cleared my throat. "Over here," I said from the shade of one of my dad's stumps. What, did you think I was just going to wait in the car?

Mrs. Miller's finger whirled in my direction even as her head turned back towards my dad. Since this had her hand going in one direction and her head going in the other, she looked a little like Linda Blair in *The Exorcist*.

"Are you *aware* . . . ?" she began, then trailed off, as if she'd forgotten how to say the word yet again.

"Gay," I called from the shadow of the stump. That's me, always eager to help.

Before my dad trashed the computer, I'd read a few stories online about what happened when kids my age told their parents they were gay. It wasn't all bad. We were well into the new millennium, after all. *Will and Grace* had been in syndication for almost a decade. There'd been *Brokeback Mountain* and

Queer Eye, and it was more or less a requirement since the second season of *The Real World* that every reality show had to have at least one gay guy in it. Even the governor of New Jersey turned out to be gay, and it seemed like some senator or rock star was getting caught *in flagrante delicto* every six months or so. But those were all adults. Things were different for kids, and they were especially different for kids in places like Kansas. There were still groundings-for-life, trips to shrinks, cult deprogrammers, and Christian re-education camps, not to mention a surprising number of beatings and, in some ways the worst of it all, simple rejection. Teenagers kicked out, locks changed, phone numbers too. Refusals to acknowledge the son or daughter when the rest of the family passed him or her on the street. Given the alternatives, I thought my dad and I handled it pretty well.

That didn't mean he liked talking about it.

That didn't mean *I* liked talking about it either.

My dad looked down at the drinks in his hands, as if they might have the answer he was looking for (he often looked at drinks this way, so that's not saying much). Finally he poured one drink into the other, set the empty glass on the table beside the front door (which table was really the seat of a chair, but whatever) and put his newly freed hand on Mrs. Miller's shoulder.

"Before I get too drunk to walk," he said, "I'd like to show you my collection."

And, steering her rather more effectively than either Mrs. Miller or myself could steer a car, he led her into his stumps.

Mrs. Miller's hair fell down her back like a frothy blonde waterfall. As I watched, my dad's hand disappeared beneath it, as if Mrs. Miller was a puppet he was taking over—as if, instead of talking to her, he was going to make her say the things that couldn't come out of his own mouth. Of course, I hoped he would say something like, "I support my son no matter what his lifestyle is," but I was afraid it was going to be more like "Maybe you and I can figure out how to fix him together," so I went in the house instead. I kept my eye on them though. Watched through one window, then another, just as I'd watched my dad the day we first moved here. Living room, my bedroom, bathroom (I had to climb into the shower stall to keep them in my line of vision) then my dad's room, where I kind of got distracted from what was going on outside by what was inside. The bed was unmade, the carpet hidden beneath a trampled layer of old clothes. Books and glasses in a roughly 1:3 ratio covered the dresser, and flies staggered drunkenly between the sticky bottoms of the latter.

As I looked around the mess, I found myself wondering what Mrs. M. would think if she saw it. Take his pegboard. It covered one whole wall of the room. It was that nice darkbrown pegboard color, its soft, fuzzy-edged holes advancing left, right, diagonally from floor to ceiling and corner to corner. On this wall hung a tortoise-shell shoehorn with the address and phone number of

ick's

arber

hop

printed in letters that had been worn away by who knows how many heels; a white rabbit's foot keychain; an uninflated former helium balloon, yellow and wrinkled like a scrotum, that said

HAPPY

BIRTHDAY

IRENE!

when it was blown up; a burgundy graduation tassel (not my dad's); six keys (three brass, two silver, one translucent green plastic); a sand dollar with a hole in the center; the top half of a crow's skull; a plastic American flag about the size of a Dairy Queen napkin; a Dairy Queen napkin; three feathers (one is definitely a peacock's and one is probly a crow's, and I think the last one's from the ostrich farm on 69th); a policeman's badge (#26703) from one of the Greenvilles in one of the states in this great nation of ours; a SIM card with

BOB

magic-markered onto it; a coupon for $5 off an oil change the next time my dad filled up* at the Kwik Shop (the * indicating that the fill-up had to be with Premium Unleaded); the scissors my dad had used to cut the coupon out of the *PennySaver*; the *PennySaver*; a long reddish-brown chili pepper; a Polaroid so sun-bleached that all you could see was a bluish-black circle that could've been an eye, or an oil slick, or the opening at the end of a gun; and then, all the way down on the floor, so that you had to lie down in the narrow space between the bed and the wall to read it, seven fortune-cookie fortunes that had been stacked on top of each other so that they read:

He who throws dirt is always losing ground.

Build your house on solid rock, not shifting sand.

Judge not according to appearances.

Failure is the mother of success.

Your mother has the answers you need.

The truth is slippery, but lies are sticky.

THAT WASN'T CHICKEN!

This pegboard had always seemed like a pretty accurate diagram of my dad's life. Kind of random, kind of boring, kind of crazy. But random and boring and crazy in a very specific kind of way, and so describing exactly how limited and repetitive his life was. But what would it look like to someone else?

Would it look like he couldn't tell the difference between junk and things worth holding on to? Or would it look like nothing at all? Like my dad wasn't really a person anymore? Wasn't capable of making his presence felt in the real world, but could only scavenge from it, let the world know how he felt through tattered, second-rate symbols and the occasional drunken outburst? And why was I thinking about all of this now, when all I'd ever thought about was getting cash out of him, or the car? Why all the sudden did I want him to be, I dunno, *happy*?

The next thing I heard was the sound of the front door opening. There was one of those giggles followed by one of those expressions ("Don't I just know it!") that made me wonder what my dad had just said. By the time I got to the living room Mrs. Miller had sat down in the chair beside the front door. There was a lopsided but still sort of triumphant grin on her face, and at first I thought it was related to the leafy garland my dad had wrapped around her forehead (not itch ivy, phew) but then I realized it was just her body that was lopsided, the left side being slightly higher than the right. My dad stood half beside, half behind her chair, looking at the top of her head so intently that I wondered if maybe he was checking for ticks.

"You're sitting on a glass," I said to Mrs. Miller.

For a moment Mrs. Miller looked like she was trying to figure out what I meant, like maybe "sitting on a glass" was some new teenage slang she hadn't heard, possibly a dis. Then, realizing I was speaking literally, she reached her left hand under her left thigh and came up with the glass my dad had set there when he first opened the door.

"Why, so I am." She looked around for something to set it on, but basically all there was was the loveseat and the floor.

After a moment she handed it to my dad. It seemed to me we'd gone full circle, save that now the two glasses in my dad's hands were empty instead of full, and we were all trapped inside the way too cramped confines of our living room.

"Well, I'm pretty sure I'm not drunk enough for what's about to happen. Excuse me, Janet, while I freshen up our drinks."

I'm not really sure why my dad said "Excuse me," since the bottle was on the dining room table, which is also the kitchen counter, which is also the end table for the loveseat, which was all of five feet away from where he was standing, but Mrs. Miller waited until he was symbolically out of the room before she said, "So. Sprout. You really want to write about being gay?"

Her voice had calmed down, but it wasn't the calmness of alcohol, which usually made her confused. She'd worked something out while she walked around with my dad. She'd come up with—*cue scary organ music*—A Plan.

"Why don't you get him to write about all the time he spends in the woods?" my dad suggested from the kitchen, which is to say, from the other side of the room, which is to say, from about five feet away. "Or, you know, that *hair*."

"It's not really a good story," Mrs. Miller said without taking her garland-shaded eyes from me. "Sprout wants to write about something more . . . interesting, doesn't he?"

It's one thing to talk about something with your writing coach when you're alone in a car and you don't have to look her in the eye because you're driving. It's another to talk about it when she's sitting in your living room and your dad's five feet away pouring her a Long Island Iced Tea.

"C'mon," my dad said, walking over to the chair with the

drinks. "Four years, the same color. One whole quarter of his life. You gotta admit, that's pretty interesting."

Mrs. Miller touched one of the leaves in her own hair, as if she could feel the green. "At first, when I saw the vines on the house, I thought he was trying to express a connection with you. But now I think it's just his way of indicating that he feels different on the inside. But, since he doesn't have any other way of expressing it, he has to find a way to let the world know what's going on. It would be different if he'd actually *done something*. But you haven't yet—or have you, Sprout?"

If you could take that squirmy feeling you get when you have to pee at a packed movie theater, but you're sitting in the middle of a row and plus on top of that the pseudo–teenaged lovers on screen are just about to either do it or else get done by the knife- or axe- or flamethrower-wielding bad guy, and then multiply that feeling times, I don't know, a *supernova*, then you'll just sort of be at the lower edge of the please-God-let-me-melt-into-the-ground panic this conversation was giving me. I couldn't even nod this time, let alone speak. Mrs. M. took my motionless-ness as a yes, rather than assuming I'd been turned into a statue, which is what *I* was thinking had maybe happened. She took the drink my dad gave her, then plucked one of the leaves from her garland and put it stem first in the glass like a garnish.

"So, what?" my dad said. "You're saying that when he starts getting cornholed he'll stop dying his hair?"

"You don't know," Mrs. Miller said in the lightest, most reasonable voice you can imagine. "*He* could be the one doing the cornholing."

I was starting to wonder if maybe it was true. Maybe homosexuality really was a sin, and these weren't my dad and my writing coach, but a pair of demons masquerading as them, and just getting started on a torture that was going to last for the rest of eternity.

My dad shook his head. "I thought the young ones were always the ones who, you know—"

"I think the term is 'passive,' Bob. Or 'receptive.'"

Great. Before she couldn't say the word "gay." Now that my dad was around, she knew *all* the vocabulary. Although I bet none of these definitions was in my dictionary.

"And anyway," she continued, "what if there are *two* young guys? Someone has to be, how do they put it, Sprout? The top? And someone has to be—"

"I HAD SEX WITH IAN ABERNATHY!"

My dad's drink slipped out of his fingers and fell to the floor. Short fall; shag carpet; the glass already drained; nothing broken or spilled: i.e., as a reaction, it was pretty superfluous. I, by contrast, took the two steps to the square of linoleum that marked the kitchen, took the coffee cup I'd filched from Mrs. Miller's cabinet out of my pocket, and smashed it to the floor.

Mrs. Miller looked at the shards for a moment, then brought her own glass to her lips, sipped, and returned it to her lap.

"I'm guessing the coffee cup was supposed to be a distraction."

"Did it work?" I said hopefully. And then: "Um, yeah," I answered myself. "I didn't think so."

There'll be no dirty parts in this chapter, so don't get your hopes (or anything else!) up

It happened the first week of seventh grade.

Oh, and then it happened again in eighth grade, sometime during track season.

Then three times in ninth grade.

In tenth grade . . . well, in tenth grade it became kind of a thing. Not a regular thing, but not really an irregular thing. Not after four years. By then we'd discovered the janitors' closet on the first floor, between the cafeteria and the gym. The door had a lock on the inside, and Ian came up with the plan of smoking half a cigarette before we got started, so that even if we were discovered we could pretend we'd just gone there to smoke, and then of course afterwards we had all the supplies we needed to clean up any trace of what we'd done. We never did get caught, although one time Ian got busted for bringing cigarettes to school, and was given detention, which is pretty damn funny if you think about it.

The cigarette should've been my first clue, I guess. That Ian was thinking about what we were doing, even when we weren't doing it.

. . .

It seemed like he followed me everywhere that first week of seventh grade. Part of that had to do with the fact that our lockers were about six doors away from each other, and part of it had to do with the fact that he followed me everywhere that first week. Every time I turned around, there was Ian's Yankees cap and Josh Hartnett smile.

"Hey, newbie!"

"Yo, Long Guyland!"

"Der, what's up, doof-butt!"

We only had two classes together. One of them was first-period homeroom, where Miss Tunie did a pretty good job of keeping him under wraps. The other, however, was gym. Depending on your attitude, or whether your name was Ian Abernathy, Mr. Balzer was either the dream gym teacher or a total nightmare.

"Girls, I see that many of you have begun developing. I want to let you know, first of all, that a sports bra is *not* acceptable outerwear, and secondly, that having your period is *never* an excuse for sitting out class."

"Mr. Bradford, I don't know how they do things in New York City, but in Kansas we wear the proper attire to gym class. Proper attire does not mean blue jeans and canvas loafers—especially not ones with writing on them. Now drop and give me ten."

"Yo, Abernathy, wassup my man! Are we gonna take Nickerson this year or *what*?"

Mr. Balzer wasn't really the problem however. I actually liked gym. I used to like team sports, but when enough people aim a basketball at your face (or a football at your crotch) the shine kind of goes off them. That's why I took up cross country. When Mr. Balzer—who also coached the track team—saw

86

how fast I ran the mile, he pretty much let me alone, and nobody else could catch me. But no matter how fast I ran, how far, I always ended up back in the locker room forty-five minutes later. Let's face it, the only thing worse than being teased with your clothes on is being teased when you're naked, and the only thing worse than being teased when you're naked is being teased when you're naked and in a communal shower surrounded by fifteen other naked guys.

"Hey, newbie, I think I dropped my soap. Why don't you pick it up for me?"

"Yo, Long Guyland, my good friend Beanpole Overholser dropped his soap. Why don't you pick it up for him?"

"Der, doof-butt, looks like we all dropped our soap. Why don't you crawl around the floor on your hands and knees and pick up *every single bar*? Don't mind that yellow streak. That's just some Gatorade I drank, oh, about a half hour ago."

But as bad as all the public harassment and humiliation was, it wasn't nearly as bad as when Ian got me alone.

It happened that first Friday of seventh grade. Ian had gotten detention from Miss Tunie for picking on me, and I had gotten detention from Mr. Balzer for having the first three letters of the most unacceptable of all four-letter-words written on my left shoe. The rule at Buhler was that at least one of the detention-giving teachers had to stay with the detention-given students. Mr. Balzer sauntered into Miss Tunie's classroom about ten minutes after school let out.

"Yo, Abernathy, wassup?"

Like gym teachers the world over, Mr. Balzer liked to walk around the halls in his shorts, as if to rub in the fact that all the other male inhabitants of BGS, students and teachers alike, had to wear long pants, even though the school didn't have any air conditioning and September temperatures often broke the 100-degree mark. Now he hooked one of his bare, tanned, sweaty legs over the edge of the desk where Miss Tunie was impatiently tapping her nails, his shorts riding up and exposing an inch of milk-white thigh.

"Hey, Brenda. So. How shall we work this out?"

Miss Tunie rolled her eyes and reached into her purse, brought out her car keys and a quarter. "Let's flip for it, Norberto. Heads I win, tails you lose."

"Sounds like a deal," Mr. Balzer said. "Tails."

Miss Tunie flipped the coin and let it roll on the floor. While Mr. Balzer scampered after it like a puppy, she walked towards the door.

"Tails!"

"Huh," Miss Tunie said. "You lose." And she was gone.

Mr. Balzer spent about five minutes trying to figure out what happened, then shrugged it off.

"Yo, Abernathy. They're waxing the gym floor today, and if I don't supervise they do a half-assed job." He winked at Ian. "If I catch you trying to sneak out before 4:35, I'll tie your butt to the chair with a jump rope."

And then he was gone too.

I looked out the window. The last buses were pulling out of the parking lot. The sound of badly tuned diesel engines faded like distant thunder, giving way to the electrical whine of cicadas as they shrieked their way through their twenty-four-hour existence. I wondered how I was going to get home. My dad hadn't bothered to put in a phone yet, and we lived five miles away.

A more mechanical drone added itself to the cicadas' whine, and I felt a faint vibration through the soles of my now-banned

Vans. I was hoping it might turn out to be an earthquake, but then I realized it was just the buffers that were putting the wax on the gym floor.

For a while that's all there was, the cicadas and the buffers and the inescapable tingle of dust in my nostrils, and then I heard a quiet thump. Even though I knew I shouldn't have, I looked over at Ian. Miss Tunie had seated us a few rows apart in those dumb grade-school desk-chair combos where the chair and the desk are welded together so you can't ever get comfortable, since you can neither scoot your seat in nor shove it back. Now I saw that Ian had stood up a couple of inches without getting out of his chair, so that the desk part rested on top of his thighs and the four rubber-soled legs floated just off the floor. Scooching around, and making sure to hit as many desks as possible, he crabwalked his way across the room until his desk was right in front of mine, where he set it down with a final ominous clunk.

"Don't mind me, newbie, I just have to do my exercises." He pushed his Yankees cap back on his head, as if it might get in the way, and then he started making big exaggerated kissy faces at me, pursing his lips so that he looked like Mick Jagger after a fresh round of collagen, then opening his mouth so wide that he looked like the stretchy faces from that old Soundgarden video, or maybe Terrance and Phillip on *South Park*. In between pursing and stretching, he would stick out his tongue and waggle it up and down and back and forth like he was trying to pick an imaginary lock.

Of course, what I should've said was, "What're you doing, *practicing*?" But instead what I said was, "What're you doing, *practicing*?" which might look like the same thing, but it's not. Not when *your* voice cracks, and *you're* the one who ends up blushing.

89

"Uh," Ian said, which I think was supposed to be "Yup," although maybe it was "Duh." It's hard to make consonants with your tongue sticking three inches out of your mouth. "Uh ay-ees *uv* ih." I'm guessing that was "The ladies love it," but you'd have to ask Ian to be sure.

I tried watching the clock over Ian's head, but how long can you stare at a clock—especially one that doesn't have a second hand? I tried looking out the window, but it was Kansas, so there wasn't much to look at. And plus Ian added slobbery noises to the weird facial movements. I tried staring him down, but Ian turned out to be a master at staring contests. Before I knew it my eyes had slipped to his spittle-bordered lips. He must've been getting tired, because his mouth wasn't opening quite as wide now, and the lip pursing wasn't quite as exaggerated and gross. It looked less like a cartoon, I mean, more like he was yawning, or maybe hungry. Hungry, and blowing kisses at me.

The only thing worse than saying something that makes you blush is blushing when nobody's said anything, because then only your *thoughts* can be the cause. Ian suddenly stopped making kissy faces and squinted at me from beneath his Yankees cap.

"What?"

"What?" I parroted, but I could still feel the heat migrating across my cheeks, crackling and popping like tiny electrical charges.

Ian stood up out of his chair and hooked a leg over my desk just as Mr. Balzer had with Miss Tunie's. He was wearing pants, though, not shorts, and the denim pulled tight around his thigh from the knee all the way up to the top of the well-worn inseam. He leaned over my desk and used the bill of his Yankees cap to tap me on the forehead, twice.

90

"*What?*"

"Nothing," I said. Except, since I still had my Long Island accent at that point, I heard myself say "Nuttin'," which only made me blush more.

"I think it's *sumpin'*," Ian hissed, doing a not-very-good imitation of my accent. "I think there are dirty little thoughts swirling around beneath all that wavy brown hair of yours, aren't there, *newbie*?"

I could hear the meanness in Ian's voice, but I could hear something else too. Curiosity. But not regular old garden-variety curiosity. No, this was something more. This was almost . . . *salacious.*

Curse that dictionary.

"Let's see if we can find out what's sprouting beneath that mama's boy haircut, a'ight newbie?" Before I knew it, Ian had wrapped me in a headlock with his right arm, was using his left knuckles to give me what used to be called an Indian burn in pre-P.C. days, and what is now usually called an Indian burn, because most twelve-year-olds don't really care if what they say is P.C. or not. I stumbled out of my chair, but because it was fastened to the stupid desk I ended up tripping and falling to my hands and knees, and this allowed Ian to straddle my waist as though we were playing piggyback, and, well, how can I phrase this so this book doesn't get banned not just from BHS, from every high school in America?

I felt something.

Felt something besides Ian's fist on the top of my head, I mean, which was burning into my scalp like a hair dryer blowing on one spot for way too long. Still, I tried to focus on that, so I wouldn't have to focus on that other thing. The thing that I was feeling on the small of my back, about two inches above my belt—assuming my belt was still where it was supposed to be, and hadn't slipped a few inches south. Ian too, seemed to direct all his attention on the Indian burn, as if he was afraid to pay attention to anything else that was happening, but at the same time his thighs had locked around my waist, and his hips started rocking back and forth as though I were a mechanical bull. "Yee-haw," he called out, "ride 'em, cowboy!" which, when you get right down to it, is possibly the most embarrassing part of the entire afternoon.

After what seemed like maybe the whole of recorded history, Ian suddenly relaxed his legs and arms and I fell to the floor. I landed on my hip, rolled over slightly, so I was facing him. The top of my head felt like it was on fire, but most of my attention was focused on that warm spot on my back, which was now cooling rapidly as it pressed against the cold, gritty, vibrating linoleum (the buffers, remember?). Ian was panting, and I was too, and when I looked up I saw that his face was every bit as red as mine felt. We stared at each other for a long time, as if waiting for someone to come and interrupt us. But no one came, which meant that we had to decide what to do on our own.

In the end gravity did the work. You've probly noticed by now that I have a hard time looking at one thing for a very long time, but have to keep shifting my focus from place to place. This was especially true of Ian's eyes, which were not so much asking me a question as just . . . asking. After a lifetime of silent pleading, my eyes finally fell away from his. Fell to his nose first, the nostrils flared and white-edged, and then to his mouth, slack and sucking in air, and then to his chin, his corded throat, the slanting lines of his collarbones coming together at the top of the hard, sweaty seam that ran all the way down his chest and stomach to his belt buckle, which had two words written on it: "Dodge" and "Ram."

What can I say? I chose the latter.

At some point I felt something soft encircle my head. At first I thought it was Ian's hands, and can I tell you something? That's when I knew I was gay. Because I wanted it to be Ian's hands. Wanted to feel the hands of the handsomest boy in school running through my light brown hair even as I labored at something that both of us knew the name of, but had never connected with real life. But then I realized that Ian had just slipped his cap on me, and even as the brim cast its shadow across my closed eyes (and nose, and cheeks, and mouth) I knew he'd put it on my head so that he wouldn't have to look at what we were doing either.

Then, later, when all I really wanted to do was disappear:

"How're you getting home?"

"I guess my dad'll pick me up."

"Jew call him?"

"Um . . . ?" It took me a moment to realize he'd said, *D'you* call him? "We don't have a phone."

So his mom gave me a lift, the ten-minute drive filled with her constant patter about how was I finding Kansas and had I seen *Cats* before I moved away from New York and did I miss the ocean, the mountains, traffic jams? She drove a pickup—I won't tell you what make—and we all had to crowd on the single bench seat, and just to drag the ride out an extra five minutes she missed the turn at 81st and had to drive down to 69th. "*Dios mio*," she said, presumably in response to the three crosses that marked some accident or other, although maybe she was just put off by the lavender-and-chartreuse paint job of the house on the corner, and then she asked me if it was true that Israel was behind 9/11, not Osama. Her voice died away in a single "Huh" when she pulled into our clearing and saw the shimmering green cocoon of our trailer. It was her son, Ian Carlos Abernathy, his right leg pressed up against my left from hipbone down to the muscle of his calf and his left leg similarly pressed against his mother, his thatch of rock-star hair ensconced beneath the brim of his Yankees cap still damp with my sweat, who took one look at the house my dad had chosen to raise me in, and said in a perfectly calm, completely honest voice:

"*Cool.*"

The first time I did it, it hurt. A lot.

The second time I did it it hurt even more, because I had a rash from the first time, which broke open, and bled.

I waited a while before I did it a third time.

I even wondered if it was worth doing again, but eventually—uncontrollably you might say—I gave in. I went to Ruthie for advice though, because she'd been doing it for years. But Ruthie said what I was doing and what she was doing were two com*plete*ly different things, and passed me off to her mom. Mrs. Wilcox was "on the market," which meant she had every kind of health and beauty aid you can imagine (and some that, well, you can't). She gleefully filled me in on all the "tricks of the trade."

"Nowadays people prefer to use a water-based lubricant instead of vaseline, but I think a petroleum product is *crucial*—absolutely crucial. And *always* shower beforehand. I mean, not only does it improve the effect, but, well, you're a teenager. An extra shower is never a bad idea."

Mrs. Wilcox had one of those shower nozzles on a long bendy hose, which was a lot better than having to use the little sprayer attached to the kitchen sink (not to mention about a bazillion times less messy). If she was home when Ruthie and I went at it, she'd even lend a hand.

"Don't worry," she'd tell me afterwards, bending me over the tub and rinsing me clean with smooth, practiced sweeps, "I've done this for longer than I care to remember, let alone admit. We'll make you look like a regular leprechaun."

Why leprechaun? Because leprechauns have green hair, *pervert*. Get your mind out of the *gutter!*

The bleach was the hard part. In the first place, it stung like crazy, and if it dripped in my eyes it felt like acid (probly because it *is* acid, duh). That's what the vaseline was for: you smear a thick border of it from ear to ear, just under the hairline, to keep the bleach from dripping down your forehead. We'd stick one of those granny showercaps over my head too, but even then the fumes leaked out and my eyes would water and my head would itch and all in all it felt as if a colony of fire ants was eating its way into my brain. This lasted for at least a half hour. You had to leave the bleach on long enough that all the pigment in the hair was leeched away, but not so long the strands became brittle and broke like dead grass. A couple of times I ended up with bald patches that I had to color in with green magic marker, and one time when Ruthie and I got sucked into a particularly bloody episode of *The Ultimate Fighter* we left the bleach on so long that I just had to shave my head, and went to school with an eighth of an inch of green fuzz clinging to my scalp like moss on the north side of a tree. In fact moss grows on every side of a tree, but we'd just read *Huck Finn*, and there was that question the Judith Loftus character asks Huck when he's dressed as a girl, and, um, why did I bring this up? I can't remember now . . .

Anyway, after about a year we had it pretty much down to a science, and from then on my head was covered in three to five inches of bright green hair. Although I could do it on my own, I went to Ruthie's house whenever I could, not just because the Wilcoxes had better facilities, but also because it gave Ruthie a chance to play hairdresser, which she enjoyed. In addition to dying my hair, she'd usually give me a trim, and then she'd experiment with different looks: gelling it flat and combing thick lines into it like a well-manicured golf course, or using a combination of mousse, hairspray, and spit to sculpt it into a fauxhawk or liberty spikes (as opposed to what I did at home, namely, rubbing a little goop in with both hands until basically my head looked like a shock of wheat left in the field so long that the wind has blown it half to pieces). Ruthie called this my "topiary look." I didn't bother to point out that a topiary is a hedge that's been clipped and shaped to look like *something*, and it would've been more accurate to call it my "untrimmed topiary look" or my "overgrown topiary look," or maybe just my "messy" look. Or maybe just messy. But hey, just because language is my thing doesn't mean I have to shove it down everyone else's throat.

Then there were the stains.

The stains were *ev*erywhere. Let's start with my face, my neck, my hands. The first time I did it, I ended up with an olive forehead, a limy neck, and hands that looked like they'd been sifting through a pile of freshly mown grass for a dropped housekey or a contact lens or something equally hard to find. Ditto the second time. The third time Mrs. Wilcox taught me the vaseline trick, which kept the dye from running down my skin, and she gave me latex gloves too. But even then I ended up with a green forehead and neck and hands, because I didn't do a good job rinsing the dye out, and when I ran my hands through my hair the color spread like a virus in a kindergarten classroom.

In fact, it was pretty much impossible to get all the dye out. I learned to wear bandanas—green bandanas, duh—for a day or two after I dyed my hair, but I guess I'm a nervous person, or, who knows, maybe dying my hair makes me nervous, or, you know, self-conscious, because I was pretty much always running my hands through it, which meant that I pretty much always had green palms, and fingers too, and wrists, if I did a particularly bad rinse job. Sometimes when I wake up in the morning I can tell where I've been touching myself (again I say: get your mind out of the gutter) because of the pale green streaks and smudges on my skin. The collars of all my shirts are green, and my pillowcases, and the headrests of the passenger seats of my dad's and Ruthie's and Mrs. Miller's cars, and then the fronts of most of my pants too, since that's where I usually wipe my hands when I notice there's dye on them. Bathroom towels're pretty much a wash, and doorknobs, and the wall just beside the door, which is where your hand actually lands a surprisingly large percentage of the time, especially when it's dark. Ditto the toilet handle, light switches, papers and books (especially my dictionary), the lock on my locker, the edge of my desk, shoelaces, the keys on my computer (before my dad broke it), the remote control for the TV (before my dad broke that too, about which more soon), the flag on the mailbox, and any mail I might pick up, and, well, just about everything else I touched that wasn't washed immediately afterwards.

By now you're probly thinking that if I had a normal mom and dad they would've made me stop dying my hair a long time ago, and who knows, maybe you're right. But my dad took a different view.

"It's like a record of your path through life. All the things you touch in the course of your daily routine. Like your toothbrush, or the cereal box, or that bottle of schnapps you tried to hide in number 22."

Did I mention my dad numbered his stumps? He numbered his stumps.

"I didn't—"

My dad pulled the flat bottle out of his jacket, and there were the telltale green fingerprints obscuring the unreadable gothic script on the label. It'd been dark when I snuck it out of the house, so I hadn't seen them.

"Don't worry, I'm not mad. And at least I know you didn't drink any."

"How d'you know I didn't drink any?"

My dad winked. "I have ways of leaving my mark too."

In fact I hadn't drank any—but I *had* poured some for Ruthie, and then added water till the bottle was filled back to its previous level. If I'd waited a bit, I could've just poured Ruthie's drink back in the bottle, because she took one sip and spat it out. Schnapps is *gross*. Fortunately, years of hard drinking had pretty much burned out my dad's sense of taste (both the oral *and* aesthetic kind), so it didn't really matter.

That "fortunately" was ironic, by the way.

Duh.

And so yeah anyway.

The stains.

Everywhere.

And everyone noticed them.

But no one noticed I was having sex with Ian Abernathy. Not even when one time Beanpole Overholser saw a couple of green smudges around the base of Ian's cap and asked Ian if I'd *dared* to snatch it off the top of his head.

"Nah," Ian didn't even blink. "The wind blew it off, and I made ol' Saladhead here run after it for me, him being such a fast runner and all. Right, Saladhead?"

"Suck an egg, Abernathy."

No one noticed, that is, except Mrs. Miller, who might not've known the *who* but somehow figured out the *what*. I gotta hand it to her. She was good. I gave her dead mom, drunk dad, cross-country move—everything she asked for, plus crazy friend and the eccentricities of dictionary and dye job, and of course my *thoroughly* disarming wittiness, and she saw right through me. Made me wonder what else she might know about me—maybe things I didn't even know about myself. Tell you the truth, it scared me a little. Scared me a lot actually. So much that I skipped our last summer session, and then school started, and then, well . . .

Then everything changed.

(She was wrong about the cup though. The one I stole from her cabinet and broke on the kitchen floor. It wasn't a distraction. Wasn't just a distraction anyway. But first things first. Or, well, in this case, second things second. I.e.:)

This is the second part!

Superman: Easy, miss. I've got you.
Lois Lane: You've got me? Who's got *you*?

Wake-up call

Seven A.M. Sunday morning.

Who in their right mind would call at such an ungodly hour?

"Mmmmyello?"

"I'M STILL ON GREENWICH MEAN TIME!" a foghorn blared into my ear. "MY BRAIN THINKS IT'S ONE IN THE AFTERNOON!"

I mentioned that Ruthie's dad took her to England for two months, right? They went on "a motor tour of the historic British countryside" (that's the brochure talking, not Mr. Wilcox) for July and August. Before she left I predicted she'd return with a fake accent. Sure enough, the voice on the other end of the line made Madonna sound to the manor bjorn. Ruthie's consonants were sharp enough to cut butter. Her vowels floated along the roof of her mouth like helium balloons trapped in the gym after a dance.

Fortunately, I'd prepared for this.

"*Scouse* me?" I said in the worst British accent I could muster, given the hour and my general lack of interest in all things English. "I *Kent* understand you."

(Ruthie's dad bought Google, by the way. Not a lot, but

enough to let him spend two months in the middle of the summer "motoring acrost" the British countryside. Oh, and he's a lawyer. That's how he was able to afford Google in the first place.)

"You are *such* a dork. D'you want to do your hair?"

"Say again? My Cockney's stuck in my Middlesex, and I'm just about to Cumbria."

A groan rumbled over the line while I inspected my roots in the mirror on the other side of the living room. It was hard to focus—my face was all warped and wobbly for some reason. At first I thought it was distance, or darkness, but our trailer's only seven and a half feet wide for one thing, and plus it turns out the sun is pretty much up by seven in the morning. Who knew?

Then I remembered we didn't have a mirror in our living room.

I squinted. The thing hanging on the wall was actually one of those big-ass chrome rims you see on *Pimp My Ride*—judging from the size, it had come from an Escalade, or one of those Suburban/Yukon/Denali clones. You gotta hand it to my dad. He could always surprise you. The rim had a few dents, so my guess is he found it by the side of the road.

"Hell-O?!" Ruthie apparently felt the silence had gone on too long. "School starts tomorrow, and we need to review our schedules." She dropped the accent on everything but the last word, which came out "shed-yules," albeit in a quiet voice, already half-defeated.

"Shed-yules?" I looked around for the three cottonwood bark paintings that used to hang where the rim now protruded from the wall. Saw that my dad'd made a mobile out of them, hung them over the dining room table, i.e., the kitchen counter, i.e., the end table for the loveseat, i.e., the place where we keep the phone. I.e., they were about three inches in front of my face. (Hey, I was just waking up.) I blew on one of the paintings and it spun in a gentle circle until it tapped me on the forehead. "Is that anywhere near Egloshayle?" I said, working the accent as hard as I could. "Sheepy Magna perhaps?"

"You made a list, didn't you? Funny English town names."

"On the contrary. These are recognized English dialects recorded by the University of Leeds during an eleven-year study conducted between 1950 and 1961. Unlike whatever the hell *you're* speaking."

Long, defeated pause. Then:

"I can't decide which I hate more right now. You or Wikipedia."

I glanced at the rim. "Hey, don't hate the playa. Hate the game."

Ruthie's snort sounded like Transatlantic static. "I'll be there in fifteen. Don't keep me waiting. Those stumps still give me the creeps."

One hundred twenty-three minutes later, Ruthie pulled up in her mom's hand-me-down BMW convertible. Her hair was in three braids, two of which stuck out from the right side of her head, one from somewhere towards the crown. The British flag was painted on her jeans—and on her tanktop, her right shoulder, and, most disturbingly, her sunglasses.

"Um, can you see through those?"

Instead of answering, she took them off. "Look what I can do." Her left eyebrow climbed an inch up her forehead while the right stayed motionless. "I was practicing my expressions. This one's 'perplexed.'"

Turned out Ruthie had read an article or an interview or a

blog or something that said aspiring model/actresses need to spend a lot of time looking at themselves in the mirror and practicing various expressions for the camera. Since looking in the mirror just happened to be one of Ruthie's favorite activities, she was able to throw herself wholeheartedly into her task.

"You look like a stroke victim."

"Stroke victims are often perplexed. Hey, it took me all summer to learn how to do this. It's a real skill."

"Carpentry is a skill. Sharpshooting is a skill. Making a double macchiato with two pumps of caramel and a foam cap is a skill. Raising an eyebrow"—I pointed to the thing wiggling just below her hairline like a fuzzy caterpillar—"not a skill."

"Oh god, coffee!" Ruthie threw the car in reverse. "England's got America beat on the culture front, but until they get a Starbucks drive-through, I'm staying right here!"

As we sped towards town, I noticed that her eyebrow was still pinned high up her forehead. I wondered if it was stuck there.

Ninety-eight minutes later, I was stretched out in the old recliner in Ruthie's mom's basement "rumpus room" (why no, we never *did* let her live that one down). Bleach was frying my skull beneath a plastic showercap and I probly would've dozed off on a vapor high if Ruthie hadn't been standing on an old sofa and screaming.

"Ohmygodyour*dad*? AndMrs*Mil*ler?! Ican'tbe*lieve*it."

"They've been inseparable for like two weeks. He doesn't even come home most nights."

"Gross! No, wait. Ger-ross! No, let me try again: Ger-row-oh-*oss*!"

"*Some*body tried to chase her jetlag away with too much

caffeine." I giggled. "Are you suggesting you're repulsed by the thought of my dad and Mrs. Miller engaging in—"

"Ix-nay on the ex-say alk-tay!" Ruthie's bellow rattled the windows in their casements. But then a funny look came over her face. I'd call it whimsical, but really, Ruthie's not that deep. "D'you think maybe, well, *you* had anything to do with the two of them hooking up?"

"Whaddaya mean?"

"Well, you know. The stuff you wrote. I mean, you did make them out to be kind of made for each other. Two lonely, mildly eccentric alcoholics bonding through the medium of one lonely, mildly eccentric green-haired boy."

My mind flashed on one of my sessions with Mrs. Miller. Sometime in July. We'd finished working and were just "enjoying the afternoon," which was Mrs. Miller's euphemism for sitting around until she was sober enough to drive. "Tell me about him," she'd said in a funny voice. Not the voice a teacher uses to a student, or even an adult uses to a child, but the voice one lonely person uses to another. "Who?" I said hoarsely, "Mr. Sprout?" "Before that," Mrs. Miller said. "Before you moved here. Before—" "Before my mom died," I finished for her, and she blushed slightly, then nodded her head.

I shook my head to clear it now, felt the sting of bleach on my scalp.

"At this moment my hair isn't green," I said. "It's white, if it hasn't actually burned off."

Ruthie pulled the showercap from my head, checked the bleach's progress.

"I mean, did you know you were playing matchmaker? Or was it unintentional? And before you answer, you should know I won't believe you if you say it was unintentional."

I stared at Ruthie, thinking about how I'd stared at Mrs. Miller the same way. Nervous without knowing why. My heart pounding in my chest. Wanting to say just the right thing, but not knowing what that thing was because I didn't know what I wanted to happen.

"I was just wondering, cuz maybe, you know, you can write *me* a boyfriend. I'd like a cross between a pre-*O.C.* Adam Brody and Krusty the Clown. Gosh, that sounds a little like *you*, doesn't it?"

Actually, that's not true. Not what Ruthie said (but really, Adam Brody? isn't he, like, four feet tall?) but what I said. What I thought, I mean, what I wrote, whatever. About not knowing what I wanted. I knew exactly what I wanted. I just felt guilty about it. So guilty I couldn't even write it, let alone say it. So all I told Mrs. Miller was, "He was the same before, except he didn't drink, hoard trash, or live by himself in a vine-covered trailer." Mrs. Miller's reaction surprised me. She gave me a half-embarrassed smile as if she'd been caught smoking outside the cafeteria, then placed a hand on my knee. "He doesn't live all by himself," she said. "He lives with you."

"Sprout?" Ruthie's voice pulled me out of my head. "You still there?"

"Whuh? Sorry, bleach-fumes blackout."

"Whatever." Ruthie dug into a pocket of her jeans, pulled out a piece of paper that was remarkably unwrinkled, given that her pants fit her like a condom. "D'you bring your shed— I mean, *sked*ule?"

"Can we rinse first? The bleach is burning through my scalp."

"I just checked, you're fine. This'll take five minutes. So: what've you got first period?"

I pulled out my class list, tried to focus my eyes, which really were watering from the fumes. "Burdett. Calculus."

"Oh! What a mean way to start the day!"

"Are you referring to Mr. Burdett, or mathematics in general?"

"Either. Both." Ruthie shuddered, glanced down at the paper in her hands. "I've got study hall."

"Which means you won't be getting in till second period."

"Bingo! What've you got then?"

"History."

"Crap, I've got that after lunch." There was a beat, during which neither of us mentioned that the after-lunch class was American history—a.k.a., the basics—whereas second period was world history, i.e., advanced. I did, however, pretend to adjust a mortarboard, which pantomime went right over Ruthie's head, who thought I was trying to point out my burning scalp.

"Don't worry, we're almost done. So, I've got studio second period—"

"Which means you won't be getting in till *third*—"

"—which is . . . psychology. C'mon, everyone has to take psych."

"I took it last year, remember? I've got Spanish third period."

"Well, that's the morning. What've you got fourth?"

"Twentieth-century fiction."

"Do what?"

"En-glish," I said. "It's-the-lang-gwage-that-al-lows-us-to-com-mu-ni—"

I shut up when Ruthie brandished the bowl of dye threateningly.

"I've got arithmetic," she said.

"A.k.a. Math Is Your Friend!" I tried not to snigger. "Fifth?"

"History."

"Oh, right." I choked back a guffaw. "I have civics."

Ruthie put her hands on her hips. "Is there something in your throat?"

"I'm fine. Sixth period. What've you got?"

"Is it the bleach fumes? Cuz I can kick you out and you can walk the *fifteen miles* back to your trailer to rinse it out. Don't let me keep you if you're not feeling well."

I tapped my form. "I-have-in-de-pen-dent-stu-dy-sixth-per-i-od. What-have-you-got?"

"Does it matter?" Ruthie crumpled her schedule and threw it across the room. "We don't have a *single* class together!"

By this point I was pretty sure the bleach had not only burned off all my hair, but the skin beneath it.

"There, there, drama queen. Madonna's career bounced back after *American Life*. We'll get through this too. Now, can we please rinse the bleach out of what's left of my hair?"

(Over the past four years, Ruthie had revised her position on the whole Madonna v. Cyndi Lauper question. She now acknowledged Cyndi had brought about her own demise by acting as a muse for professional wrestling—"Although really, she was ahead of the curve by twenty years if you think about it"—and Madonna deserved points for "longevity," if nothing else.)

"*American Life* sucked, it deserved to tank," Ruthie said as she unceremoniously bent me over the sink. "This year's gonna suck too." She blasted my burning skull with a jet of cold water.

"Hey! This isn't prison! Go easy on me."

"Oh, settle down, you big mary." Ruthie combed her fingers through my hair to keep it from tangling. The fact of the matter was, after four years she was pretty good at this. She cupped one hand over my forehead to shield my face from bleach-tinged water, used the nails on the other to scratch lightly at my skin, restoring sensation. I closed my eyes, started to relax into the scalp massage, but Ruthie's next words made me snap my head up and hit it on the faucet.

"You think Abernathy's in your Spanish class?"

There was very little I'd kept from Ruthie in the course of our friendship—there was very little a person *could* keep from Ruth Wilcox, if she wanted to find out—but I'd never breathed a word to her about what went on between me and Ian. Keeping my voice as nonchalant as I could, I said,

"Probly. It's the only thing that keeps his GPA high enough for him to play sports."

"Oh right, his mom's from Chilly. Ugh, he's so gross." She grabbed a towel and rubbed it into my hair. "But," she said almost whimsically, "I would *kill* for his permatan." She pulled the towel off, let out a little shriek. "Oh my God, your nipples are *rock* hard."

Did I mention that I was shirtless? I was shirtless, so the dye wouldn't get on my shirt. Duh.

"It's the water. Brrr."

Ruthie pinched the left one, and I yelped and did my best not to jerk out of the sink. By now she was slathering green dye on my head, and it would've gone everywhere. Somehow I had the feeling she'd planned it that way. I crossed an arm over my chest like a virgin guarding her modesty.

"So, uh, why the sudden interest in Ian Abernathy?"

"Oh nothing. It's just that I think I need to sleep with him."

The dye in my hair felt like a thousand-pound weight when

111

all I wanted to do was look up. I turned my head, squinted one eye open. "You think you need to . . . ?"

Ruthie nodded. "Sleep with Ian Abernathy." Like all she was telling me was who she would vote for, if she was old enough to vote.

She finally slipped the showercap over my gloopy hair and I was able to stand. A line of cold water ran down my spine, but that wasn't why I shivered.

"Ian *Abernathy*?"

"I'm six*teen*, Sprout. It's time I joined the club."

"Um, what club would that be?"

"*Um*, the I'm-not-a-virgin-anymore-and-thank-the-god-damned-*Lord* club?"

I shrugged. "What about France? Last year?"

Ruthie smiled, one-quarter guilty, three-quarters pleased. "I kind of exaggerated that whole thing a little bit. Right before Jean-Claude and I could've, you know, done it, it occurred to me that he was probably uncircumcised, and I was afraid I might laugh or, I don't know, puke."

(In fact, I'd pretty much figured out Ruthie was lying about losing her virginity one day when we were fooling around with a box of condoms we'd found in her mom's bedside table. Ruthie tried to put one on a banana—hey, it seemed funny at the time—but she put it on inside out, and then couldn't figure out why it wouldn't unroll.)

"Okay, fine," I said now. "But: why *Ian*?"

"Look, I know he's got this thing with always picking on you and getting you detention and stuff, but come on. You must've clocked by now that he's *smokin'* hot."

Thank God my head was covered in green dye. Ruthie

probly couldn't see my blush, although my cheeks felt so hot I was surprised the water didn't steam off them.

"But you just said he's gross."

"I meant his *personality*, what he *stands* for, all that Nazi jock stuff. I mean whatever. I don't want to have his babies. I just want to . . ." It was Ruthie's turn to shrug.

"Join the club."

"Look, when I crack my first VH1 hot list—you know, the top twenty-five under twenty-five, the twenty-five thinnest celebs, whatever—I want them to flash a grainy image of Ian's yearbook photo across the screen so that everyone at home says, 'Damn, he was hot, I wonder what he's doing now?' when they all know he's probly pumping gas or flipping burgers or sitting on a tractor with his love handles spilling over his Wrangler's. My fans—"

Ruthie broke off when she saw the dubious look on my face. Since I didn't study my expressions in a mirror the way she did, I achieved this effect by pointing both index fingers at my face and saying, "This is me, looking dubious."

"Whatever, Sprout. This is Buhler. Choices are limited."

"You're telling *me*? At least you *have* a choice. Ever since my dad broke my computer, I don't even have the internet at home, let alone a real live—"

I stopped. A real live what? Gay friend? Boyfriend? What *was* I looking for?

Ruthie's eyes went wide with sympathy. "Oh, I know, baby, you're horny too. Hell, I've got more than a decade before I reach my sexual peak but you're practically at the summit right now." She touched my knee sympathetically. "I told you, you need to try that bar down on east Sherman. My mom's hairdresser said it's totally gay on Wednesday nights. Mostly gay. Well, he's there anyway."

"Your mom's hairdresser is like forty!"

"He keeps himself in good shape though."

"Ugh! I'm going to *puke*!"

"Whatever," Ruthie said, "I don't get why you don't just come out at school. It's not like everyone doesn't know already."

"Why? Did you write it on the bathroom wall or something?"

Ruthie rolled her eyes. "Total guy thing. Girls just smoke in the bathroom. But I don't need to tell anyone. People, you know, *know*."

"Then why do I, you know, *need* to tell them?"

"I don't know. Cuz maybe you'll inspire someone who's not quite as clued into himself as you are. Maybe Jack Wallace—"

"Ew!"

"—or Campbell Dillon—"

"Double-ew!"

"Or, whatever, someone. You can't be the only gay at Buhler. I mean, doesn't the captain of one of the sports teams always turn out to be a big 'mo? Hell, look how much time Ian spends on his hair. I would totally not be shocked if he turned up at our five-year reunion with a cute Puerto Rican boyfriend named Diego or Amir or something."

"Okay, one: gay is an adjective, not a noun. Two, I thought we agreed to send a video of ourselves to every high school reunion until we could afford to charter a helicopter like Sandy Frink in *Romy and Michele's High School Reunion*. And three, Amir is an Arabic name, not Spanish. Oh, and four—"

"And four, don't change the subject. You need to come

114

out at school, Sprout. You're not gonna get laid, let alone find a boyfriend, until you do."

Suddenly all those things Mrs. Miller said to me last summer when I told her I wanted to write about being gay came back to me. I'd pretty much rolled over on the whole subject, and I realized now that I hadn't put up too much of a fight because on some level I must've agreed with her. I mean, when you thought about it, I was already doing what she advised, wasn't I? Taking the easy road? The high road even? By which I mean: keeping the focus on my green hair (and the brain underneath it) rather than on areas a bit lower down my body, if you know what I mean.

"Look," I told Ruthie now, "I don't want to be that guy, okay? The gay guy. The token homosexual. The school fag. I don't want to have to try out for every stupid school musical, wear pink triangle pins, and start a letter-writing campaign to bring my boyfriend to the prom. I just want to be *me*."

"Okay, my turn to count. One: you can't sing. Two: pink triangle pins are *so* over. And three: you've gotta *have* a boyfriend before you start worrying about bringing him to the prom."

"Ruthie!"

"Fine, fine. We should rinse anyway." She shooed me towards the sink. There was a long pause and somehow I knew what she was going to say before she said it. "What about—"

"Don't *even*."

A jet of water blasted against my head.

"Yeah no, I guess that's crazy." She adjusted the temperature, cooling it slightly, as if she knew my scalp was still tingling from the extra-long bleach treatment. "Still, I'd be, you know, curious. To see how it all works."

"Yeah? Then why don't *you* go down there?"

115

What Ruthie was talking about (in case you're curious) was Carey Park. (See also pages 63 and 64, and Ruthie's soliloquy on Madonna v. Cyndi Lauper.) You might remember that a man had walked by towards the end of Ruthie's monologue, and she'd chucked her cigarette in the pond and driven us home. At first I thought it was because she was afraid of getting busted for smoking, but in fact it was less paranoid than that. Well, maybe not less paranoid, but at least more serious: about six months before I moved to Hutch, the dad of one of the kids in eighth grade had been picked up in Carey Park for "loitering with intent." Apparently Carey Park was where Hutchinson homosexuals went to meet each other and, well, do the things homosexuals do when they meet each other. In parks. Apparently the dad of the kid in eighth grade had approached some guy who was only nineteen (the dad was forty-seven) and, while this is not illegal, it's still pretty ick, and gave rise to a bunch of rumors about predators and that sort of stuff. Even though none of those rumors were ever proven, twelve-year-old Ruthie was still creeped out enough to want to jet. But after I told her I was gay she did a complete about-face, and started pestering me to hang out in the park and find out if there was any truth to all the stories. I was like, no thanks. I'd just as soon remain sexless as get it on with someone old enough to be my dad. Ruthie had argued that if there were old guys looking for young guys then that meant that there had to be young guys, right? I could just hook up with one of them? The scary thing about this was that her argument made some kind of sense—make no mistake, Ruthie Wilcox could be diabolically clever when she wanted to be. But still. Trolling a park in search of a kid who was so desperate to get his rocks off that he'd risk being picked up by a middle-aged pedophile (or, for that matter, a cop) was not how I wanted to take the next step on my sexual adventure. Not that Ruthie knew anything about the first step, of course. But I was pretty sure that even if I hadn't fooled around with Ian I still wouldn't be horny enough to work Carey Park.

While all this was going through my head, Ruthie was rinsing my hair. She pressed the strands between her index and middle finger, expertly squeegeeing out the excess dye without tugging at the roots. I closed my eyes, let out a long, tired sigh. Talking to Ruthie could be so exhausting. If only she could just rinse my hair forever, we'd get along great.

In fact, she continued to run her fingers through my hair for so long that I risked opening one eye. The water running into the sink was clear, which meant that she'd drifted off, and I knew she was imagining what it would be like to have sex with Ian. Which is kind of ironic when you think about it, since I was doing the same thing.

I closed my eye again and smiled to myself, wondering what Ruthie would think if she knew I'd beaten her to Ian Abernathy. It was nice to have one thing to myself. Not just something she didn't have, but something she didn't even know about.

Turns out I was wrong about that.

On both points.

Like that girl in the pink coat in *Schindler's List*

At BHS the lunch period is spread out over the course of seventy-five minutes. Classes come in at ten-minute intervals and get thirty-five minutes to eat, nap, study, make out, play video games or band together in marauding packs to pick off the glasses-wearing outcasts and top-button-buttoned pariahs and overly-afflicted-by-acne future internet millionaires. In addition to not having a single class together, it turned out that by some cruel twist of fate Ruthie went in on the very first shift of this byzantine schedule and I went in on the last. Normally we spent the first week of school lunches deciding which of the new freshmen were going to lose their virginity to upperclassmen and which of the seniors were going to be pregnant by graduation. On the first Monday of our junior year, however, our entire lunchtime interaction consisted of her warning me to avoid the "hamburger"; on Tuesday, she advised me not to sit anywhere near the northwest corner of the cafeteria, where one of the Special Ed kids had puked up the twenty-three Jell-o cups that the football team had been "kind" enough to give him; and on Wednesday all we had time to do was link pinks as we passed each other in the lunch line.

"I'll never let go, Jack," she solemnly intoned, "I promise!"

"A woman's heart is a deep ocean of secrets," I responded, and then, *Titanic* style, we sank into the stygian depths of the rest of the school day.

And now, how can I say this so I don't come off sounding totally disloyal? The plain truth was, I was kind of glad. Well, not glad, but relieved. I'd enjoyed spending July and August with my notebook and pen, being my own muse instead of hers, which is pretty much impossible anyway. After four years of churning out monologues, performance pieces, and soliloquies for Ruthie to perform for youtube videos or school talent shows or regional beauty pageants (Ruthie had been last year's runner-up in the Miss Reno County pageant, which was pretty amazing given that she wore an evening gown for the swimsuit competition, and a swimsuit for the evening gown competition) the only thing I'd ever written that met with her approval were those first three words. "Oh my God," she said whenever I showed her anything else, "you make me sound *so* self-involved!" Ruthie'd been right when she told me all the way back in seventh grade that she'd inspire me: there *were* a lot of things I wanted to write about her. Just not a lot I wanted to write *for* her. And, once that was stripped away, our relationship mostly consisted of her doing my hair, or me following her around the mall while she shopped with her mother's credit card.

Not that eating lunch alone was so much fun either. For three days I put up with people beaning me with peas, carrots, cauliflower and the occasional soggy, ketchup-dipped French fry (a true mark of disdain, since French fries are to high school what cigarettes are to prison). On Thursday, I decided that if my peers *were* going to throw things at me, I might as well get to throw back, by which I mean that the guys usually got a game of touch football going in the gym during lunch, and I decided—what the hey—to join in. I got in line to be picked, purely as a formality, of course, since on the rare occasions I did something like this (usually against my will) I was always picked last. Still, it was kind of fun, in an anthropological way if nothing else, to see Ian Abernathy and Troy Bellows try to balance the fact that they didn't want me on their respective teams with the fact that they didn't want me on the *other* team because I was the fastest kid in school. And of course it was a completely different kind of fun to watch Ian *not* watch me, which I have to admit he was a master at. Just lifted his Yankees cap and pushed his unruly mop of dark brown hair off his forehead and wedged it back on (in the process giving anyone who wanted to look a glimpse of the green stains that ringed the inside of the cap), then pulled a coin from his pocket and flicked it a good twenty feet in the air.

"You call it, Troy-boy. You're gonna need all the help you can get."

Troy's voice cracked when he called tails, which elicited a snicker from Paul "Beanpole" Overholser. Troy blushed, but before he could say something another voice cut him off.

"Language, Mr. Bellows."

I whipped around. Mrs. Miller was just taking a seat on the bleachers. I didn't know if she was gym monitor that afternoon, or if she just—

"Hello, Sprout. May I speak to you a moment?"

Well, that answered that one.

There was a faint *thwick* and then a louder *sptt* as Ian caught the coin and slapped it on the back of his hand.

"Heads."

"Sprout?"

"Yeah, um, I don't want to lose my place. I might end up—"

I did a quick count to see if there was an odd or even number of players "—on Ian's, um, team."

At the mention of Ian's name, Mrs. Miller's eyebrows raised dramatically, and she blinked rapidly. My blush was the red-rose version of Troy's carnation pink, and I glanced in Ian's direction to see if he'd noticed. An expression flickered over his face so quickly that I couldn't tell what it was. Fear? Hatred? A muscle spasm? But all he said was:

"Don't worry, Brussels. I'll save a spot for you. Railsback, get your ass over here."

"Detention, Mr. Abernathy," Mrs. Miller said, all traces of summer-friendliness squashed beneath her formidable teacherly authority. "Sprout? You don't want me to give you detention with Ian, do you?"

After a brief moment in which the world stopped turning on its axis, the gym floor split open and a demon from the underworld reached one long tentacle out and pulled me down into the depths of hell, I realized Ian hadn't heard what she'd said. Sighing half in relief, half in consternation, I shuffled over to her.

"Mpmf?"

Mrs. Miller's eyelids were still twitching. I wasn't sure if this was because of what I'd said, or because of the cinnamony eye shadow she'd applied so heavily that it dusted the inside of her glasses with an iridescent powder. It was the first time I'd seen her since she started dating my dad, and I noticed that, in addition to the new eye shadow, her bangs hadn't been tortured quite so much with the curling iron either. Most frightening of all, her blouse, usually strapped in by a belt that made her stomach pooch out on either side, was casually—insouciantly even, positively brazenly—untucked.

Ah, synonyms.

"I just spoke to Principal Stickley. In light of your excellent grades, not to mention your role as the school's representative in the State Essay Contest, he's agreed to allow you to take senior English with me, instead of Mrs. Whittaker's more, shall we say, remedial class."

Like most English teachers, Mrs. Miller has a kind of, you know, English teacher way of talking. However, the strategic deployment of not one, not two, but *three* dependent clauses told me she'd rehearsed this sentence before she said it, right down to that seemingly spontaneous "shall we say, remedial" at Mrs. Whittaker's expense.

"But what'm I gonna do next year? Take your class all over again?"

A grin curled up one side of Mrs. Miller's lips, whose usual layer of cracked pink lipstick had been replaced with a subtler yet—God, it *kills* me even to write this—more sensual sheen of gloss. "Do you really think you can learn everything I have to teach in one year? Oh, don't worry," she said before I could answer, "we'll arrange an independent study for your senior year, possibly even let you take a class at JuCo for college credit."

I closed my mouth. That *would* be cool. But the past Saturday—the day before Ruthie got back from England—I'd spent my allotted day with the car driving all around town, until eventually, totally by accident, com*plete*ly by chance, I ended up driving by Mrs. Miller's house, where I'd seen my writing coach and my dad dancing arm in arm in her too-many-shades-of-yellow living room, which might as well have been the interior of the sun, given the strangeness of what was happening inside it. The idea of spending an hour a day with the woman who waltzed to Patsy Cline with my dad was just too much.

"Look, I—"

Mrs. Miller waved a hand. "Let me save you the trouble of thinking up one of your *bons ripostes*" (which she pronounced *clever retort*). "This isn't a request. My class. Tomorrow. Fourth period. And, since you're coming in late, you'll need to read the first twenty pages of *In Our Time* tonight."

"Janet—"

"School's in session, Sprout. It's Mrs. M."

She grinned, and it was hard to tell if she was trying to soften the blow or rub it in, but as she walked off I could swear she somehow managed to make the click of her low heels sound victorious, if not simply smug. Sanctimonious. Pusillanimous even, but still triumphant.

Damn those synonyms. Or, I dunno, adjectives. *Words.*

"Yo, Alfalfa."

My head jerked back to the court. Apparently Ian was working a vegetable conceit today.

"You playing or what?"

I took one last look at Mrs. Miller, then sighed dramatically. "Last again," I said, and trotted towards Ian's team. But then:

"What am I, invisible?"

Sometimes things happen in your life and you just know everthing's going to be different afterwards. Sometimes it's pretty obvious, like the day when I was ten years old and I came home from school to find my mom smoking her first cigarette in more than two years, and she asked me if I knew what the word "metastasize" meant. Sometimes it's a little more obscure, like the day my dad came home with that first stump rattling on the back of his trailer, and I sensed that he'd found the person he was going to be now. And sometimes it's just a feeling, a premonition I guess, that only the passing weeks and months will confirm. And for whatever reason, when I heard that strange voice say,

"What am I, invisible?" I knew even before I turned and looked at the speaker that something important had just happened.

So. My head jerked to the right. A kid I'd never seen before was standing on the sideline. Crewcut, dark eyes, prominent zit in the crease between lower lip and chin. He was short enough that I wondered if maybe he was a freshman, but something in his stare—aggressive, but also amused—seemed a lot older than fourteen.

"I mean, I know my hair ain't green. But on the other hand, hey, my hair ain't *green*."

White buttondown shirt, gray polyester pants, a cracked patent leather belt that was *at least* twice as big as his waist. And the shoes. The shoes were . . . dude, I don't even *know* what they were. They were from *Sears*. Sears brand. Ultrasuede uppers the color of dirt, with big bulbous rubber soles that looked like they'd hold you up if you tried to walk on water. The killer detail though—the detail that let me know that after two years of High School Hell I'd finally climbed from the bottom of the social ladder to an eminently respectable one rung up: a pocket protector. From the local Stuckey's. The *t* had been worn off by the repeated passage of a pen handle or, I don't know, an air-pressure gauge, which was why Troy Bellows sighed like a punctured tire and said:

"I guess I'll take Suckey's."

Beanpole Overholser snickered, and for the first time in my life I was tempted to join him.

It turned out Mrs. Miller really *was* the gym monitor that afternoon, and her victorious—cum-smug—cum-sanctimonious walkoff meant that twenty-two teenaged boys playing flag football had been left unsupervised before an audience of about fifty teenaged girls, which is the long way of saying we played shirts versus skins, so at least half of us could show off for what Troy Bellows called, in a completely unconvincing appropriation of hiphop slang, "the shorties." He whipped off his shirt with a flourish, exposing a surprisingly thick growth of hair curling over his chest in the shape of Croatia. One by one the members of his team did their version of the half Monty, equal parts blush and braggadocio, futzing and flexing—and one seriously shocked *ouch!* when Carl Peterson's navel ring caught on his shirt—until it was the new kid's turn. The whole gym was staring at him. No, scratch that. The whole gym was staring at him, and doing that bump-and-grind music that strippers, you know, strip too. But all the new kid did was roll his eyes, undo the top two buttons of his clerk-in-a-video-store shirt, and pull it over his head. Dropping it on the floor, he looked Troy Bellows in the face.

"Yo, Sasquatch. Let's play already."

Giggles erupted from the girls on the bleachers. Not because the new kid had a bad body or anything—his skin was stretched tightly across the wiry muscles of his chest and abs—but because he had the absolute worst farmer's tan I'd ever seen. His neck and his arms up to the middle of his biceps were light brown, but his shoulders and the front and back of his torso were so white they were almost blue. The line between the white and the brown was so neatly drawn you could almost believe he was wearing a T-shirt, if it weren't for the freckles spread over his torso, and two nipples the size of pink Skittles, and a nervous little outie that poked from his stomach like a piece of chewing gum stuck on a radiator.

After that I lost sight of him. Indoor flag football is fast and rough. The end zones are a hundred feet rather than a hundred yards apart, and, with no monitor on duty, blocking involved a lot of stiff-arming, tripping, and headlocks. One time Troy Bellows even tried to pants me, but I'd cinched my belt in for precisely that contingency, and all he exposed was a little cheek. He kept shaking though, till finally Ian Abernathy called,

"Hey-yo, Troy. I don't wanna put words in my wide receiver's mouth, but I don't think you're his type."

"I heard you put something else in your wide receiver's mouth," Troy muttered.

I couldn't help looking at Ian to see if he reacted.

"Yo, Green Day," was all Ian said, "heads up." A brown speck left his hands and grew rapidly larger. I'm not sure if he was throwing the ball *to* me or *at* me, but a second later it bounced into my chest and I took off, not so much towards the end zone as away from the dozen hostile boys who converged on me like a horde of zombies going after that girl in the *Resident Evil* movies (or the *Dawn of the Dead* movies, or *Shaun of the Dead*, or *28 Days Later*, or any other film franchise where hordes of bumbling zombies chase the fleet-footed good guy). For about four and a half seconds there was nothing but my breath and my legs and the sound of forty rubber-soled shoes squeaking over freshly waxed wood, and then Ian's voice cut through it all like a siren:

"Touchdown!"

I know you're supposed to feel some kind of rush when you score in football, but the truth is I always feel let down. For me, it's all about running—the chase, the dodge, the feint, the leap—and I would've kept going if there'd been room. But we were inside the gym, and there was the wall, its white-painted cinderblocks covered by a big paper banner that said

We're ALL Crew-saders!

The words stretched over a We Are the World/Hands Across America—type sea of smiling faces, each crowned by red or yellow or black or good old mouse-brown hair. There was a bald one, and a pink one (I'm pretty sure that was supposed to be Ruthie, since she was taller than everyone else in the poster) and even a black one, by which I mean a black person, despite the fact that there were no black students at Buhler, but not a green one in sight.

"*Dude*. Good one."

Ian was jogging up to me. For some reason it was hard for me to look at his face, and I looked down at the ball instead, saw a drop of green-tinged sweat already beginning to disappear into the panoply of grass stains dotting the nubbly Naugahyde. I looked up again. Saw Ian's cap. Saw an identical smudge of green under the brim.

I jerked my thumb at Troy. "Hey, uh, thanks for the save back there."

Ian looked over at Troy, who was assembling his team in an all-butts-out huddle. Shrugged, then turned back to me.

"Go wide," was all he said. "I'll hit you again."

I tried to play it down, but during the usual round of hut-ones and hut-twos I was practically bouncing on my toes. I nearly jumped the line of scrimmage before Fred Lynch *finally* snapped the ball and the gym erupted in squeaks as Troy's team launched themselves forwards. I ducked right, leapfrogged (leapedfrog? leaptfrog?) over a sweaty back, headed for the sideline. Go wide, Ian'd said, I'll hit you again. So okay. I was going wide. I was going to get hit—

Something smacked me in the side of the head, almost knocked me over, which task was accomplished by a half dozen defenders jumping on me like a horde of toddlers fighting over one lone lollipop. They pulled at my shirt, belt, pants, hair, crushed me to the wooden floor. And then, when everyone cleared, there was Ian, his glowering eyes shadowed by the stained rim of his cap.

"You might as well take a seat, Vomithead, cuz there ain't no way you're seeing this ball again."

For the last ten minutes of the game I could have been running drills for all the action I saw. In fact, I zoned out and *did* start running drills, and I would've gone at it till the bell rang if Beanpole Overholser hadn't run past me at one point on his crazy giraffe legs, the breath whistling in and out of his freakishly elongated body like an out-of-tune saxophone.

"Hey, Mouse," he panted. "Nice *shoes*."

"My name's—" I started, but then the new kid ran past me—the kid with the farmer's tan and the zit in the middle of his chin, not to mention the ridiculous shoes, which is when I realized Beanpole Overholser must've been talking to him. Mouse? I thought. He's here four hours and he already has a nickname? It took me a full *week* to get mine.

"Hey, Beanpole," the new kid shot back. "You know what's worse than these shoes?"

I wondered how he knew Paul's nickname, even as Beanpole did his best to hunker down and make himself, I dunno, thicker.

"Huh?"

"Having the kid who's wearing 'em steal—your—*ball*." And, diving in front of Beanpole, he intercepted Ian's pass and ran it all the way to the other end of the court, his funny, fat-soled shoes squeaking like a worn fan belt with each and every footfall. He reached the endzone and spiked the ball, which bounced up just in time to catch Beanpole Overholser in the face. The spokes of Beanpole's arms and legs jangled around like wonky TV antennas, and the gym echoed with the sound of laughter. When he finally got a hold of the ball he heaved it at the new kid. The shot went wide, but before I knew it a rain of footballs and basketballs, soccer balls and kickballs was flying through the air. The new kid stood pressed up against the "Crew-saders" banner at the back of the gym and didn't even bother to cover his face, as if he knew it was his lot in life to suffer through the time-honored hazing rituals of the American secondary school system.

At some point a ball bounced wonkily in my direction, and I lunged for it and caught it because, well, that's what you do when a ball bounces in your direction. It was a tetherball of all things, a U of hard, solid rubber poking from its surface where the rope normally went. I wondered how much it would hurt if that U was the part of the ball that made contact with your thigh or your gut or your cheek. If it would leave a welt instead of just a red burning patch like Ian's football had left on my head. But the new kid was hidden behind a wall of bodies, and every time it seemed like I had a shot someone would get in the way. Before I could do anything the bell rang, and sixty or seventy screaming kids disappeared the way only high school kids can, scattering like leaves shunted by a leaf blower.

Brown, orange, white, striped, and pentagonally patterned balls came to rest like a field of psychedelic mushrooms around the new kid, but all by himself he was a surreal sight. His farmer's tan had disappeared: the bare skin of his upper body, from the off-white stretched-out waistband of his granddad underwear to the golden peach fuzz covering his head, was a swirling splotchy field of angry pink and bitter red and birthmark purple, with here and there the blue-veined spiderweb of a bruise just beginning to swell up. His torso was like a human-shaped flame spouting from the nerdy base of his polyester pants and his wrinkled tube socks and his stupid, stupid, *stupid* shoes. The only part of him that was still white was his teeth, which were bared in a wide, taunting smile—and aimed, out of everyone else in the gym, at me.

"Yup," he said. "My hair *still* ain't green."

All at once the tetherball in my hand felt as heavy as a cannon shot. I bent down, set it on the floor so it wouldn't bounce or crash through the freshly waxed boards to the locker rooms below. It seemed to me that the dozens of balls between me and the new kid were evidence that everyone had taken a shot at him except me, but when I let go of the ball I saw that it was covered in green—fingerprints and handprints and a million sweaty-palmed smears, a clear indictment of the eager, almost desperate way I'd waited for my own chance to throw. To make sure it really hurt. To make sure it left its mark.

By the time I stood up the new kid was gone, and instead it was Ian Abernathy again. He nudged the stained tetherball with his toe. The expression that had flickered over his face at the beginning of the game was back again, and this time I saw it *was* fear and hatred. But it wasn't me he was afraid of, me he hated.

"You wanted to," he said, "didn't you, Sprout?"

For a long time I just stared at him. And then, surprising even myself, I reached out and flicked his green-stained baseball cap to the floor.

"Yeah?" I said. "Well, so did *you*."

Welcome to the jungle

Time passed.

Specifically, eight days passed, but it could've been five years. It was what Mr. Schaefer, the world—i.e., advanced—history teacher would've called an "epochal shift." One age was ending, another was beginning. We just didn't know it yet.

The first sign of the change was that afternoon in the gym. Well, in fact the first sign of the change was actually that afternoon before school started, when Ruthie told me she was interested in Ian. The second sign was that day in the gym. I thought the change had something to do with Ian—like maybe Ian was going to turn out to be straight after all—but it turned out Ian was just a distraction. This was made clear by the third and final sign, namely, a pickup truck rattling down 82nd Street's washboard ridges. It was a Tuesday, around four; I was getting in my after-school run, and I hung back a little from the intersection so I wouldn't have to wade through the truck's cape of dust. I had my pretend ipod on, a pair of old earbuds plugged into the waistband of my underwear, and I did jumping jacks while singing along with the song in my head.

"Oh Mickey, you're so fine, you're so fine . . ."

(I'd try to make an excuse here, but really, there isn't one.)

The truck was dark and funny-shaped. Everything rounded, bulbous, protruding, concave. Running boards, flared wheel wells in front and back, a windshield curved like a bow. The hood stuck out like the snout of a bloodhound and the engine made a sound like a dog stuck midbark. A shadow filled the window on the driver's side. On the passenger's side, a head and arm hung out like a balloon on a stick.

"Oh Mickey, you're so fine, you're so fine you blow my mind, hey Mickey!"

(Like everyone else, I only knew that one line of the song. Oh, and also? I have a *terrible* singing voice.)

As the truck grew closer, I could see that the arm hanging out the passenger window was thin but wiry. Corded muscle lay over bone, under skin. What little fuzz remained on the shaved head had gone white-blond under the sun. The cheek-bones were sharp, the jaw pointed, but I didn't recognize him till I saw the zit on his chin. Sometimes I wonder if I really saw that pink pinprick—he was in a moving truck, after all, enveloped in a cloud of dust. I found myself wondering if he recognized me too. I imagine my green hair was pretty much a giveaway.

His eyes were already looking at mine when I met his. I felt my mouth move, saw his lips pucker and curve. If it hadn't been for the name each of us voiced, you could've thought we were blowing kisses at each other.

"Mouse . . ."

". . . Sprout."

And then the truck was gone.

It seemed like I didn't stop running till I found him the next day in school.

"Hey."

"Hey."

Later, we argued over who said "hey" first. Never did agree.

"Was that you yesterday?"

"Yeah. That was you?"

"That was me."

The words could've come from either of us. Our first conversation: we both had the same questions, the same answers.

"You live around there?"

"Yeah. With my dad."

"Me too."

"I didn't know there was anyone my age in the hood."

"Me neither. I never saw you before."

"I never saw you either."

My heart thrilled. Never had a lack of connection made me feel so connected.

"It sucks living out there. No one around."

"Yeah. But school sucks worse, right?"

"Right. Damned if you do—"

"—damned if you don't."

We had cursed together. We were friends for life.

"Ty," he said, and stuck out his fist.

"Daniel," I said, and touched his, knuckle to knuckle.

We argue over who said whose name first too. But I know: it was him. It was him, because I'd've never said what I said if he hadn't said what he said first. Never would've said Daniel, I mean, if he hadn't said Ty.

I noticed his zit had popped, faded.

One of us said, "I gotta get to class."

"Yeah, me too," the other said.

We walked down the hall then, side by side, and didn't say anything.

Over the course of three lunch periods, eleven breaks between classes, two chats before school and a couple more on the way to our respective buses (and one time when I ran into him outside Stickler's office, during which all we said was "Hey"), I learned that he lived on the other side of Tobacco Road, which is the next road over from the one I live on. I'd probly gone past his place a hundred times but never once noticed the house. Like all the land on the west side of Tobacco, Ty's dad's property was pretty much tree-free, but it was hilly (or what passes for hills in Kansas), the house set back from the road a good quarter mile, and built into a south-facing slope to boot. The asphalt shingles had worn to the color of the dusty fields surrounding it and sported a few wisps of grasslike hairs on an old lady's chin. When you got close enough to see it (by which I mean when you crawled under the padlocked gate that barred the entrance to the driveway and made your way past a half a dozen signs informing you "Trespassers WILL Be Shot") you didn't think *house* as much as *storm cellar* or *bomb shelter*, or maybe just *bunker*.

This wasn't an accident.

It turned out Ty's dad was convinced the Russkies, China-men, Islams, or Aussies (I know, random) were going to start Armageddon any day now, and he'd built his house accordingly. Metal shutters flanked the narrow windows and the concrete-walled "sub-basement" held more canned food than a supermarket, not to mention an armory of pistols, shotguns, deer rifles, semiautomatic weapons, and a couple of compound bows and military knives in case the ammo ran out. Mrs. Miller says to avoid hyperbole when characterizing bad guys or else they become satirical, but it's hard not to sound O.T.T. when you're describing a man who has a sign on his front door that says:

God Bless Our Home
And CURSE the Homes of Sinners!

complete with a picture of a mushroom cloud in the background. All this, *and* a picture in the living room, right where some people put pictures of their family and other people put needlepoint aphorisms and still other people put bark paintings or chrome rims. The picture showed a pasty, slightly pointed face (not unlike Ty's actually) scowling above one of those police-number boards you get when you get arrested. The caption read:

Timothy McVeigh
A REAL American hero

All this makes it sound like I actually met Mr. Petit, but that didn't happen until later. Ty told me up front that if his dad caught a glimpse of my green hair he'd forbid his son from coming near me (what he actually said was that his dad would forbid him from visiting my grave, since Mr. Petit would shoot me on sight), so the only times I went to Ty's place were when the house was empty, which, not coincidentally, were the only times I let Ty come to *my* house, because I was pretty sure that if *my* dad saw Ty he'd forbid me from going near him too, if for entirely different reasons—reasons that had a lot to do with the condom he left in my bedroom one day, along with the note, "I don't want to know. But I don't want you dead either." What gave the gesture added significance was the fact that my dad'd taken the condom from the box he'd bought when he started dating Mrs. Miller. Touching, right? Not dysfunctional *at all*.

But I'm getting ahead of things. Before we get to sex we

have to get to Ty's house, and before we get to Ty's house we have to get to the forest, which was the neutral ground we chose to have our first out-of-school meeting. Which just about brings us to:

"Hey. You found it."

You'd think his play clothes would be different from the slacks-and-buttondown ensemble he wore to school, but nope: he was dressed as he was every day, from the weird shoes right up to the collar of his shirt, still buttoned tightly against his Adam's apple. The end of his belt had come free from the loops, hung down like the rope a monk uses to cinch his cassock.

In the sunlight beaming down on the Andersens' pasture he was as bright and indistinct as a candle flame. A stiff breeze swayed the branches and the world pixilated like a screensaver. For a moment I was afraid he would disappear, but the crunch of leaves beneath his feet testified to the concrete existence of his body. I could tell from his expression that I was looking at him the same way he was looking at me: as if he were nothing more than a dream.

"We, um, we don't have trees like this on our land," he said when I continued staring at him as if he were a ghost or Pamela Anderson or something equally improbable. "I, um, I used to sneak over here when I was a kid. I'd crawl through the fence and hop over that branch you're sitting on, and when I was done I'd go back over it too, even if it was way out of the way and I ended up being late."

As it turned out, I knew the tree Ty was talking about it. I even knew the *branch* of the tree he was referring to, and not just because I was sitting on it. It splintered off from the tree's base and sloped upwards like a staircase for a good twenty-five or thirty feet, where it poked from the forest's edge over the

Andersens' pasture and gave you a view for miles in three different directions. In fact, I'd read so many books in the crook of this particular branch that I'd even given it a name. Originally I called it the Northern Branch of the Hutchinson Public Library, but, in addition to being stupid, that name was also unwieldy, so I shortened it to the Lending Library, which, though also stupid (hey, I was twelve) was easier to say. But, stupid or not, I'd been right to think there was something special about this particular tree, this particular branch, because Ty'd noticed it too. Now, though, you could see he was wondering if there wasn't something "special" about me too, and not in the good way.

"So, um, yeah. When my sister June got her period my dad pulled us out of Buhler and sent us to Central Christian. He said he didn't trust her in a 'heathen school' now that she had the 'blood of Eve' on her. Said boys wouldn't be able to resist temptation. Of course June had her period for like a year before he noticed, but whatever: he pulled her and me and L.D., that's my oldest brother, L.D., he pulled us out of Buhler like it was Sodom and Gomorrah or something. Sodom *or* Gomorrah, I guess. One or the other. Me, I didn't give a crap, but L.D. only had a year of school left and had to give up all his friends. June finished three years later and that left just me, at which point my dad said he was tired of fighting with Central Christian to keep them from expelling me, and so whatever, if I wanted to go to hell, it was my own business. Buhler was cheaper than private school anyway. Christians suck," he said, presumably to explain why his last school tried to expel him, and then he shoved his hands in his pockets.

The silence was so loud the leaves bumping against each other sounded like a thirty-car pileup on the highway. One fell to the ground. I guess it was the foliage equivalent of a Mini or a Prius.

Ty's eyes followed the leaf to the ground, stared at it for another whole minute or so. Finally he looked back at me.

"So, uh, are you ever gonna, you know, *talk*?"

Of course I *wanted* to talk. I mean, I'd talked to him a dozen times in school. But now, away from all those other distractions, all those other people, I felt completely paralyzed, like I was caught in one of those *in medias res* beginnings of a music video and had to wait for the action to catch up to the opening scene so I could figure out what was going on. I looked around desperately, as if the ability to speak were something I'd dropped, a golf ball, a house key, and all I had to do was find it. But all I saw was a crabapple tree growing at the edge of the Andersens' pasture. At some point they'd wrapped the fence wire around it, and bark bilged over the steel tourniquets like a kinked rubber hose filling with water. See, those were the kinds of sentences that were running through my brain: over-articulate, pointless observations that, if I said them aloud, would've probly made me look even worse than my Marcel Marceau impression.

"Daniel? Earth to Bradford. Are you there?"

The ground beneath the crabapple tree was dotted with dozens of mushy green balls. I glanced at Ty, then hopped off the branch and walked over and picked one up. It was spongy beneath my fingers, gave off a sweet yet acrid smell, like a bowl of sugar that's been peed on.

"Daniel Bradford. I swear to *God*. I will feed you your own ba—"

My shot caught him square in the chest, and even as the green goo exploded over his shirt I was off, my feet following a trail I'd worn into the underbrush over the past four years. Ty's ridiculous shoes were loud in my ears, along with his curses and death threats and general promises of bone-breaking, life-ending, gender-altering revenge.

As I ran, I wracked my brain, trying to visualize the terrain around me. South was out. The clearing lay that way: the stumps, the trailer, my dad, all the other things I didn't want Ty to see just yet. Suddenly I remembered a large catalpa about a hundred yards to my right. Its low branches were perfect for a speedy ascent. Better yet, it linked up with an adjacent tree at a fairly good height above the ground, so I could go up one tree and, when Ty followed, clamber down the other.

"I'm gonna *kill* you!" Ty screamed, punctuating his threat with a series of curses.

I veered off the trail. Immediately my footsteps grew louder, as tamped mulch gave way to years of dead leaves and sticks. Branches slapped my face, vines tangled my arms and legs. I heard my own screams, and my mind flashed back to my first day at Buhler, when I'd heard the little kids screaming and thought they sounded more like they were dying than having fun.

"I will *bury* you, Bradford! Right up to your neck! And then I'll drag a cow over here and get it to chow down on your stupid grass-colored hair until it rips the brains right out of your skull!"

I saw the tree I was aiming for, sprinted the last fifty feet, launched myself at its lowest limbs. I'd climbed it countless times, knew instinctively where to place my hands, my feet. By the time Ty reached it I was safely out of reach. He took a moment to walk symbolically around the trunk, as if to emphasize that the only way down was past him. Or, who knows, maybe he was just trying to catch his breath.

"Rookie mistake, Bradford. You're trapped now." He looked up with an evil grin on his face. "Your ass is *mine*."

He heaved himself into the tree gracelessly, his slick-soled shoes slipping against the bark of the trunk, his hands grabbing at branches that were obviously too thin to support his weight. A twig snapped off in his fingers and he swung by one hand, legs kicking wildly.

While he was distracted, I transferred to the second tree. It was a tricky business: I had to shimmy out on the proverbial limb, which quivered beneath my weight in a way that I didn't remember from the last time I'd done this (growth spurt, I guess). I reached for an even thinner branch growing off the second tree. Once I had hold of it, the only thing to do was swing free and loop my legs around the new branch—a relatively easy monkey bars—type maneuver, but complicated by the fact that the branch I was grabbing swung beneath my weight like a fishing pole with a great white on the line, and plus too I was thirty feet up in the air, and between me and the ground were several thick branches that didn't look like they'd break my fall so much as break my neck. I half wished Ty wasn't stuck twenty feet down, so he could see how gracefully I pulled it off. (Hey, like I told Ruthie: don't hate the playa. Hate the game.)

Once safely on the new tree, I climbed closer to the trunk, made my way a couple branches higher so Ty couldn't see where I'd gone across. I sat down then, and waited.

Assuming I was trapped above him, Ty concentrated on his climb. God, those shoes. You'd think they'd been sprayed with WD-40 or something, they were so slippery. The fact that he'd outgrown his pants at least a year ago didn't help, and his shirt, in addition to the big green splotch in the center of it, was soaked with sweat.

"What the—"

Ty suddenly realized I was no longer above him. He looked around wildly, finally found my smirking face a dozen feet over from his.

"That damn hair. It's like camouflage." Then: "How in the *hell* did you get over there?" Instead of waiting for an answer, he began making his way towards me. He stood up, held on to a branch above him for balance, and tightroped away from the trunk. The branch he stood on was too thin to support his weight, and before he'd gone a half dozen steps he was bouncing up and down. This seemed to amuse him, and he *sproing*ed up and down until one of the branches, either the one he stood on or the one he held, cracked in protest.

He looked over at me again, then looked up and down for an alternate route. The branch he needed was actually off to his left; but by this point in the season the catalpa leaves were as big as sheets of printer paper, and I doubted he could see it. But just to make sure he didn't look too hard, I began throwing sticks to distract him. I'd broken off about fifty while I waited for him to get up here, so I had more than enough.

"Jesus Christ, Daniel, what's up with you and the *throwing*?" He broke off a stick and threw it at me, but his perch was so unsteady that it sailed ten feet wide.

"Hmmm," he said, as if he were thinking aloud. "This *is* a pickle." He pursed his lips, furrowed his brow, tapped his temple with the index finger of his right hand. "What *will* I do?" The next thing I knew he was reaching for his belt, slipped it free of the loops in one long flourish. The kinked, cracked length of patent leather hung from his hand like a dead snake, or maybe just a snakeskin. It had to be at least five feet long.

"My dad always buys clothes we can 'grow into.' I think he went a little overboard with this, don't you?"

He leaned towards me. For a moment I thought he was actually falling off the wobbly branch he stood on, but then I saw he was reaching for another branch about three feet in front of his face. This branch was a bit thicker than the one he'd been holding on to, about as big around as his upper arm.

I remind you that his upper arms were not particularly thick.

His upper arms were, in fact, particularly thin.

His body was at an incline now, like a trapeze artist caught midair in the jump from one bar to another. As I watched, he looped his belt around the new branch, pulling the end through the buckle and tightening it so that almost the entire five feet hung free. He yanked on the belt several times, testing to make sure it would take his weight. Then, looping the end of the belt around one hand, he suddenly stepped off the branch into empty space—not like a trapeze artist at all actually, but like a yo-yo in the hands of a skill-less yo-yoer, his spasmodic bounces gradually flattening out until he hung thirty feet above the ground.

"Ty!"

My voice reverberated through the vibrating branches.

"It speaks!" Ty said, his own voice thin with the effort of holding on to what was proving to be a slippery liferope.

"What are you doing? Get back on a branch!"

"I intend to. Just not"—Ty's voice disappeared when he kicked a leg out and began swinging back and forth—"the one"—*kick*—"I was"—*kick*—"*on.*" He was swinging a full 180°

now, a violent yawing motion like the pendulum on a grand-father clock that just happened to be caught in an earthquake. The branch his belt was tied to creaked ominously, and other, smaller branches broke as he kicked them out of the way.

"Ty, c'mon. Enough already. Get back on the tree."

"*I'm—gonna—get—on—your—tree—in—STEAD!*"

How he did it I'll never know. Hell, *what* he did I'll never know. Well, I mean, I know what he did: he jumped. But how he jumped, and how he managed to grab the end of one of the branches growing out of the tree I was on, is a complete mystery. Ty's feet swung forwards and upwards till they were higher than his head, and then, when they swung back, he hoisted himself up so that his waist pressed against the branch, his hands hip-width apart, his arms rigid, the muscles of his chest straining against the crabapple-splattered buttons of his shirt.

One of his ridiculous shoes slipped off his foot and, like a bird that leaves the nest too soon, bounced off one branch after another before thudding, dead, to the ground. His foot was surprisingly small, his sock *phenomenally* dirty.

"Daniel? What're you looking at?"

What I was looking at was a distant silver shadow just visible though the forest, a plastic dome beneath which huddled all the furniture we'd brought from Long Island that hadn't fit in the trailer. For five fantastic minutes I'd forgotten every stupid thing in my life, but that shiny blob was a reminder that it would all be waiting for me as soon as Ty went home.

"Daniel?" Ty said again, his voice curiously gentle. "Quick. Gimme the name of a famous gymnast."

I looked at his hands, gripping the branch. His muscles, corded with effort. His face, purple as a pokeberry.

"Um, Nadia Comaneci? Mary Lou—"

And then the branch broke.

"Sh

    ih

        ih

            ih

                ih

                    ih

                        ih

                            —*OW!*—

                                ih

                                  ih

                                      it!"

His voice and body bounced off one branch after another. He didn't manage to grab onto any of these branches, but at least they broke his descent into a series of three- or four- or five-foot drops instead of one thirty-foot plunge, which is why this book doesn't end here, but still has another hundred pages to go before it reaches its (dramatic and deeply satisfying) climax.

He hit the ground with the kind of dull thud that a fifty-pound sack of dogfood makes when you drop it off the roof of your house (did I mention that we had a German shepherd named Fang for three weeks? For three weeks we had—oh, never mind, it's not important right now), and then he just lay there, unconscious, and, as far as I could tell, unbreathing. His belt hung limply from its still-swaying branch, the frayed end of a gallows rope after the hanged man has been cut down.

"Ty?"

His mouth was open, and there was a brownish bubble of blood below his right nostril. His arms and legs splayed out from his body, but none of them was obviously broken or twisted out of socket. I stared at his chest for I don't know how long, trying to see if it was moving, if he was breathing, before I suddenly realized that if he *wasn't* breathing it was more likely I could help him down on the ground rather then up here in a tree. I started descending, cautiously at first, then faster and faster, more or less falling the last ten feet or so, then running towards him.

Just as I reached him he shot up from the ground with a huge gasp, eyes wide, arms thrown out as if to ward off a blow. I could've almost thought he was faking it, save for the single word he screamed out:

"Holly!"

The pure aching empty *need* in Ty's voice could've stopped traffic, distracted soldiers in the line of fire, caused a stream of lava to split and run around either side of him. I don't know if there'd been any birds singing before, but they weren't singing afterwards, and the only sound was my last footfall before I reached him, thudding against the earth like a boulder falling off the side of a mountain. Don't get me wrong. I'd've stopped too, at the sound of his voice, but momentum worked against me, and I more or less ran into him.

His hands clutched my legs blindly, pulling me into him. He slammed his face against my knees, his choked breaths tearing from his body like pages ripped by the handful from a book.

"Ty?" My hand hovered above his head for a moment; then, as delicately as I could, I placed it on his crewcut, matted now with bits of leaf and bark and dirt. "Are you okay?"

He stiffened, shuddered, then relaxed. He let go of my legs and, shakily, sat back.

"That—" his voice caught in his throat, he coughed. "That knocked the wind outta me."

"It knocked you *out* is what it did." My voice was almost as raspy as his.

"I'm fine. Just—" He coughed again. "Have to catch my breath."

"Who's Holly?"

He reached for his oversized, ugly shoe, pulled it on.

"Hollis. My brother. My other brother."

"Oh. Does he have green hair?"

Ty looked up at the sky then. No, not the sky: the trees. His belt.

"Screw it," he said, though it didn't seem like he was talking to me. "Least this way he can't hit me with it." Then, standing unsteadily: "No," he said. "He didn't."

The difference a tense makes. Not *doesn't. Didn't.*

"Hey!" Ty did his best to make his punctured voice sound cheery. "What's this?"

He pointed to something on my chest. I looked down, and he smacked me in the face, nearly peed himself laughing, then nearly choked to death coughing.

"I gotta go," he said when he could talk again. And, coughing and crashing, he ran off through the trees.

But he found me before first period the next day, still wearing yesterday's green-stained shirt. The little bubble of blood below his nose had swollen into a fist-sized pink and purple bruise that stretched from his cheekbone down to the corner of his mouth, and he was limping too, his left foot half sliding out of his oversized shoe with every dragging step—which was weird, since he hadn't been limping yesterday. From a distance he looked like the old battered jockey in the Hemingway story we'd read for Mrs. Miller's class, but when he got closer I saw that his smirk, though shrunken by the bruise on his face, was even more self-satisfied than usual.

"*Dude.*" He lifted up his shirt (which was covered with hay for some reason) to show me a black and blue mass laid over his ribs like the 72-ounce porterhouse at Amarillo Andy's. "That was *awesome.*"

We know the sound of two hands clapping, but what is the sound of a hormone?

The Andersens' St. Bernard had acquired legendary status two years earlier, when it pulled down a six-tined buck whose flight had been hampered by snowdrifts from a recent blizzard (it almost never snows in central Kansas, but when it does it tends to dump a foot or two, which the wind whips into four- or six- or eight-foot drifts that're a lot of fun if you're a kid, but apparently less so for things like rabbits and deer). According to Vernon Andersen, his St. Bernard ripped the buck's throat out and fed on the rotting carcass for almost two weeks before he—Vernon, not the dog—was able to get a rope around its—the deer's, not the dog's—antlers and haul it away. I suppose I should mention that this story came to me through my dad, who heard it from Vernon at the 4th Street Tavern, the bar my dad went to on the rare occasions he wanted to drink with other drunks. Among other things, the 4th Street is actually on 5th, so it's hard to trust any bit o' wisdom that manages to stagger out of its door (although my dad told me the name/address discrepancy is just to throw wives off the track of wayward husbands, but whatever): my point is, however vicious the Andersens' St. Bernard was, he still wasn't the major obstacle preventing me from visiting Ty's house.

"Oh—my—*God*," Ty laughed so hard a pea flew from his

mouth, landed on my thigh, disappeared into the sea of green stains. "When my old man saw my shirt he kicked my ass from one end of the house to the other. Course, we live in a pretty small house, which when I pointed that out he kicked my ass back to the *other* end, and then kicked me out the front door. I had to sleep in the barn."

"I guess that explains the hay," I said, although what I was looking at was the bruise on his face, the others concealed beneath his stained, straw-covered shirt.

Ty picked a piece of hay off his shirt. "You kind of like pointing out the obvious, huh? When you don't got nothing to say? Anyway," he cut off my protest, "here's the plan: cut around the southern edge of the Andersens' pasture to avoid that stupid dog—"

"Do we know the stupid dog's name, by the way?"

"Do we care about the stupid dog's name, *by the way*?"

"It's just easier than calling it 'the dog,' or 'the Andersens' dog,' or 'Vernon Andersens' stupid—' "

"What's *easier* is if you shut up and listen to the *plan*, so that way you don't get your head shot off by my *dad*."

There was a pause here, while I waited for Ty to laugh, and Ty waited for me to realize he wasn't going to laugh. Something—talking or chewing—had caused the cut on the side of his mouth to open, and after a moment he touched a finger to his lip, looked at the blood, licked it off. My eyes flickered to the bruise on his face. Noted again that it was the size of a fist, with knuckle-shaped scalloping following the line of his cheekbone like lace at the edge of a bra.

"Okay?" Ty's eye twitched a couple of times above his bruise, less wink than tremor. A flush had pinked his cheeks, and for a minute I thought he might actually cry. But all he did was say:

"So." He gulped. Then: "So," he said again, "follow the Andersens' fence all the way to Tobacco, then walk up the road till you get to this line of hedge on the west side. There's a sign on the fence that says it's electric, but that's a lie. Go through it, but make sure to keep the hedgerow between you and our house. When you get to the end of the hedge you're gonna have to cross this big open field, kind of a valley like, with a couple of little willows and mesquite at the bottom you can use for cover, if you make it that far. My dad's usually in the barn when we get out of school, so make sure he don't come outside, cuz that's only about a hundred feet away from the field and he keeps a thirty-ought-six hanging by the door in case of terrorists or taxmen. Anyway, once you get across the field, you have to make your way up the hill to this linden tree that grows about halfway up. It's the only tree, you can't miss it. It's half dead cuz it's so dry up there, but it's tall enough that you can use it to get over the fence, which *is* electric, even though there's no sign on it. There're a couple of places you can go under, but my dad'd probly spot you before you found 'em and then, well, then you'd be dead, and we wouldn't get to have no fun. So anyway, get yourself over the fence and then go far enough down the other side that no one can see you from our property, and then wait for me. And try not to make too much noise, or you'll rouse the ostriches."

In the time it'd taken Ty to say all this a spot of blood had welled up on the side of his mouth and then run down his cheek. It didn't run straight down, however, but veered left into the hollow between his lower lip and then spiraled around the point of his chin. It seemed just about to drip onto his white shirt when he suddenly finished talking and wiped his face on the back of his hand and, after inspecting the smear of blood with an almost proud expression, licked it off. I was so transfixed by the blood's progress that I missed most of what he said, and in fact only really remembered the last word, which, since I couldn't think of anything else to say, I now repeated:

"Ostriches?"

"The back of our property butts up against the Regiers' ostrich farm. You seen the sign? 'GOOD MEAT OSTRICHES'?"

"Uh, yeah. I've seen it."

"They'll rip your throat out if they're in a mood. There's a pretty thick stand of sandhill plums just over the hill. If they come at you, just go in there, they can't get in. At least I don't think they can. Whatever you do, don't try to outrun 'em. They can do forty miles per, easy."

"Wipe your chin," I said, and then: "You ever tried ostrich meat?"

Ty wiped; looked; licked. Shrugged. "My dad shot one once. He told Regier that it got on our property, but that was a bald-faced lie. He said if God wanted ostriches in America, He'd've put 'em here Himself, so he—my dad, not God—was really just staving off the Apocalypse, which a Methodist like Willy Regier should thank him for, since he's just gonna end up in hell when that happens." He licked his lip without wiping first. "I thought it was okay."

"That he shot it?"

"The *meat*. Jesus, Daniel, keep up." Ty took a breath. "So. You got all that?"

I stared at him. We'd started out with *cave canem* and ended up with the horsemen of the Apocalypse, except they were ostriches, not horsemen, and then something about plums and Methodists. And of course all that blood, and the fact that every time Ty licked it my mouth filled with water. Of course that too.

151

"JFC, Ty, this is more complicated than the plot of *Ocean's Eleven*."

"What's that?"

"Um, George Clooney, Brad Pitt?" When he still looked at me blankly, I said, "Julia *Roberts*?"

"I meant, what's JFC?"

"It's like OMG, but JC instead. With an F in the middle."

Ty looked at me as though I was speaking Greek. Then: "Julia Roberts played the whore, right? They burned her picture in our church so we'd know what was going to happen to her in hell. The preacher said hair the color of flames deserves to go *up* in flames."

Ty's voice went a little fire-and-brimstone, and I tried to imagine what it must be like being raised to believe that everyone in heaven is going to have brown hair, maybe a few blonds, but no redheads and probly no green-haired atheists either. (I asked him one time about people with black hair and he said, "You show me a person with black hair, I'll show you a Catholic or a Muslim").

He'd lifted up his shirt now, pressed on his bruised ribs until he started coughing and laughing, and then the bell rang and we had to go to class. I caught up with him in the break between fifth and sixth periods, worked out one more kink in the plan ("You'll see a metal thing that looks kind of like a great big TV antenna or a really small jungle gym. Whatever you do, don't touch that"), and then, just before we got on our separate buses, he saluted me and said, "Go with God, my son." I started to walk away, but he called me back.

"I just got it."

"Huh?"

"What the F stands for."

"The F?"

"In JFC. Dude. Good one."

Ty was waiting in the Regiers' pasture by the time I got there, had already picked a couple of plums, one of which he tossed me. I dodged it instead of catching it, I guess thinking of the crabapple from the day before, which made Ty roll his eyes.

"*Food*, doofus? You eat it?"

I looked at the plum on the ground, lying a few feet from something I'm guessing was an ostrich turd, which looked pretty much identical to the plum, right down to the shininess.

"Huh." I let the plum lie where it'd fallen.

Ty had already turned and was marching west. He skirted the plum thicket, which clung to the bottom of the field like a dense green cloud, and headed up the opposite hill. I was half tempted to pick up the plum and throw it at him, but instead just followed.

In the shallow valleys the air was hot and still, but on top of the hills the wind needled us with a powdery grit that collected in the corners of our eyes and nostrils and lips. Ty led me up one dusty rise after another, only speaking to point out this or that cottonwood or willow or patch of sumac we could use for cover if the ostriches got wind of us. I thought about pointing out that ostriches had a pretty crappy sense of smell (I'd googled them in the library that afternoon) but figured that would be obnoxious, and so I just nodded. At some point I realized that Ty didn't have a destination. Or, rather, that this walk was the destination. That he was showing me his childhood stomping grounds—the dry Kansas plains—just as I'd shown him my forest yesterday, or at least the parts I was willing to share.

And so we walked. Up one hill, down another. Up one

hill—the ever-present wind, the dust and the grit—and down another, to the hot bowels of the earth. Up one hill. To the left, right, forwards, more of the same. Down another, to another prairie hollow. Clumps of grass grew from a parched lunar landscape imprinted with the tracks of coyote, deer, snakes, ostriches. Thickets of sand plums picked clean by larks and starlings and blackbirds; ditto blackberries and raspberries. A bone, anonymous as a paper towel tube, lay bleached and white in the lengthening shadows. A few ants gnawed at the memory of marrow in its seams.

After nearly an hour of walking, my throat felt coated with dust, and I regretted abandoning that plum. I didn't have enough saliva to spit, instead swallowed what seemed like a mouthful of grit.

"So, uh"—I had to swallow again—"you never mention your mom."

"I got one." Ty didn't bother turning around.

"Got," I said, "or had?" Thinking of his *doesn't*-not-*didn't* of the day before.

"Don't know." Ty kicked a tumbleweed off its stalk, sent it on its endless rolling way. "Don't care." His back was ramrod straight, and he forged ahead like a periscope rising out of sandy soil, purposeful, directed, the very opposite of the tumbleweed, which rolled lopsidedly heels over head down the hill.

I finally managed to spit, a big brown lugie that landed on the ground with an audible splat, then immediately disappeared as the dry soil sucked up the moisture.

"My mom died."

"Everyone knows that."

Something about his voice. All I could say was: "Huh."

"Everyone knows Sprout Bradford's mom died of cancer,"

Ty went on before I could think of something else to say, "and Sprout Bradford's dad is a drunk, and Sprout Bradford dyes his hair green because he thinks he's special, and Sprout Bradford gets drunk with Mrs. Miller because she don't got no kids and he don't got a mom cuz she died of cancer. Tell me something I *don't* know."

Ty rattled off his list, but all I could hear was Ruthie's voice. *It's not like everyone doesn't know already.*

Ty whirled around. "Not all of us like to talk about it, okay? Not all of us like to share every last endless detail of our lives like we're a character in a book, or—or a *writer*, Mr. State Essay Contest."

For a moment I just stared. Then:

"You'd be surprised what you don't know about me."

"Yeah, I bet I wouldn't."

"People see this," I said, running my fingers through my green hair, not smoothly like Ian Abernathy, but making it stick out in every direction like a tumbleweed. "They think they know me. But they don't know me. They just know I have green hair, cuz that's all I want them to know. But I have secrets. *I have secrets*," I repeated, as if repeating it might make it true.

"Yeah? Then how come everyone knows you're—"

I felt the blood drain from my cheeks, felt the wind blow its grit against my pale face as though it would flay skin from bone. I waited for him to say it. Waited for him to say what he knew, then waited for him to tell me to get the hell off his land and never bother him again. But, well, it wasn't his land, and all he said was:

"It's not so easy for some of us, Daniel. It's not, Oh, my mom died, feel sorry for me. It's, My mom took off cuz maybe she didn't give a crap about her kids or maybe her husband punched her in the face one too many times, or maybe, you know, maybe she was just a whore, and not no Julia Roberts kind of whore neither, but the kind of whore who sneaks out in the middle of the night and climbs in the cabs of truckers who park their rigs down at the end of the driveway. *Listen*," he cut me off when I opened my mouth. "Don't talk. *Listen*. Don't try to make sense of it, cuz it's not something you can make sense of. It's not something you can *tell*. It's just something you got to live with. She's gone, okay. My mom's gone, and my brothers're gone, Holly's dead and L.D.'s working full time and my sister went and married the first goombah who'd get her out of our house, but my jerkwad of a dad is still here, and so am I. *Me*, Daniel. *Ty*. I'm—still—*here*."

There was a moment then, just the wind blowing grit in our faces and some movement on the horizon I was hoping was a distant stand of trees or the smoke from a burning field and not an army of ostriches come to rip the guts from our bodies. The idea that we might be set upon at any time by a troop of eight-foot-tall, five-hundred-pound birds added a slightly surreal edge to what Ty was saying. A comic edge, I want to say, despite the desperation in his voice. Or, I don't know, maybe it was just the smile that cracked his dust-ringed lips, the cough that barked out of his mouth.

"Ow," he said. He rubbed his sternum gently. "My ribs."

"Let's see," I said, and he unbuttoned his shirt, showed me how the bruise was spreading across his fish-white skin like an oil slick dispersing in the ocean. "Does this hurt?" I said, and jabbed a finger right in the center of the dark pool.

"Mother—" The rest of the word disappeared in a cough, and I turned to run, but he tripped me before I could get away, then fell on me in a rain of punches so hard I wasn't sure if we were wrestling or if he was really trying to kill me. But even as we began to roll downhill, strangling, elbowing, scissor-kicking and otherwise aiming ninja death blows and Ultimate Fighting—style submissions against each other, I knew it was a game—a life or death game, maybe, but that was how Ty did things. That was how he played, and I was discovering I liked playing that way too. Or at least I liked playing that way with him. Every jab, every parry was a bone-hard reminder that I finally had someone else to measure myself against, to find out what was me and what was beyond me. By which I mean: I got him in a rear-naked choke and squeezed as hard as I could. Ty didn't bother to try and pull free, just went straight for my groin with the big fat heel of one of his shoes, which, when my boys exploded in what felt like about a gallon of blood, suddenly seemed less ridiculous than a masterpiece of offensive engineering. Spots danced in front of my eyes, and when I could see again Ty was behind me, his arms looped under mine and his hands pressing my head forwards in a full nelson. My shoulders screamed as Ty attempted to rip my arms from their sockets, and plus too our heads were knocking together because—remember?—we were still tumbling down the slope, which was baked hard as concrete yet powdery at the same time, battering us and coating us in dust, breaking bones and choking the last breaths from our bodies and Ty doing his dead-level best to snap my arms out of their sockets, until suddenly something green and spikey caught my eye.

"Cactus!"

By some joint navigational effort we managed to veer off to the right just in time to avoid the needled paddles of a nest of prickly pears, but:

"Crap!" Ty said, which might've been a pun, since what he was exclaiming at was a big pile of ostrich turds, nestled together like a basket of plums, or dinner rolls maybe, or cupcakes (though why they only reminded me of food is anyone's guess). We stopped then, since otherwise we'd've had to roll uphill, and we were too exhausted. Ty loosed his nelson and fell off me, and we lay side by side on our backs, panting, coughing, spitting, staring up at the blue-brown sky, occasionally turning our heads to the side to spit. At one point Ty turned his head my way, and I slitted my eyes against a glob of brown spittle, but all that came out of his mouth was:

"You think this is what Adam looked like? When God first made him out of dust?"

I turned and looked at Ty head-on. A brown patina covered his skin from top to toe, and you could almost believe his blinking eyes were opening for the first time, taking in the vastness of the physical world and the even vaster sky that hung above, empty and endless and blank.

"You believe all that stuff?"

"I want to believe. I wanna believe that there's a heaven and my dad's gonna go to it, and that there's a hell I can go to too, so I don't never have to see his ugly face again."

I looked over to see if his lip had started bleeding. The bruise was covered in dust, but I could still see the shadow of it. Fist-sized. Right there on his cheek. He saw me looking. Looked away.

"You miss her?" His voice was hard, defensive, like someone holding up a tennis racket to protect his face rather than actually trying to return the ball.

"Who?"

"*Duh*. Your mom, doofus."

"Oh. Her. Yeah, sometimes."

"Sometimes I wish my mom was dead. Then I could stop wondering if she's ever gonna come back."

"And rescue you?"

Ty coughed, then cursed. "That's what *I'd* say to her," he said, "if she came back." He spat out the wad of phlegm that had come up with the hard *k* at the end of the particular curse he'd picked out. "That's what I'd *do* to her."

"I, um." I didn't know what to say. "I don't know what to say," I said, and then I threw in, "Maybe she had her reasons?"

Ty's lip curled away from his teeth, half sneer, half snarl. It was scary how quickly he could go from being mad at someone who wasn't around to being mad at the person who just happened to be in front of his face.

"You were doing better when you had nothing to say."

"Look, Ty—"

"*No.*"

Ty's word shut me up like a punch to the throat.

"If you leave your home—your *kids*—you don't *get* to have reasons. You don't *get* to come back. *Ever.*"

I just stared at his stomach then, rising and falling heavily. His shirt was unbuttoned, remember, and the bruise seemed to expand and contract with his anger. Then suddenly he stood up. "Hey! Follow me!"

He was already running across the hard soil, grit and grass crunching beneath his shoes, leaving me no choice but to stagger after him. How he knew one shallow hollow from another in that featureless world was beyond me, but somehow he made a beeline directly for, well, for—

"Uh, what *is* that?"

Ty looked at me like I'd incorrectly identified a gamepad

as a joystick, confused Black Eyed Peas with the Fugees or called a Ford Bronco a Chevy Trailblazer.

"Duh. It's a coyote den."

"It" was a hole in the ground. Or rather, a pair of holes: a shallow trench covered by about eighteen inches of earth. There were no tracks, no bits of bone or fur. How Ty knew it was the work of coyotes and not erosion was anyone's guess. But, you know, he was a Kansan, and a Petit besides: I figured he'd probly shot it. But I could've never predicted what he said next.

"Let's make one!"

I stared at the trench. I tried to connect it to what we'd been talking about a minute ago: his mother, and abandoning your home and your kids. I could see the symbolism in it, I suppose, the concept of shelter reduced to its most fundamental sense, but the idea of making a human-sized version—of excavating it from this rock-hard soil in hundred-degree air—seemed less romantic than, well, stupid.

"C'mon, Daniel," Ty sensed my reluctance (probly because I said, "I'm reluctant"). "It'll be cool."

"Dude. Scoring a copy of *The Grey Album* on Pirate Bay is cool. Getting a new car is cool. Digging . . . a . . . *hole*? Not cool, dude. Not cool at all."

"Enough with the dudes, dude. Now come on, let's get a couple of shovels. We'll dig our way straight to hell."

By "hell" I assumed he meant the place where people who never wanted to see their dads went. I wasn't quite as mad at my dad as Ty was at his, but still. If hell was where we could be alone, far away from fathers and teachers, and friends who weren't really friends, and enemies who weren't really enemies, then, well, toss me a shovel.

The hole story

We spent five weeks on it. Not because we worked at it every day, but because we didn't.

In fact I almost never hung out with Ty two days running, because every afternoon he spent with me translated to one or two or six afternoons that his dad invented a whole slew of chores to keep him busy. "It drives him *crazy* that he don't know where I am. He thinks I've got a girl somewhere cuz I lost my belt."

Ty reported this gleefully, but what he didn't report was the source of the fresh bruises that replaced the ones on his cheek and ribs, the archipelago of black-and-blue lumps that floated on his back, the welts that tracked up and down his legs like tire treads. When I tried to ask him about them, all he said was:

"Check this out."

He lifted up his shirt. His dad had run a length of rope through his belt loops to replace the strip of patent leather that'd been there before. He'd even—may God strike me dead if I'm making this up—poured hot wax over the knot, so he'd know whether the rope'd been untied.

"I was like, Dad, I don't have to take my pants off. All I have to do is—" and he pulled down his fly, exposing a sliver of not-quite-white undies framed by the angry teeth of his zipper. It made me think of that scene in *There's Something About Mary*— I'm sure you know the one, although Ty, not surprisingly, didn't.

"Mary who?" he said, dropping his shirt over the waxed rope. "Whatever," he waved away my answer. "He like to knock my head off."

Judging from Ty's fat lip, it looked like his dad *had* knocked his head off. But that was the one injury Ty did tell me about.

"That lard-ass Mike Weise." Ty poked his swollen lip so hard that it brought tears to his eyes, which in turn made him laugh until he started coughing. He squeezed his bruised ribs and let out a string of curses. "Man," he said when he could talk again. "I am a *mess*. But you should see *him*."

In fact, Mike Weise was in first period calc with me, and I didn't recall a scratch on him. But I didn't mention this to Ty.

In fact, I always knew when Ty got in fights, because he didn't show up for lunch. Apparently Mr. Petit'd convinced Principal Stickley that Ty absolutely had to come home right after school to work in the family business, and so whenever Ty got in trouble (i.e., two or three times a week) he had to spend lunch period in the front office.

I only ever saw him fight once: Chad Paglia, who, besides being the only kid in school with an Italian last name (besides his sister Christina, I mean) was also the welterweight star of the school's wrestling team. That's 184 pounds if you don't know wrestling weight classes; Ty weighed about 125. So you kind of get how it went down: Chad beat the holy royal crap out of Ty, or he would have, if Mr. Pollack hadn't told them to knock it off. Actually, Mr. Pollack told them to knock it off, and Chad was totally like, whatever, I wasn't really fighting anyway, but Ty kept swinging at Chad until Mr. Pollack, who just happened to be the assistant coach of the wrestling team (and one-time All-State heavyweight), put Ty into some kind of headlock. Even then Ty was struggling to throw himself at Chad, lifting both feet off the ground so that Mr. Pollack was more or less holding him up by this throat, and it was hard to say which of them had the redder cheeks.

"Step to me!" Ty half screamed, half choked (though God only knows where he picked up a phrase like "step to me"). "Step to my face and say it to me!"

"I already said it to your face," Chad Paglia said, doing that fake dusting-off thing with his shirt and jeans. "Your friend is a faggot."

"I'll hunt you down!" Ty spat. "I'll find out where you live!"

"We're the only Paglias in the phone book," Chad said. "Come by any time you want to get your face broke." He turned and strolled down the hall then, and Mr. Pollack dragged Ty to the principal's office, kicking and screaming the whole way.

"I'll kill you if you go near him! You hear me, you piece of trash? I—will—kill—*you*!"

Meanwhile:

The dog days of September metamorphosed into the why-yes-it-really-*is*-autumn chill of early October. Fall was a tricky time for me, because that's when the leaves started falling off the trees (that doesn't even *deserve* a duh), and the heretofore impenetrable Trojan Wall of foliage that protected our house from prying eyes was suddenly revealed to be nothing more than a thin strip of trees that, because they'd been planted in straight lines, almost seemed to point your eyes towards our dingy little trailer choking inside its net of vines. Not that the leaves had fallen, yet. They'd just gone limp and brown around the edges, maybe one or two blowing to the ground like shoppers trying to beat the Christmas rush. The sun set earlier too, bringing with it cold breezes that seemed to blow off the snow-covered Rockies five hundred miles to the west. It was barely light when I got up for school, which made it that much harder to wake up, and then it wasn't light at all, and the only thing that got me out of bed was the thought of seeing Ty at his locker before classes started and then seeing him for a whole twenty-five minutes at lunch and then again for one final chat outside his bus, where, like a cheating spouse, he would tell me whether or not he thought he could get away to see me that night.

So. The hole. Our original intention—to build a human-sized coyote den—faded pretty quickly, and what we ended up with was, well, a hole. But a covered hole: if it ever actually rained on the plain we would've been protected, or at least our heads would've been, although I'm sure our butts would've gotten soaked since, well, it was a hole, and holes tend to fill up with water when it rains, don't they?

What I can tell you for sure is that it was a filthy job. *Filthy*. Every night we went there we emerged coated with dirt that our sweat had turned to mud, which is fun when you're five or six or seven or eight, but a little gross when you're sixteen. At the same time, however, the fissure opening up in the earth's skin seemed to promise so much, as if, if we kept at it long enough, we would make a tunnel to a place far from Kansas and broken dads and missing moms and a school full of kids who hated us and we hated back. Or maybe the ambition was smaller: maybe it was just the idea of making a space that was ours and not theirs, no matter how small and dingy it was. Or, who knows, maybe it was the labor itself. What I mean is, the work was sweaty and close. It was impossible not to rub against one another in the cramped quarters. Ty had this way of taking me by the hipbones and guiding me to one side or the other as we squeezed past each other in the entrance. I was shyer, would use my shovel to steer him out of the way as though he were roadkill I didn't want to touch—but then, as I stepped by, I would pretend to trip and fall against him and wrestle him to the wall.

There was a lot of wrestling.

There was a lot of lying next to each other after wrestling.

There was a lot of lying next to each other.

I thought of what Ty'd said the first time we'd lain next to each other, about Adam opening his eyes and taking his first breaths, and I remembered how Adam was lonely because he was the only one of his kind. But I didn't know if I was lonely or not, because I didn't know if Ty was my kind or not, and after a minute or two, when the silence seemed to float above us like some impossibly huge thing, a Borg cube or the Death Star, I'd get up and grab my shovel, and Ty would get up and grab his shovel, and then we'd squeeze past each other in the narrow entrance to the hole, hips rubbing against each other, chests brushing, hands touching bare skin in ways they could've never done in another context, but which was innocent here— *clean*—precisely because we were so dirty. Because we were digging a hole, and that's all we were doing.

When we finally stopped, the hole was ten, maybe twelve feet deep and half as high, narrow enough that our knees touched when we sat cross-legged inside it. We built a fire—it took us an hour to gather the firewood and two to set it alight—and toasted marshmallows and then we never went back again. Sometimes Ty would bring it up, wondering if maybe a hundred years in the future somebody would come across it and find the ashes and the faded plastic marshmallow bag and think it was, "like, historical." I wondered if maybe the top would fill up with snow during a blizzard and then a deer or a coyote or maybe even an ostrich—we never did see one the whole time— would fall into it and be trapped there, and would slowly starve to death. Ty said maybe we should fill it in, but we never did, and we never went back the following spring either, to see if there was a half-rotted corpse in the bottom. If you believe in Schrödinger's cat then these possibilities are probly interesting to you, but me, I'm a dog person, and only good with what's in front of my face.

I mentioned that we had a dog, right? The German shepherd? Fang? It was a good dog. A smart dog. How do I know it was smart? Because it knew enough to get the hell out of our house, that's how.

"Creepy," I said to Ty, after the marshmallows were gone and the fire'd burned out.

"What's creepy?"

I looked up at the dark walls hemming us in, shovel cuts prominent as whip marks, the sliver of sky visible around the bend of earth.

"It feels like we're sitting in our own grave."

A stricken expression twisted Ty's face—the same look he got when he grabbed the Regiers' electric fence on a dare— and then he got up and walked away.

You know that expression, "mo' money, mo' problems"? Yeah, that's pretty much crap. I mean, I know Biggie got shot and all, but Ty was living proof that the less you have the harder it is. Compared to him I was rich. Compared to me he was the most miserable boy in the world.

I followed him up and down the usual hills. Again, I don't know how he knew where he was going, how we'd never been here before, but there was something different on the other side of this hill. Truth be told, it was just mud. The valley was a little lower here, which made the water table a little higher. The resulting bog—an eighth of an acre at most—was black and churned by two-toed ostrich prints, with here and there standing puddles of water three or four feet in diameter. In a minute I'd kicked my shoes off. The mud was cold and thick like cream cheese just taken out of the refrigerator—but black cream cheese, foul and fecund at the same time. Strong and resistant when you stepped in, tightly gripping as you tried to step out. I made it six steps before I fell onto my hands and knees. I had an urge to lie down and roll around in it, but before I could Ty screamed.

"Daniel!"

The panic in his voice: I thought something had happened to *him*, but it turned out he thought something had happened to *me*. When I turned I saw that he'd kicked his stupid shoes off but hadn't actually ventured into the mud. Instead he paced its edge like a sandpiper skirting the tide back on Long Island.

"Jesus, Ty. You scared the crap out of me."

"You should get out of there. It's not safe."

Still on my hands and knees, I looked around at the expanse of mud. My body had already acclimated to the chill and my fingers kneaded the clayey goop. Ty's fear made me think of the La Brea Tar Pits, but only in a hey-aren't-I-a-good-student-to-remember-the-La-Brea-Tar-Pits-(just-like-I-know-about-Schrödinger's-cat)? kind of way. There were no sinkholes or pools of quicksand in Kansas. Just mud so thick we could've made pottery out of it, ashtrays or blobbies or voodoo statues to take down our enemies: Ian Abernathy and Troy Bellows and Beanpole Overholser, either of our dads. Both of them for that matter.

"Dude," I said to Ty, "calm down. It's just, you know, mud."

Ty wrung his hands like a nervous monkey. "You don't know. There could be holes. You could sink in, I couldn't reach you in time. You should get out, Daniel. You should get out now."

Something in his voice told me this wasn't the time to reason with him. I stood up awkwardly, made my way to dry ground, lurching in the thick soup. I fell once, and he stifled a yelp. When I stood up again I held my goop-encrusted hands in front of me like the Swamp Thing, lurched stiff-legged the last few feet. In my best old-time horror-movie voice, I said:

"What strange creature lumbers forth from the infernal blackness, its external appearance human, but unspeakable desires lurking deep within its breast?"

"Cut it out, Daniel." Ty stepped back as I stepped towards him. "You get that crap on me and I'll kick your ass."

I dropped my hands.

"Sorry to spoil the tea party, Mary Jane. Just give me a moment to spread my tablecloth and then we'll have some poppy seed muffins with black currant jam."

Ty cursed. It wasn't the word, wasn't even the accompanying

finger gesture, which was reflexive more than angry. It was the look on his face. As if I was a ghost and he wished I was the real thing, or that I'd stayed dead.

"Dude. What's up?"

Ty turned, started walking away. "Nothin'."

By now I knew that when Ty started dropping his g's somethin' was up. Ty hated rednecks, and hated sounding like one even more.

"Ty!" My voice was sharper than I'd intended. I reached out for him, saw my mud-encrusted hand and pulled back just in time. "Hey. It's me. It's Daniel."

Ty took three more steps, then dropped to his knees as though the great puppeteer in the sky had released his strings. He cursed again, his voice wet with that clot of mucus that collects at the back of your throat when you're swallowing back tears.

I wanted to touch him on the shoulder, or maybe trace the line of his ear or the hairline at the nape of his neck, but my hands were covered with mud, and anyway boys don't touch each other like that. But I told myself it was just the mud.

"My brother," Ty said.

I started slightly. For a moment I'd thought he meant me. I thought he was calling me his brother.

"L.D.?" I said, even though I knew he didn't mean L.D.

"No." Ty made a blustery, whinnying sound, and I knew he was fighting with all his might not to cry. "No. Not L.D."

"Holly."

He nodded. "Holly."

Suddenly I had one of those $1 + 1 = 2$ flashes. I remembered what had set Ty off in the first place, which was my comment about our hole being like an open grave, and I remembered his *didn't* not *doesn't* of our first day in the forest, and then I turned and looked back at the muddy bog. I stared at it for a long time, then looked down at my hands, my feet, my knees.

"Aw, crap," I said, and began flinging and scraping the mud off my skin as well as I could. "Crap crap crap. Here," I said to Ty. "Really? *Here*?"

Ty nodded miserably. When it seemed like I'd gotten all the mud off that I could without a fire hose, I walked in front of him and sat down.

"Here."

Ty's cheeks were red and puffy. "I dunno why I'm getting so worked up. It was a long time ago."

"He was your brother." I turned to the mud again. "Quicksand?"

Ty let out a little blubbery laugh. "Nah, no quicksand." He pointed to a line on the surrounding hills. Tufts of grass fell over an eroded patch of bare dry soil like bangs combed forwards to cover a receding hairline. Ty's arm traced a wide circle around us, and as it traveled I could see the area fill up with water, making a small pond.

"In wet years that's how high the water gets. It was our swimming hole."

The line Ty pointed out was three, maybe four feet above the valley floor. The pond would've been smaller than our clearing, as shallow as a hot tub. Shallow enough that I felt compelled to ask:

"He . . . drowned?"

Ty nodded his head, then shook it. Then nodded again. "Oh, man. I've never said this out loud before. Man oh man."

It took all my strength not to put my dirty hand on his knee.

"It's okay. If you tell me. I won't tell anyone."

"It didn't make any sense." Ty pointed at the waterline again. "It wasn't but three, four feet deep."

"How—"

"Tall was he? 'Bout, four, five feet."

"—old was he?"

Ty turned from the mud and looked at me for a moment. He shook his head, let his eyes fall.

"Ty?"

Before I knew what was happening Ty had thrown his face in my muddy lap and his sobs echoed eerily in the wet valley.

"He was my twin, Daniel! He was my twin brother, and he drowned himself and left me all alone!"

He was younger by eighty-two minutes. That's a long time between twins. He didn't want to come out, Ty said. The doctor had to go in and get him.

Technically they were identical but you'd've never known it. Holly was always smaller than Ty, shyer. Hid behind his bigger brother, did whatever he said. He took it hardest of all four children when their mom disappeared—they were only seven, but Holly always acted as though Ty knew something he didn't. Knew where their mom had gone, when she was coming back, or when they'd escape their dad's house to join her. As the years passed and she didn't come back or send for them he stopped talking about her, but Ty knew he thought about her all the time. He liked to draw, but their dad thought drawing was sinful, so he drew in the dirt. He drew stick figures, with a stick, a woman with a boy on either hand, and afterwards he'd rub them out with his bare feet. When he forgot to wash his feet before he went in the house his dad would whip the blackened soles with an electrical cord.

Ty said Holly always forgot to wash his feet.

By the time he was eleven, he'd become a recluse. Ty had to get him out of bed in the morning, make him shower, dress, eat. Nothing caught his brother's attention, roused him from his stupor, not even the threat of a whipping. He just stood there and stared at Mr. Petit as if willing him to do the thing they both really wanted him to do. But it's no fun hitting someone if it doesn't make him suffer, so their dad took to ignoring Holly instead. He'd pass plates of food over Holly's head at the table, hand out playing card–sized Bible verses to L.D., June, Ty, but leave a blank card in front of Holly. Holly didn't protest, didn't even seem to notice. He used his thumbnail to etch stick figures of a woman and two boys into the blank laminated cards and stare at his empty plate in silence unless Ty put some food on it, put a fork in his hand, said, "Eat." Which is why, Ty said, he didn't notice Holly wasn't in bed that night.

"He put clothes under the sheets. You know, like a person. He even—" Ty moved his hands through the air, traced a shape. When I didn't understand he showed me with his body. Curled up on the ground in a fetal position with his knees only inches from his snuffling nose, caked with dirty mucus. "Like a baby," Ty said, "cuz that was how he slept."

Ty said: "No one realized he was gone till the next morning."

"We didn't find him till the day after that," Ty said.

"He was on his back," Ty told me. "On the water, on his back. Everyone said it was like he'd gone to sleep on the bottom of the pond and floated to the surface. But I told them he didn't sleep on his back. He slept on his side, like a baby."

Ty drew a stick figure in the ground beside him, arms and legs akimbo.

"He was like that," he said, and then he rubbed out the drawing with his feet.

He showed me the gravestone. The Petits had a scraggly cedar break planted west of the house to check snow drifts in the winter, and Holly's ashes were buried beneath them and marked by a single brown brick. Vitrified, ferrous, crenellated: not even the fanciest adjectives in the world could disguise the fact that Mr. Petit had marked the final resting place of his youngest son with a leftover brick from the construction of his dingy subterranean house. Two brass letters had been set in the top.

H.P.

Ty brushed dirt and needles off the brick.

"The crows had eaten his eyes by the time we found him."

His voice was nearly inaudible, as if the crows that had eaten his twin's eyes had taken his tongue as well. With the light coating of dust covering his body, he could've been Adam standing up for the first time, his earthen heart pumping a river of mud through his veins, but his eyes remained as lifeless and empty as still water, reflecting only what passes in front of it.

Well, what would you have done? I put my hand—still dirty, but dry now—on his shoulder. But before I could pull him close he threw me off.

"I'm not gay, Daniel. Dammit, I'm not! I'm not!"

He ran for the house then. It was a good hundred yards

away, and I could've caught him easily, but the field was open to the house's windows. I didn't know if his dad was home, but I knew that if his dad saw me everything would be that much worse. Not for me. For Ty.

I waited though, in case he turned around. He didn't turn around.

The door slammed.

I continued to wait, in case the door opened. It didn't open.

A light came on in a back window.

I kept waiting.

"Oh hell, Sprout," Mrs. Miller said when she got to the end of what I'd written. "Is *this* where everything was going? I could've told you all this on the first day of school, if you'd've just come to me."

Oh.

Yeah.

Mrs. Miller.

You might remember her as the inventor of such cocktails as the mojitorita and the margarinha, as well as the hanger of the front-door plaque "God Bless Synonyms, Metaphors, and Euphemisms too!" Oh, and the seducer of my dad. Let's not forget that.

You didn't think she'd let me off the hook just because I was being "sullen and uncooperative," did you? (That was me by the way: "I'm being sullen and uncooperative," I told her when she walked in on me trying to raise my left eyebrow without moving my right, which is harder than it looks. "Really?" Her own eyebrows had gone up in unison. "I thought you looked perplexed myself.")

As the weeks ticked by, she reminded me with ever-increasing frequency that she'd "staked her reputation on a junior," and even though she now came to school in untucked, unbuttoned blouses, she was as uptight as ever where the State Essay Contest was concerned. Since time trials weren't working (I could fill more than a dozen sheets of paper with the word "No" in five minutes) she assigned me weekly papers instead. At first I thought I'd blow those off too. But, well, things with Ty were just so strange. He'd moved into my life and pushed everything else aside, yet hadn't given me anything concrete to take the place of what was gone. Not that there'd been a lot for him to replace. Ruthie. *Shove*. Ian. *Flick*. My dad. *Ping*. All gone. That left just me.

Me and Ty.

I dunno. Maybe Mrs. Miller'd had more of an effect on me than I realized, or maybe I'd just become infatuated with my own linguistic prowess. But every Sunday night a blank page sat in front of me on the table, and, well, *something* had to go on it (besides my name, I mean, and a few green smudges, Sunday being the night I usually touched up my hair). I wrote hesitantly at first, afraid of revealing too much, but before I knew it I'd produced as many pages about the month and a half I'd spent with Ty as I had about the first sixteen years of my life. But this time I wrote not to reveal something about myself, but to discover something about Ty. Some crucial fact I'd missed during our F2F encounters. And when I say "with Ty," I mean just that: I didn't write a word about the strained fifteen-second chats I had with Ruthie when she caught me in the lunch line, the post-its on my locker I didn't answer or the bazillion and one phone calls I dodged. Nor have I mentioned the various and pretty much transparent attempts Ian made to lure me into the janitors' closet, or get us both detention, up to and including pretending to share his answers on a history quiz, which made Mrs. Coulter laugh so hard I thought she was going to pee herself (the funny thing is, I *had* been copying his answers, because I'd hung out with Ty the night before and hadn't read the assignment). And, when you find out that I've left out the academic warning I got in civics (you'd think after twenty-four or twenty-five constitutional amendments they'd just start over, but *no*, they keep adding more), it probly won't come as a surprise that I also skipped over the fact that I got booted from the cross-country team (you're not allowed to suit up for sports when you're on academic probation at Buhler, and since I'd already missed like 90% of the practices Coach Greene went ahead and gave me the ax). And so anyway, after all that I doubt it'll come as a big shocker that I haven't bothered to allude to the truly magical hour I spent with Mrs. Miller every day in fourth period, let alone the "bonus session" on Fridays when she pulled me out of independent study to go over my writing assignment for the week. This was sixth—i.e., last—period, and Mrs. Miller generally ignored the 3:30 bell, my peers screaming their weekend plans up and down the hallway outside her door, the throaty rumble of buses as they lumbered south on Main Street with their sardine-loads of high school-ers. "I'll just drive you home," she always said, a big smile on her face, like she was taking me to the mall or a water park or, I don't know, a strip club. But of course it wasn't just *me* she was taking to my house: it was herself, and by the time we turned on 82nd Street I'd become little more than a passenger. I ground the back of my head into the already-green-stained headrest of her Civic while she touched up her lipstick and eye shadow and foundation or blush or whatever it is you call the makeup women put on their cheeks. She drove with one hand, the rearview and vanity mirrors angled so she could see both sides of her face at once, and every once in a while I'd scream "Cow!" or "Deer!" or "Ostrich!" just to make her jump. When

177

we reached my house I climbed out and my dad climbed in, his hair as neatly combed as mine was messy, his shirt tucked into his belt in a way that somehow complimented Mrs. Miller's untucked blouses. "S'a jar-a cream corn on the counter," he'd joke as we passed each other. "Make it last till Monday." In fact there was usually a twenty-dollar bill on the counter, and the car keys, and of course my notebook—which pretty much brings us back to where this paragraph started about two pages ago. I.e., Mrs. M., reading slowly, occasionally commenting on my "esoterical grammatical constructions" or "nonlinear narrative progression" or "over-reliance on irony as a distancing technique," and even though she often looked at me over the tops of her glasses with that skeptical expression she'd thrown my way when she first recruited me at the end of sophomore year, she never did ask the one question that, you know, *I* also wanted the answer to, even more than she did. Namely:

Was Ty gay?

On the one hand, there was our need to be with each other as much as possible, and the more or less constant excuses we found to touch each other. On the other was the fact that Ty pretty much talked about girls nonstop (which comments I haven't reproduced here because, first of all, the world really doesn't need one more catalog of teenage boys talking about girls' bodies, and, secondly, it's the kind of stuff that would 100% definitely get this book banned from the BHS library).

And then too there was that last thing he said. I.e.:

"I'm not gay."

That seemed pretty, you know, assertive. Definitive even.

And yet.

And yet, he'd said it without me asking him. Said it when

he was showing me his twin brother's *grave* of all things, and I'd put a hand on his shoulder to comfort him, which suggested Ty was thinking about the subject as much as I was—more even, since, although I admit I'm a little socially awkward, not even I am uncouth enough to make a play for someone at a moment like that. And let's face it: Ty wouldn't be the first gay person to deny his homosexuality: Ricky Martin, meet Doogie Hoswer. And so yeah but anyway (by which I mean what*ever*, mary): after a month and half of hanging out with him, not to mention fifty-some pages of well-observed scene-setting and exposition (that's Mrs. Miller's evaluation, by the way, not mine, although of course I'm forced to agree with her), I felt like I knew even less about Ty than when I'd first seen him standing red-skinned against the back wall of the gym. Felt like I had even less of an idea what he wanted from me than when he'd sneered, "At least my hair ain't *green*." It's kind of funny when you think about it. When I started writing about myself, I waited as long as I could before I told you I was gay, because once you reveal that, it seems like it's all anyone can think about. Look at the way my dad trashed our computer when he found out I'd been looking at gay sites (as opposed to just forbidding me from looking at certain stuff like the parent of any heterosexual kid would do) or how Mrs. Miller had to grill me on what I had or hadn't done sexually, as opposed to just giving me "the talk" that every other teenager gets. But with Ty, everything I knew about him seemed to float in the air, and the only thing that would keep it from blowing away like a Kansas tumbleweed was knowing whether or not he was gay. Knowing whether the amorphous feelings that hovered between us were going to solidify into a bridge that would bring us together, or a wall that would keep us apart. And like I said, I'd've thought Mrs. Miller would've asked me about this, but all she said was:

"The teachers call it day-tention."

I took my essay from her outstretched hand.

"Huh?"

We sat in the office behind her classroom. The walls were lined with melamine shelves that sagged beneath the weight of graffiti'd textbooks and dusty stacks of once and future tests, and below the counter-slash-desk thingy that ran around all four walls sat bags and plastic boxes and two-drawer filing cabinets whose drawers looked rusted shut.

"Day-tention. Detention during the day. Oh, and 'first recruited'? Redundant."

"One thing at a time, please."

"Haven't you noticed Ty doesn't have to stay after school, even though he gets in a fight just about every other day and pretty much never does his homework and has a mouth like a truck driver crossed with a marine sergeant?"

"I'm pretty sure that's a variety of specialty porn," I said, and then, while Mrs. Miller blushed, I threw in, "Ty told me he doesn't have to stay late because he works for his dad."

Mrs. Miller rolled her eyes. "As far as I know, Phil Petit's only source of income is stealing copper from construction sites and selling it to the scrap metal yard down in South Hutch, which why that doesn't violate the eighth commandment is beyond me. *Look*," she silenced me with a semi-parental voice. "The school has known Phil Petit beats his children ever since the oldest one, what's his name—"

"L.D."

"—ever since L.D. first went home with an F and came back with a black eye. But if you try to talk to them about it they deny everything. Mr. Stickley and Mr. Philpot thought maybe the girl—"

"June."

"June." Mrs. Miller shook her head like, *June*, what a *Seventh Heaven* kind of name. "The Phil-bot and Sticky thought maybe June would fess up, but instead she started dating boys from the south side of town, and, well, when you have three kids—"

"Four."

"Oh!" A slightly embarrassed smile flashed across her face. "The other one."

"Holly."

"Right. Hollis." Her eyes softened and she shook her head sadly. "What was I saying?"

"Four kids."

"Right. When you have four kids—"

"Three."

Mrs. Miller sighed heavily.

"When the children deny their father mistreats them, there's pretty much nothing the school can do. So we push their F's to D's, their D's to C's, whatever it takes to pass them through to the next grade, and we invented day-tention, because if we make them stay after school they come in the next day with a fresh set of bruises. Assuming they come in the next day at all."

"Oh!" I said like I was just getting it. "Day-*tent*-ion." I over-enunciated the *t*, ended up spitting on my paper. "I thought you were saying day-*tens*-ion, like, you know, a really *tense day*, or *ten*-sion during the *day*time."

Mrs. Miller glared at me. "I didn't make up the term, Sprout."

"Yeah, but you use it. You do it."

"Actually, I've never had a Petit. They're not exactly what you'd call honor students." I must've made a face, because she raised her hands helplessly. "What do you want me to do? Call Child Protective Services and say hey, I think this guy beats his kids, even though they claim he's the bestest dad in the whole wide God-fearing world? Maybe I should just go to his house and tell him he's a bad, bad man?"

"I think you should stop"—*BLEEP BLEEP BLEEP*—"ing my dad." I broke off, stared at Mrs. Miller in surprise. "Was that a *cell phone*?"

Not only did Mrs. Miller not carry a cell herself, she was said to have once made a girl hand-copy the entirety of her user's manual when her phone went off in class—including the Spanish, French, German, and Japanese versions. Mrs. M. blushed now, but a smile flickered across her mouth, a little proud, a little defiant, a little hopeful too. She rolled her chair backwards to the opposite side of the room, a move that would've come off better if the casters hadn't tangled in the half-shredded industrial carpeting and almost tipped her over. She used her heels to drag herself the last couple of feet, pulled a TJ Maxx shopping bag from beneath the counter. A tangle of black cords protruded from the bag, plugged into a power strip. She tipped the bag towards me. It was filled with dozens of Sonys, Sony Ericssons, Nokias, Motorolas, LGs, even a Black-Berry. Blue, gray, silver, pink, green, some cracked and scratched, some covered with FUCT and OBEY and R★ stickers, others shiny and new. There'd been a second *BLEEP BLEEP BLEEP* as she scooted across the room, and now a closed Samsung clamshell let out a truncated *BLEEP BLEE* and then presumably went to voicemail.

"Twenty-nine," Mrs. Miller said before I asked. "Eight years of confiscation by Mr. Johanson and I."

"Mr. Johanson and *me*. You keep them plugged in? Really?"

"Freddy and I got curious. We wondered how many students deactivated their phones after we took them away, as opposed to how many were too embarrassed to tell their parents that their phone'd—their phone *had* been confiscated. So we picked up a few chargers, rotate them to keep the batteries powered up. You'd be surprised. Some of these puppies have been yipping away for more than a year. And the buzzing." She moved her thumbs like she was texting. "It sounds like a sarcophagus full of scarab beetles."

I thought about asking what a scarab beetle was, but figured I could just google it Monday. The Samsung *BLEEP*ed, announcing a new voicemail, and Mrs. Miller chuckled. "That's Vicki Watkins'. I took it from her yesterday, so it's been busy."

"She's a popular girl."

"She's a slut, is what you mean."

I shrank away from the overladen shelves as if they might fall down like the walls of Jericho. For a teacher to call a student a slut—on school property, no less—was a bit like wearing a hooded black robe in a Baptist church at Christmas. But then Mrs. Miller wheeled back across the room and took my hand and said, "I've missed you, Sprout," and I suddenly realized the word and the hopeful look in her eyes had more to do with me than Vicki Watkins (who *was* a slut, when you got right down to it, which most of us would be if we had the guts for it, or, in her case, the ass). Mrs. M.'s use of the word "slut" was the equivalent of leaving me alone on her patio so I could pour tequila into my margarita, or dissing Mrs. Whittaker's English class as *remedial*. She wanted to prove she was still on my side, not theirs, whether *they* were cliquey girls or square teachers.

I looked down at my hand in Mrs. Miller's as if I was just noticing it sat in a pot of boiling water, but I didn't pull it away.

"You've had me in class every day."

Mrs. Miller held my hand a moment longer, then let go. "I have Peter Bowen in class too. And—ugh!—Samantha Hardy, and that Loomis girl." She barked a brief, bitter laugh. "For her paper on Booker T. Washington and George Washington Carver, she wrote Booger and Carter, every time, I swear to God."

"That was probly spellcheck."

"That was *probly* laziness, if not simply stupidity. That is *def- initely* what I have to deal with around here, ninety-nine days out of a hundred, with ninety-nine percent of my students, and ninety-eight percent of my colleagues." She sighed again, but it was less plaintive, more wistful. "I've *missed* you," she said again. "Missed this. Our little talks."

"Hey, no one asked you to start dating my dad."

"Really?" Mrs. Miller said, and you could tell the word had come out before she'd taken the time consider it. I remem- bered Ruthie's question from the day before school started, about whether I'd intentionally played matchmaker, or whether it'd merely been unconscious (okay, she didn't use the word "unconscious," but it's what she meant).

Mrs. Miller drew a line in the air with her hand.

"I'm not going to talk to you about my relationship with Bob. That's a discussion for him to begin, not me. What I would like to talk about—" she tapped the paper on the counter between us "—is this."

Somehow I didn't think she meant the essay. The language,

I mean. "Esoterical grammatical constructions" and "nonlinear narrative progression" and all that. But once again she threw me for a loop.

"Do you know what a clitic is?"

"No, but it sounds dirty."

"A clitic," Mrs. M. said, tapping my essay again, "is a particular form of a word that doesn't have any real meaning until it attaches to another word. The simplest example is the contraction. The apostrophe-M in *I'm*, or the double-L in *I'll*. Or that little e in *email*. A clitic has lost its ability to be independent, can only exist when another, stronger word comes along to prop it up."

"Um?" I said, cuz, like, what else was I going to say? "I liked it better when I thought it was dirty." But as I stared cluelessly at her finger tapping my essay, I noticed that it was covering and uncovering the word "Ty," and one of those lightbulbs went on in my brain. Well, it didn't go on as much as flicker a bit, but I thought I sort of understood what she was trying to tell me.

"You're saying Ty is a . . ." The lightbulb flickered out. "Contraction?"

"*Clitic*," she said. "Good lord, Sprout, you work some complicated metaphors. Give me one of my own."

"You—think—Ty—" the words dropped out of my mouth one at a time, as I tried to figure out what she was saying "—is—dependent—on—*me*?"

"Think about it. A twin who lost his brother. A boy with no mother, no friends, no future. It makes sense that he'd latch onto anyone who'd let him."

"You're saying—" I gulped, struggling to keep my voice level "—you're saying Ty's friendship with me isn't *real*? That I'm just, I dunno, *handy*? A *prop* or something?"

Mrs. Miller shook her head rapidly, her long blonde unhair-sprayed locks swishing back and forth like a Clairol commercial. "It's *real*, Sprout. Of course it's real. I'm just not sure it's what you think it is. What you hope it is." I started to say something, but she waved me silent. "Look, it's not Ty I'm concerned about here. It's you."

"Why? I thought he was the clitic. The apostrophe-M. I'm just the good old noun."

"Pronoun." Mrs. Miller allowed herself a grin. Then: "It takes two to tango, Sprout. Or, in your case, to wrestle, fall out of trees, and dig holes in the ground. Since you've met him, your one stable friendship has fallen apart, you've been kicked off the cross-country team, and you're on academic probation."

"Don't forget that I've started shooting heroin and dismembering small animals."

"This is serious, Sprout."

"The only reason I did well in school was because I had nothing better to do. I'm as smart or as stupid as I ever was. I'm just not regurgitating it on some test."

"Well, what about writing? Don't tell me that was just a way to fill up time. You were too good at it not to care."

"I'm *still* good at it!" I tapped the essay on the counter. "Don't tell me this isn't good, cuz I *know* it is."

"Sprout—" Mrs. Miller's voice fell. Up till then she'd sounded stern yet pleading. Now she just sounded defeated. "Of course it's *good*. It's great. But—you know you can't write about this."

"About what? Ty?"

"Not Ty. Not exactly. About—"

"What? About being *gay*?"

Mrs. Miller shrugged helplessly. "You know the state you

186

live in, Sprout. If you turn in an essay like this, an essay *about* this, the judges aren't going to see your inventiveness, your humor, your compassion. They're just going to see your sexuality. And they're not going to like it."

"And that's a good reason not to write about it? Because some bigot in Topeka will be offended?"

"No. Because some bigot in Topeka will keep you from winning the contest you deserve to win. From getting the scholarship that'll help you go to the college of your choice, and heading towards the life you deserve to have."

I started to protest again, then closed my mouth. It was so confusing. On the one hand, there was what I'd said to Ruthie about how I wouldn't come out at school because I didn't want everyone to think of me as the gay kid. But on the other hand there was this feeling that if I couldn't write about being gay for the State Essay Contest, then I wasn't actually representing myself. And even though I understood that it wasn't *my* fault people got all bent out of shape when they saw the words "gay" and "teenager" next to each other in a sentence, still, I knew I wasn't doing a very good job dealing with the problem.

So what'd I do? What anyone would, I guess. I changed the subject.

"I don't need the scholarship. My dad put aside money—"

But Mrs. M. was shaking her head. "There's no money, Sprout."

"What are you talking about?"

"I asked Bob. He says he doesn't know where you got that idea."

"I got the idea from him telling me he put money aside. When he sold our house on Long Island."

"If he ever said that, he doesn't remember." Mrs. Miller's

raised eyebrows acknowledged that there were probly a lot of things my dad didn't remember about the last four years. "At any rate, there's almost nothing left. He's looking for a job now. You don't think he's shaving for me, do you?"

I ignored her weak attempt at a joke.

"But how am I going to pay for college?"

"By getting good grades. By winning this contest, and getting the scholarship you deserve. By giving up the idea of saving Ty, and concentrating on yourself."

"I don't want to—" I stopped. I was a lot of things, but I wasn't a liar, and I knew just as well as Mrs. Miller that I really *did* want to save Ty.

Mrs. Miller let the silence sit between us another moment, as though it were cementing our agreement. Our alliance. Then she glanced at her watch. "Oh dear, look at the time. I need to be getting you home."

"Yeah, um, sure."

"Don't forget this." She tapped my essay like it was one of the twenty-dollar bills my dad left on the counter for me.

"Sure," I said again, stuffing the pages in my pocket. "Whatever." I stood up slowly, followed her out of the office.

You'd think the day would've thrown enough at me by that point, but apparently the universe still had one more surprise up its sleeve. As we stepped from Mrs. Miller's classroom, I saw a pair of figures halfway down the hall, their bodies glued together at lips, hips, and ankles.

"Ahem." Mrs. Miller did that fake clearing of the throat thing, and then said, "Ahem" again, because whenever you do that fake clearing of the throat thing you usually end up having to clear your throat for real.

The figures separated. Not that I needed to see their faces to know who it was.

"Oh, hey Sprout." Ian Abernathy rubbed fuchsia lipstick off his mouth with what looked like a sigh of relief. "Haven't seen *you* around in a while."

I ignored him. Ian and I'd had two classes together that day, like we did every day. My eyes were glued to the second person, who was busy reapplying the lipstick she'd smeared all over Ian's lips before she actually looked at me.

"Oh, *hey* Sprout," Ruthie Wilcox said, her voice brighter than all the lighters at a Pearl Jam concert when they sing "Jeremy spoke in class today-ay." Her and Ian's fingers tangled together like a pair of mating octopuses. "I'm *so* glad this happened. Now we can finally tell you our big news."

"—and I mean well of course I *knew* him. How could I not know him? My folks got divorced when I was six and my mom and me moved to Prairie Dunes that summer, so I started first grade at Union Valley and of course Ian here"—shoulder squeeze, in case I didn't realize which Ian Ruthie was referring to—"this big ol' hunk-a soccer-playing beefcake-in-the-making lived on north Lorraine and already went to UV. And so anyway, yeah, I guess I've known him for a whole *decade* now. Ten long years, yet somehow I never saw his best qualities. Who knows? Maybe it was just"—*BLEEP BLEEP BLEEP*—"I mean, ever since I got *these* babies"—Ruthie took her hand from Ian's shoulder and squeezed the same nonexistent breasts she'd brandished four years ago on the Buhler Grade School playground—"I've looked at the world a little differently. I mean, it kind of makes you wonder if biology really *is* destiny. Estrogen and cholesterol start racing through your system, and before you know it the boys you used to think were so *icky* and *like, gross* and *oh my God I'm gonna PUKE if he sticks his tongue down my throat* suddenly seem"—*BLEEP BLEEP BLEEP*—"the word I'm looking for, honey? Ian? Honey? What's the word I want?"

"Um . . . "

"Vital! That's the word! Boys just suddenly seem, like, vital for your continued existence. Like text messages, or the right shade of lipstick, or, I don't know, one of those Balenciaga bags Nicole Richie is always carrying around. I mean, Nicole Richie is so over, duh, but whatever: why was Ian the right bag for me? It's not like I even *liked* him before. Heck, I kind of hated him if you want to get right down to it. I'm not saying I spent my nights fantasizing about him driving his car into a telephone"—*BLEEP BLEEP BLEEP*—"and going through the windshield and cutting his pretty little face into Freddy Krueger hamburger or, I don't know, reaching his arm into an auger and getting it chewed off or having an engine fall off a passing 747 like it did in *Donnie Darko* and kill him while he slept. Nothing like that. But he was such a *guy's* guy. Know what I mean, Sprout? A guy's guy? The kind of guy who goes *boo-ya!* whenever someone mentions the Crusaders, and makes farting sounds when the teacher's back is turned, and has to take his whole"—*BLEEP BLEEP BLEEP*—"ing shirt off just to wipe the sweat from his forehead in gym. But, you know, off goes the shirt, and out come the abs. Show Sprout your abs, baby."

"I'm pretty sure he's—"

"*Show him your abs!*"

Ian squirmed like a nervous dog looking for a place to pee, then finally pulled up his shirt to expose a couple inches of skin.

"Pretty nice, huh? Right, Sprout? Ian's abs? Nice?"

"Yeah, they're, um"—*BLEEP BLEEP BLEEP*.

"They're *mine* now," Ruthie practically hissed, and it was hard to tell if she was acting or not. "Ugh," she said. "I hate myself, but I'm a *slave* to these abs."

Ian's face was as red as a paddled bottom, but at the same time there was an excited glint in his eyes, a half-proud, half-sheepish smirk on his face. He had great abs, and he knew it.

"But I mean he's not all abs—or biceps, for that matter, or those cute li'l dimples when he smiles."

Ian's smile, still nervous, widened, and the dimples obligingly appeared.

"He's got a great butt too!" Ruthie's laugh burst from her mouth like a cuckoo jumping out of its clock. "Kidding!" she sang. "I'm kidding! No, he's *actually* a reasonably nice guy"—*BLEEP BLEEP BLEEP*—"for-crap taste in music though."

"Hey, Daughtry is—"

"*Crap* taste in music," Ruthie emphasized, "and that whole Abercrombie look is—how can I put this delicately?—a bit homosexual mall. But his little brother has autism—"

"Asperger's—"

"—and Ian is like *totally* sweet to him. Like he helps him with his homework and plays catch with him and lets him sit on his lap to watch TV for *hours* at a time. I mean, it almost makes you wish every little kid had autism—"

"Asperger's—"

"—just so Ian could be as nice to them as he is to his little brother, and so—"

BLEEP BLEEP BLEEP.

Ruthie stopped.

Turned.

Glared at me.

"Okay, I give up. *What* is the deal with the bleeping?"

Let's pause to catch our breath, okay?

In case you haven't figured it out, we're in the back of Ruthie's mom's hand-me-down BMW convertible. I mean, *I'm* in the back of Ruthie's mom's hand-me-down BMW convertible. Ruthie and Ian are in the front, and you're just along for the ride. And so whatever: I apologize if you're a little confused as to how we ended up here. I mean, *I* ended up here. But trust me, you're not half as confused as I am.

The simple explanation is that Mrs. Miller said, "You still drive your mom's hand-me-down car, don't you, Ruthie? That BMW? A dark blue convertible?" and then she said she was running late for the hairdresser and asked Ruthie if she would take me home. That part was probly pretty obvious, right? And I mean it probly makes sense too that Ruthie was macking on Ian, since she'd told me at the beginning of the year she was going to get him. Let's not forget this is the same girl who told her parents she was going to grow a foot and managed to eke out thirteen inches: we should never be surprised when Ruthie Wilcox gets what she wants. The part I didn't understand—the part Ruthie somehow managed to leave out in her half-hour monologue—was what Ian was doing with Ruthie, since he had this look on his face like a cow standing in line at the slaughterhouse. And then there was my growing suspicion that Ruthie and Ian had been together for longer than the two months school had been in session, which suspicion was based primarily on the heart-shaped card that dangled from the rearview mirror, which bore the inscription "To us, on our quarter-year anniversary."

BLEEP BLEEP BLEEP.

Oh, and the bleeping (by which I mean the plethora of customized ring tones available to the modern aficionado of mobile communications technology): it came from Mrs. Miller's bag of phones, which I stole. Duh. It was less than an hour since school'd let out, and a Friday to boot, so they were at their peak of busyness, as high schoolers all over northern Reno County called or texted each other to find out, as one of the phones on top of the pile read, "yo where da party at???"

"The phones are Mrs. Miller's," I said to Ruthie. "Long story." And, to Ian: "I didn't know your little brother has autism."

Ian was still twisted around in his seat, his shirt still pulled up, as though showing off his abs was all he could think to do in this situation.

"Asperger's Syndrome. It's related, but, like, totally different."

"That's *illuminating*," Ruthie said to Ian. Then, to me: "Are you going to invite us in to watch youtube or something?"

Let me conclude the scene-setting by mentioning that we were in my driveway. In fact, we'd been there for about twenty minutes (it's only a ten-minute drive between my house and Buhler) but neither Ian nor I had made a move to get out of the car, since it seemed like Ruthie would do something drastic if we did. And, you know, the view from there was pretty interesting. The backseat, I mean, with Ian and Ruthie's heads framing the view. It's funny how the tiniest shift in perspective can make you see things differently. For the first time in years I noticed how small our trailer was. I mean, I make fun of how small our trailer is all the time, but the very fact that I can make fun of it makes the smallness interesting. But now it didn't seem interesting. Just small. And the net of vines covering it didn't seem interesting either. Just weird. And the stumps were weirder still. But not weird in an interesting kind of way. Who knows, maybe I was only seeing things this way because of what Mrs. Miller'd said about my college fund. I.e., that it didn't exist. Before, my house had seemed like one of those things you have to endure in order to move on to bigger and better rewards, like the bleaching process you have to go through before you can actually dye your hair. But now that it looked like I might be stuck in our little house forever, it wasn't so funny anymore.

"We don't have a computer," I said to Ruthie. "Which you know." And, to Ian: "How long have you two been dating?"

"Whatever," Ruthie said before Ian could answer. "We can watch TV or something. We haven't hung out in forever."

"We don't *have* a TV," I said, "and how long have you and Ian been *dating*?"

For the first time Ruthie's composure cracked. She turned around to face forwards, looked at me in the rearview mirror instead of head on.

"Since the summer," she said, sighing heavily. "Since you and Mrs. Miller became, like, best friends."

"You spent the summer in England."

"I spent July and August in England. I spent June with Ian, while you were in Mrs. Miller's backyard, and Ian's parents let him come visit me in August."

"London's cool, btw," Ian said. "What happened to your TV?" He was still holding his shirt up, by the way, which had gone from being funny to scary to slightly neurotic.

"Long story. Oh wait, no it's not. My dad threw my dictionary through the screen during Hurricane Irene. And why," I said to Ruthie, "didn't you tell me you were dating?"

"We wanted to tell you," Ian said. "I mean, *I* wanted to tell you, but Ruthie—" He smiled nervously, and pulled up his shirt another inch or two to make up for ratting her out. "Why Hurricane Irene?"

"Duh. His mom's name was Irene." Ruthie glared at Ian for a moment, then adjusted the rearview mirror. It's anyone's guess whether she did this so she could see me better or so I could see her better, but before she spoke she used a black fingernail to move a magenta bang that apparently wasn't exactly where she wanted it. Then:

"I told him about you."

"You—"

"Told him."

"Yes, you said that. *What* did you tell him?"

"C'mon, Sprout . . ."

"No, you come on. I mean, if you could say it to Ian, surely you can say it to me. Or perhaps Ian would like to tell me?"

Ian's fingernails dug at his stomach so fiercely they left red scratch marks. "She told me you were gay," he said finally, then suddenly pulled his shirt down and tucked it deep deep deep into his pants. He tried to turn away, but I locked eyes with him.

"I—don't—understand," I said slowly. "What does *me* being *gay* have to do with *you* dating *Ruthie*?"

Ian stared at me, a deer in headlights, a rabbit transfixed by a rattlesnake. His mouth opened and closed convulsively, but nothing came out. Ruthie's stare fell on us like a wave of hot air from a suddenly opened oven, but I didn't look in her direction. I could see the desire to just come out with it in Ian's eyes, and for a moment I actually thought he was going to. In some ways, this didn't really surprise me. Ian was one of the most straight-up guys you'll ever meet. Keeping secrets just didn't suit him. What surprised me more, though, was how much I wanted him to confess.

Suddenly Ruthie's arm appeared in my peripheral vision. She reached over and took Ian's hand, pulled it possessively into her lap. He jumped like she'd shocked him, then tried to laugh it off, but his knuckles were white where his hand wrapped around hers, and I thought I could actually hear bones cracking.

"It was like what we talked about the other day," Ruthie said. There was a question in her voice that she didn't quite know how to ask, and, after a confused pause, she went ahead with her own explanation. "The day before school started, I mean. When you were saying how hard it was for you to find someone to date."

Ian nodded his head so rapidly I thought it was going to fall off. "I—I mean we—we didn't want to rub what we had in your face."

Okay. Here was my best friend, telling me that she'd hidden her relationship from me because she didn't want me to feel bad about the fact that there was no one for me to date at Buhler, when in fact she was dating the very boy I'd been hooking up with for the past four years. And, to make the situation even juicier, the boy I'd been hooking up with for the past four years was present at this scene, and telling me that he didn't want to rub his relationship with my best friend in my face because he had to pretend to his girlfriend that he thought I was leading a sexually frustrated existence. I mean, I *was* sexually frustrated, but I wasn't celibate, which is really what he was pretending. It was all too rich. Or at least it was until that proverbial lightbulb went off again. Not flickering like it had in Mrs. Miller's office, but bright white light.

"Oh. My. God. You two are having sex, aren't you?"

Ian's mouth opened, but before he could answer Ruthie spoke over him.

"Well, what about *you*?"

"Um-huh-what?" I said, by which I meant: "What do you mean, what about me?" even though I knew *exactly* what she meant.

"I *mean*," Ruthie said, "what's up with you and that Petit

dork? You've been joined at the hip ever since the beginning of school."

All of a sudden—by which I mean, as soon as I tore my eyes from Ruthie's and looked anywhere but at her face—I noticed that one of my dad's stumps had fallen over. Sixteen, I think it was, although I can never remember how he numbers them. The grass had grown up around it where the mower couldn't reach, which meant that it had been on its side for a long time—like, way longer than my dad had been seeing Mrs. Miller, or I'd been hanging out with Ty. While Ruthie stared at me and Ian stared into space, I stared at the fallen stump, trying to figure out why it bugged me so much. At first I thought it was because I'd always considered myself the kind of person who picked up on things like that. I mean, I'd been writing about things like that. Writing about my house, and my life, and the people in my life, which meant I was *supposed* to notice things like that. But if I wasn't paying attention—if I wasn't writing about how my dad had lost interest in his stumps and how our house wasn't interesting or weird but just small or how Ian and Ruthie, far from feeling abandoned by me, had actually taken up with each other—then, well, what *was* I paying attention to? What was I writing about?

"Sprout?" Ruthie prompted me. "Are you two—I mean, is he, well, you know? Is he?"

And even as she spoke, I realized it wasn't the stump that was holding my attention. Wasn't just the stump anyway. It was actually a pale stillness in the trees, just visible over the stump's fallen length. In a forest, nothing is ever still, not even tree trunks, which sway in the slightest breeze. Leaves flutter, branches rock up and down, birds and squirrels and termites flit from one place to another. But right in the middle of all this movement one thing was frozen in place, staring at us. An angular white face from which shone two dark hot—*furious*—eyes.

"Ty!"

As soon as I called his name, he turned and melted into the shadows. I stood on the backseat and hopped over the side of Ruthie's mom's hand-me-down BMW convertible. Ian's eyes followed me with that same pleading look leaking out of them like X-rays, but Ruthie's mouth just dropped open.

"Sprout! What the fu—"

"Ty!" I yelled over her. "Wait!"

I didn't know how long he'd been watching, how much he'd heard. I mean, there'd been nothing to hear, really, nothing to see, yet somehow my presence in Ruthie's car seemed like a betrayal. Like I was reverting to my old way of life. My life before him. Maybe I only felt like that because Mrs. Miller'd told me that's what I needed to do if I wanted to get that scholarship, or maybe it was because Ruthie had called Ty a dork and I hadn't slugged her. Or maybe it was because of the way Ian Abernathy was looking at me with those pleading eyes. Eyes that wanted not just to reveal his own secret, but *our* secret, as if maybe something more had gone on between us than an activity we carefully shielded from ourselves with the brim of his hat. I mean, for all I knew Ian fooled around with other guys, but I didn't think so. Buhler wasn't that big for one thing. And then, well, four years is a long time to pretend sex is just sex. At a certain point you realize that it might not be just the act that you enjoy, but the person you're enjoying it with.

But all that was behind me, at least for now, and up ahead was Ty. He'd disappeared into the undergrowth, but the sound of snapping branches and crunching leaves let me track him pretty easily. He avoided the paths, made a beeline for the

Andersens' pasture, and I found myself hoping he was wearing socks or else he was going to end up with a terrible case of itch ivy. I'm a faster runner than he is, but he had a good head start and plus running through tangles of itch ivy and marijuana—er, hemp—is a lot different from running on an open road, and of course there was that stupid bag of cell phones I was carrying, which why I didn't leave them in the backyard is beyond me. And so anyway, the long and the short of it is that he made it to the Andersens' pasture and was streaking across it by the time I pulled up short at the fence. I grabbed the upper strand as though I was trying to snap the wire from its posts. You might think I'd given up or something—the fence symbolizing the barrier that had suddenly grown up between us and all that—but the simpler truth is:

"Ty! The dog!"

Ty's head jerked to the right. The Andersens' St. Bernard was barreling towards him, a yellowish-brown blur like a backhoe careening out of control. Ty almost tripped over his too-big shoes when he whirled and started running back towards me. The dog was slow and clumsy as dogs go, but it was still closing on him fast, ears flapping like bits of cloth pinned to his head, clods of dirt and cow patties spitting from beneath his paws. Like most scared people, Ty ran like an idiot, arms flailing, torso straight up and creating as much wind resistance as possible, and of course turning around every other step to see how close his pursuer was, which nearly made him trip twice. But I didn't think offering him this kind of rational analysis would help, so all I screamed was:

"JFC, Ty, *RUN*!"

I stepped on the second strand of the fence, held up the third, but he didn't bother climbing through, just vaulted it.

The cottonwood with the long sloping branch was about fifteen feet behind us, and we'd've never made it if the dog hadn't got held up by the fence. He yelped when he shoved his scarred, slobbery muzzle through it, jumped back, but then he shoved forwards again, leaving fat, blood-stained clumps of fur on the barbs, which might've made me feel sorry for him if he hadn't been trying to kill us. By then Ty and I had scrambled as far up the branch as we could go. Leaves shivered and fell off with each footfall, and the branch itself swayed like the arm of an oil derrick, but seemed to be holding our weight just fine. The St. Bernard actually jumped on the branch (it was about three feet in diameter at its base, in case you're having a hard time picturing this) but when he tried to clamber after us he fell to the ground. A little bark burped out of him when he smashed into the forest floor. Twice more he tried, twice more he fell, and after that he just stood on the base of the branch, his beady, bloodshot eyes glaring up at us, ropes of saliva hanging from his flappy jowls.

For a long time Ty and I just looked down at the dog. We'd glance at each other every once in a while, then turn back to the dog. Glance at each other, turn to the dog. Each other; the dog. Then one of the phones let out a *BLEEP*, and it was only after we jumped and let go of each other that we realized we'd been holding hands.

Our eyes flitted to our fingers in the same way they'd flitted to the dog. As though the thing we stared at was capable of ripping our bodies limb from limb. We scooted as far from each other on the branch as we could get, which is to say, about one and a half inches.

"Um," I said.

"Yeah, Ty said.

BLEEP, one of the phones said (which bleep was actually the sample from Beyoncé's "Crazy in Love").

Twenty feet below us, the Andersens' St. Bernard barked.

A distraction! I leaned over, looked down. "We should give it a name!" I said, pointing. Then I realized I was pointing with the hand that'd been holding Ty's and I shoved it in my pocket.

Ty blushed a deep, deep red. "Why? A name'll just help us remember this embarrassing moment," he said, and his hand, the one that'd been holding mine, curled into a fist.

"Well, at least we outsmarted him. We should feel proud."

"He's the one walking around. We're stuck up a tree."

I looked down at the dog, who had lifted one leg to mark our trunk. I made a mental note to climb down on the lee side, then, more because I didn't know what to say to Ty than anything else, I took one of Mrs. Miller's confiscated phones out of the bag and tossed it at the dog. I don't have a good aim even when I'm concentrating, and the phone missed the dog and hit the tree trunk instead, snapped into two or three pieces and fell to the forest floor.

When I looked up, Ty was staring at me.

"Did you just throw your—no, wait. First of all, you throw like a girl. Now: dude, did you just throw your *cell phone* at that dog?"

I nudged the bag in his direction, opened it. Ty stared at it for like five minutes with an unreadable expression on his face. He could've been looking at gold coins, or dead snakes, or a TJ Maxx bag full of cell phones.

"You know what? I'm not gonna ask." And he took one of the phones and chucked it at the dog. The dog was at that particular moment licking himself in the place only dogs can lick, and the phone bounced off his thick fur. If he even felt it, he didn't react. There being nothing else to do, we threw three or four or five or six more phones at the dog in the same half-hearted sort of way. I think the word for how we threw them is "desultorily," or maybe "perfunctory," but I didn't have my dictionary with me to check. I was about to throw the precious BlackBerry when I noticed Ty looking at me funny.

"What?"

"Nothing."

"*What?*"

"I dunno. I was just thinking maybe you're right."

"Maybe—?"

"Maybe we should give the dog a name."

I looked down at the dog. His tongue was still lapping away, accompanied by snuffling noises it was all too easy to misinterpret.

"You want to name the dog?"

"I want to remember this moment."

I let the BlackBerry clatter back into the bag. "You want to . . ." I let my voice trail off. I hate it when people repeat the last thing that's been said to them because they're too afraid to ask what the other person meant by it. "You want to remember this moment," I said finally, because when it comes right down to it, I'm a coward.

"Maybe," Ty smirked. "I dunno how it's gonna turn out yet."

"I'm pretty sure it'll get tired and go home eventually."

"I wasn't referring to the dog."

"What were you—"

Ty cut me off by sticking his tongue in my mouth. Later on I realized I didn't flinch. I'd've thought I'd've flinched (there's a lot of apostrophes in that sentence, by the way; sorry). I mean, I knew I was gay and all. But at the same time: kissing a guy? (I mean, I *hope* you don't think I ever kissed *Ian*.) Everything I knew had taught me that two guys macking on each other was weird or different or at the very least would take some getting used to. But I didn't think any of those things. In fact, I didn't think anything at all. The Phil-bot would say that it's a defense mechanism of a certain type of overintellectual personality— i.e., mine—to insulate itself from a given moment by cutting away to the past or the future in an effort to describe what the moment meant rather than what it felt like. Well, I don't remember what it felt like. What I felt. Emotionally or physically. I don't remember what I thought, don't remember what Ty's mouth tasted like or whose hands went where or how in the hell we managed to stay on that branch. All I remember is that after Ty sat back the 72-degree air—24.6 degrees less warm than his mouth—the naked breath of the forest felt ice cold on my lips, and all I wanted to do was pull him back on me.

So I did.

An image of Troy Bellows and Stacy McTaverty popped in my head, and I found myself giving them a mental high-five. Why? Because, well, kissing is *awesome*. I mean, you practice with the side of your hand, you see it on TV, your friends do it in the backseat and behind you at movie theaters and, well, wherever else they can, and, you know, you've probly had the misfortune of catching your parents at it once or twice, but, I mean: *take the hint*. It's fun. Try the Pepsi challenge. Kiss someone. Then don't kiss them. Which one tastes better?

By the time we unclinched the Andersens' St. Bernard had wandered off. Ty looked all around for it as though he almost hoped it was still around.

"I guess I better get home."

"Here," I said, brushing a finger over his lips. "Lemme wipe the lipstick off."

Ty flinched, and I jerked my hand back.

"Um," I said, "that was a joke? Cuz I'm not a girl?"

"I know that! I know you're *gay*."

In the realm of stating the obvious, this seemed to me to significantly outrank anything I'd ever said. But then I suddenly remembered the conversation he'd overheard, the question Ruthie had asked me just before I saw him.

"I didn't tell Ruthie," I said to him. "I didn't say you were gay."

"I'm *not* gay!" he practically shouted, and then he grabbed me and kissed me and scrambled down the branch so fast I thought he was going to fall and break his neck.

"Use the lee side," I said, remembering the dog marking the tree, but Ty climbed right through the wet patch and hopped over the fence.

So. A thousand years from now, after we've all died from global warming or a neutron bomb or brain death caused by reading one too many stories about Britney Spears, the aliens might come down here to check things out—or the cockroaches that have evolved intelligence, or that one lone human who survived in cryogenic suspension—and the sole survivor or the cockroach or the alien might happen across a cottonwood tree in the remnants of an artificial forest eight miles north of what had once been Hutchinson, Kansas. The tree will be dead by then, of course, probly little more than a crumbling stump, but that stump will be ringed by a half dozen indestructible plastic cell phones (not counting the one that broke against the side of the trunk, of course).

Was this the site of some minor battle in mankind's final years? A communications center perhaps? A trash heap? As our resident of the future ponders the imponderable, one of the phones bleeps.

"The ultraviolet radiation penetrating the depleted ozone layer must've kept the battery charged all these years!" is the first thing the resident of the future thinks.

The phone, which doesn't care about the implausibility of its functionality, bleeps again. The LCD screen flashes a message: ONE NEW VOICEMAIL.

The resident of the future picks up the phone and, because the residents of the future are much smarter than us, presses the right button to retrieve the message on the first try. Perhaps this will elucidate the situation, the resident of the future thinks. But all he hears is a thousand-year-old voice squawking in his ear.

"WHOO-HOOOOOOOOOOOOO!"

Liquid courage

The next morning the phone rang.

(In fact the phones had been ringing all night, or bleeping really, but this particular ring came from our land line.)

"Meet me at the end of our driveway. And bring those phones."

"When—"

But he'd already hung up. The car keys were on the counter, along with a twenty-dollar bill and a note: *At least half on gas*. It was Saturday, I remembered. My dad had promised me the car on Saturdays. Whatever else you could say about him, he was a man of his word.

The Taurus sat in the driveway beneath a sky seamed by the passage of crows following the harvest south. I put the phones in the trunk so I wouldn't have to listen to them before climbing into the musty cab. There were lipstick-smudged Kwik Shop coffee cups on the center console, a copy of *A Connecticut Yankee in King Arthur's Court* in the backseat. The slip of paper from a fortune cookie had been taped to the dashboard—not the fortune side, but the obverse:

Learn Chinese!
Friend = Peng-you

It seemed to me a faint scent of Mrs. Miller's perfume hung in the air too, although that could've just been the salsa residue in the Taco Bell takeout containers.

I know: *totally* uncalled for.

The car faked me out for a minute, refusing to turn over, but I stomped on the gas and it sputtered into life, along with a few crows roosting in the stumps, who cloffed and cawed loudly into the air. As soon as I dropped the car into reverse, though, it stalled, and after I got it started again I had to gun it for what seemed like forever until the thermometer needle finally twitched off the blue bottom of the gauge and edged towards the red. I shivered while I waited for the car to warm up. It was a chilly fall morning, but the sky was clear and it would be warm in a few hours. Kansas weather is notorious for being unable to make up its mind.

Five minutes later, I parked fifty feet shy of the Petits' gate. Five minutes after that I shut the car off. Five minutes after that I started the car again and inched past the gate, but I couldn't see anything between the sandy ridges and sumac through which the Petits' driveway wound like a dry steambed. I parked and resumed my vigil, this time with the rearview mirror. The fortune cookie paper caught my eye. I imagined my dad and Mrs. Miller listening to Patsy Cline or Garth Brooks as they drove six or seven miles an hour slower than the speed limit to prolong their time together. *Hello, friend. Ni hao, peng-you.*

"Peng-you," I said in my best Elvis voice. "Peng-you very mush."

A breeze was whipping the nearly leafless branches around, and the migrating crows moved laboriously through the air, as if dragging the threads of some vast atmospheric shroud behind them. With each minute Ty didn't show up, I imagined the sky filling with long dark lines. Right about the time the bright autumn morning had been completely blacked out and the earth plunged into everlasting darkness, a blond head flickered in the rearview mirror. My heart did something unheartlike, I swear to God. Jumped, or turned a somersault, or Morse coded the words *There he is!* straight to my spinal cord, which in turn shot the message to the top of my head, where it felt like my hair danced on end as if a balloon charged with static electricity were being waved over it. But then my hair fell and my heart sank all the way down to the pebbles and bottle caps and mashed pages of newspaper around my feet, cuz what followed the head was the snout of Mr. Petit's beat-up old pickup. Crap, I thought. His dad's caught him. His dad's taking him to one of his all-day church services (revivals, they were called, which prompted the question, who died?), or his dad was driving him to a Christian re-education camp, or his dad was driving him to some remote field where he'd make Ty dig his own grave and then shoot him. *I smelled 'im on you* is what he'd say when Ty asked him why. (I'm just guessing about the accent here, but it adds something, don't you think?) Or, who knows, maybe Mr. Petit would just say what he said when Holly died. *One less mouth to feed.* Did I mention that's what he said? He said it to the paramedics as they put Holly's bloated, eyeless body into the back of an ambulance. *Oh well. One less mouth to feed.*

Oh right. Jesus. That's who died. And now they're revivin' him.

Christians. God save 'em, ha ha.

The gate kicked open, and I saw that the shaved head wasn't Ty's. I figured it must be his brother L.D. He was a little taller than Ty (but still short), a little thicker (but still wiry), the same pointed chin and quick, almost spastic movements as he yanked the gate out of the way and his dad's truck jerked forwards like a horse at the starting post. No, not spastic. Frightened. As if he knew that if he didn't get the gate open fast enough his dad would just drive over him. In fact the pickup never quite came to a stop after Mr. Petit pulled onto the road, and L.D. (like I said, just guessing here) had to slam the gate and then run like hell to catch up. He had one foot on the running board and one hand on the door handle as gravel spat from beneath the truck's rear tires and it shot towards me.

I hunkered down in my seat, wishing I'd thought to wear a cap to cover my telltale hair, but L.D. (still guessing) was too busy getting in the truck and Mr. Petit had things to do, places to be, and then, well, neither of them knew me from Adam, right? They sped past, filling the road with a cloud of dust, at which point I assume I became as invisible to them as they were to me. Still, I kept my eyes peeled in case they turned around. At 69th Street the brake lights winked once, twice, and I held my breath until the dust settled and I saw that the truck was well and truly gone, and then, when Ty stuck a pistol through the open passenger window and said, "Bang!" I jumped so high I hit my head on the roof.

"Ty! What the hell—"

Before I could finish, he pulled open the passenger door and slipped in the car and grabbed my head and pulled it onto his. The sixteen or so hours since our last kiss—the tasteless dinner, the worksheet on imaginary numbers and the fifty pages of *The Heart Is a Lonely Hunter*—all disappeared, along with the seat cushion and the Taurus and Tobacco Road. I felt the rough branch of a cottonwood beneath my butt, wondered if every kiss would put me back there, swaying, shivering in a breeze, the guttural growls of a pink-eyed St. Bernard in my ears. The hand holding the gun was pressed against my head the whole time, but I didn't even think of pulling away. Kissing: it's that good.

"Rufus," Ty said when he pulled off me.

Somehow I knew. "The Andersens' dog? How'd you find out?"

"I asked my dad," Ty said. And then, a moment later: "Peng-you."

I headed south on 61, towards town. I made it to town. I made it through town. I headed out the other side of town. As 61 merged with 50 (and went four-lane to boot), I thought, one of us better do something, or we're gonna end up in Oklahoma.

After his initial boldness, Ty suddenly found himself fascinated with everything in the car except me. There was certainly a lot to be fascinated with, although none of it was particularly, well, fascinating. Takeout containers from about ten different fast-food and convenience-store chains, bits and pieces of months of *Hutchinson News*es, beer bottles and cans, pop bottles and cans, the associated detritus of same (caps, cartons, six-pack rings, used straws with dried brown bubbles clogging their hollowness like cholesterol-choked arteries), empty gum and candy wrappers (original flavor Hubba Bubba and watermelon Jolly Ranchers especially), half-chewed or -sucked candies, Styrofoam peanuts, real peanuts, a book of *Peanuts* cartoons. I'm just making that last one up, but you get the picture. It was just trash, and a lot of it.

"Good *God*," Ty said, as he threw one bit of greasy paper after another out the window. "Your dad is, like, *six years old*."

"Um, Ty?"

"Oh-oh-oh!" Ty's voice went up an octave. "A *dirty* six-year-old!"

I glanced over, saw that he was holding a little black square adorned by what appeared to be a pair of bodacious tatas. Though I'd never actually purchased them before, I'd been in enough truck stop restrooms to recognize the Rough Riders logo.

Ty waggled the condom wrapper at me. "*Empty*. You know what *that* means."

"Um, Ty?"

"Doing it in the *car*. Give it up for Mr. B. and Mrs. M. W00t, w00t!"

I grabbed the condom wrapper and threw it out the window. So my dad was having sex with Mrs. Miller. In the car. That was kind of, I don't know, gross and funny and even a little sweet. But still, it seemed to me that there were more important things in the car right now. Well, one thing. It was sitting on the seat, its barrel pointed alarmingly towards my leg.

"One," I said sternly, "there will be no w00ting of my dad's sexcapades. And two: what are you doing with a—Ty! What in God's name are you doing *now*?"

Cuz Ty was clambering butt over brains into the backseat, kicking me in the side of the head with one of his ridiculous shoes for good measure.

"Evidence! I want a wet spot. Crusty stains!" Bits of paper flew around the cabin and were sucked out the open windows. "Condom number two! Three! *Mint-flavored lubricant!* Oh, peng-you!" he moaned in his best orgasm voice. "Peng-you, peng-you, PENG-you!"

I was just about to grab the gun off the passenger's seat and hit him over the head with it, but at that exact moment the sides of the road just sort of fell away, and we found ourselves on the long low bridge that crosses the Arkansas River south of town. The actual channel of the river isn't particularly big—in some places only twenty feet or so—but because it floods regularly (or used to, before most of its water got sucked out for irrigation) its bed is nearly a mile wide, with a jungly border of vine-choked softwoods growing on either side, and then the dark sandy track of the river itself, which splits and writhes around hundreds of sandbars, some of which had dark campfire circles on them, or raggedy pieces of garden furniture. Silver and gold cans glinted more brightly in the morning sun than the brown water, and in a single sparkling instant the last four years of my life melted away. I was back in the passenger's seat of the Taurus and my dad was behind the wheel, my mom had just died and we had just moved here and my dictionary was open on my lap, filled with meaningful words that told me absolutely nothing about how my life had managed to turn itself inside out like a reversible fleece—blue one minute, red the next. The same, yet completely different.

And then Ty's gun appeared in the corner of my eye, pulling me back to the present.

"Blam," he hissed, and the fact that he whispered it somehow made it scarier. He pointed the gun at the beer and soda cans discarded on the riverbed, yet it felt more like he was aiming at the happy hands that had once held them, the smiling mouths that'd sucked them dry. "Blam blam blam," he fired at their phantom bodies, as if he hated even the memory of their good times.

And then the river was gone.

"Ty," I said as we descended the far side of the bridge. "What is up with the *gun*?"

"We'll make 'em pay, Daniel!" He was suddenly hollering, right in my ear. "We'll make 'em *all* pay!" But he was laughing as he said it, and then he tapped me on the head with the gun barrel. It was really, really hard. "R*elax*. You're whiter than me, for God's sake. I just wanted to do some target practice."

I waited for more, but there wasn't more. Ty looked at me with this blank expression on his face, like, Why are *you* looking at *me*? then dropped the gun on the passenger seat and went back to ransacking the debris in the back.

Well, I'll tell you: I believed him. About the target practice, I mean. Ty was just one of those people for whom guns were a part of life, the same way computers or cell phones or indoor plumbing are a part of life for other people. It was fun to shoot them, and it was fun to shoot things, but it would've never occurred to him that someone might think he wanted to shoot a *person* with them, because, well, he wasn't crazy. Angry maybe, a little bit bipolar, but not crazy. But at the same time it didn't seem to occur to him that the gun in his hand had been specifically designed to shoot people, and so maybe it wasn't so weird that someone might worry just a little bit about his intentions.

I picked it up gingerly. I'd never held a gun before, and I was surprised how heavy it was. There was no visible brand name on it. I guess it wasn't like a car or a pair of sneakers. You didn't want a big logo or a tagline on the side: "Colt Kills 'Em Dead!" or "Remington Rifles: The Sniper's Choice!" Talk about ergonomics though: I was amazed at how it just sort of fit in my hand. Without any effort on my part the nobbly grip lined itself up across my palm and my index finger was caressing the trigger, which poked from the base of the barrel like a snake's single fang. I pointed the gun towards the passenger window, was trying to think of a better line than "Go ahead, make my day," when a honk sounded behind me—I'd slowed to about 35 on the highway—and I dropped the gun. That tells you something about me. The fact that I didn't pull the trigger, I mean. That my first impulse wasn't to hurt someone, but to surrender (or maybe just hide). I ask you to keep that in mind when you get to the end of this book, cuz then maybe you won't think so badly of me.

HONK!

With a start I looked up and realized I'd drifted into oncoming traffic. I had the briefest glimpse of a big round white face before I swung the car so violently off the road that I could swear two wheels left the ground. Fortunately a dirt path angled west off the highway, heading towards the river, so I didn't end up in the ditch. I grabbed the gun off the floor and stuffed it in the glove compartment, peeked into the rearview mirror to see if anyone had followed. The coast was clear. But Ty had also disappeared.

"Um, Ty?"

There was a long pause—just long enough for me to wonder if I'd somehow thrown him out of the car when I jerked onto the dirt road—and then a long, satisfied burp sounded from the floor of the backseat. Ty's head popped back into view, and even before he said anything I smelled the sweet fire on his breath.

"Well I tell you *what*," he said, rolling back into the front seat. He held a three-liter bottle of dark brown liquid, nearly full. "I don't know what this is, but it sure as hell ain't *Pepsi*."

I drank. If you want an excuse or an apology, you ain't getting one. I'd watched my dad and Mrs. Miller enough to know alcohol had its uses.

"Rum," I said, handing the bottle back to Ty. "Trust me, we're gonna regret this tomorrow."

"Live for today, that's what I say." Which is about as completely the opposite of who Ty is as possible—he has one foot stuck in the past, the other striding blindly towards a make-believe future—but I didn't bother to correct him. Just listened to the glug-glug-glug as he took a second long drink, then accepted the bottle when he passed it my way.

I swigged again, perhaps a little delicately—rum is gross, after all, and flat pop doesn't help the taste *at all*—and handed the bottle to Ty.

"What're you, a little girl? We're getting' drunk here, Daniel, and then we're gonna shoot some stuff up. *Drink*."

"Screw you, Petit." I tipped my head all the way back, sucked so hard that the plastic sides of the bottle buckled inwards and a syrupy sweet-and-sour river coursed down my throat, inside and out. Rivulets of brown liquid streamed down the sides of my cheeks and into my green-stained collar.

"Allow me," Ty said, leaning over and slurping the residue from my face and neck, fumbling at my pants at the same time.

"Hey!" I heard myself say more harshly than I'd intended. "Don't be like, Oh, I'm so drunk, I don't know what I'm doing. You'll be really drunk soon enough."

Ty was silent a moment, then grabbed the bottle, swigged deeply. Then: "I know exactly what I'm doing," he said, and pressed himself against me again, slower this time, more deliberately, the tip of his tongue flicking at my ear, my jawbone, his teeth nipping at my collar, his fingers dancing over my T-shirt.

"Car!" I yelled. "Car! Car!"

Ty rolled off me as some kind of Oldsmobile rattled past, stayed slumped against the passenger door even after the car had disappeared behind us. At first I thought he'd been spooked, but then I looked over and saw that he was laughing so hard no sound was coming out. His face was red as a ripe tomato, and lines of sweat had broken out below his hairline and above his upper lip. Actually, I think the line on his lip was spit. My spit, I mean, not his.

"Car!" he wheezed finally. "Car, car!" His voice creaked like an old air conditioner the first time you turn it on in June. He pointed at the crows in the sky. "I thought you were imitating them! Car, car!"

"You're drunk," I said, reaching for the bottle. "Give this to me!"

"Hey," Ty took the bottle after I'd downed about half of what was left. "Just cuz I'm a straight-D student doesn't mean I'm an idiot. It's much too soon for us to be feeling the effects of the alcolol."

"Alcolol? *Alcolol*?"

"Car!" Ty cawed. "Car, car!"

Suddenly he sat up.

"Where'd the river go?"

"Whuh?" I looked around. Sure enough, the river had vanished. Since the Arkansas River is almost 1,500 miles long, this was slightly disturbing. I prodded the Taurus' cracked dashboard with my index finger. "And the GPS is on the fritz too! We'll *never* find it."

"Don't worry, cap'n, I'll be your navigator." Before I knew it, Ty'd rolled down his window and hoisted himself into the open ledge. Cold air rushed into the cabin. I felt it on my forehead, throat, forearms. Realized Ty wasn't the only one who'd started to sweat.

He hooked a couple of fingers around that mysterious handle that car manufacturers install on the ceiling right inside the passenger door and banged on the roof of the car.

"Yee-haw! Floor it, cowboy!"

"Ty! Get your butt back in here!"

"That's a negatory," he called faintly, unselfconsciously mixing his pastiches. "River's just a little ways north. There's

217

a left coming up in about a quarter mile. You need to take it."

I did take it, hard, and Ty slid even further out the window. Only his knees were hooked over the edge of the door, and his eyes went wide in surprise—and delight.

"Whoo-hoo!" he hollered, hoisting himself back up. "Thass what I'm talking a*bout*."

If I had to guess, I'd say Ty's "thass" had more to do with the rum than ebonics, but I didn't really care. I floored it, and the car sputtered up to fifty miles an hour. The great thing about old rattletraps, though, is that fifty feels like a hundred, especially on dirt roads, what with all the shaking and skittering and bouncing, and that effect is multiplied about a hundred times more when you're drunk (yes, it felt like we were going ten *thousand* miles an hour). Every once in a while Ty would scream out "Left!" or "Right!" and then he began screaming "Left! Right! Left-right-left!" in marching cadence, and I swung the wheel back and forth and the car fishtailed down the road. My eyes flickered between Ty's writhing legs on my right side and the meandering river, never more than a mile away, on my left. For some reason I felt that as long as I stayed between these two poles we'd be fine. If I didn't go near Ty's legs or dump the car in the water everything would turn out okay. The road played along, supplying a left or right turn at convenient intervals to bring us closer to the river each time it meandered away, but not so close that we ever felt like stopping and walking to it. We passed Yoder, Haven, Mt. Hope even, which is not so much a town as two houses planted a quarter mile apart. A needy-looking road sign—read me, please read me!—annouced 279th Street, and I knew we were closer to Wichita than to Hutch. I'm sure I'd've kept going all the way to the Missouri border if physics hadn't gotten in the way, or chemistry, or mechanics, or I don't know, maybe just math, by which I mean:

We ran out of gas.

Oops.

I'd never been in a car that ran out of gas, so I don't know if the experience was typical. The first thing I noticed was that the power steering disappeared, and then when I glanced down at the gauges I saw that all of them had gone to zero, and we were losing speed rapidly. The rattling was so loud that I didn't realize the car'd actually turned off, however, until Ty slid back in his seat.

"Why'd you turn the car off?"

"Whuh? I didn't turn the car off." I stomped on the gas, which did even less than it usually did. By now we were inching to a stop, and even I could hear that the engine wasn't running.

"Um, Daniel? You didn't happen to check the gas this morning, did you?"

I tried to look in my brain, but in order to do that I had to lift it out of a vat of dark fumy liquid, and even after I'd managed to hoist it up for inspection it kept dripping in my eyes, so I dropped it back in with a drunken splash. Just before the dark liquid swallowed it I remembered the twenty-dollar bill on the counter, the note that'd been with it.

"Well, that little turd."

"Who?"

"My *dad*. He deliberately ran the car low on gas so we couldn't go too far." But then it occurred to me that my dad knew nothing about me and Ty, had no reason to suspect us of getting up to anything. But Mrs. Miller did. I glanced down at the lipstick-stained coffee cups.

"Well-played, Mrs. M. Well-played."

"Um, Daniel? Who *are* you talking to?"

"Never mind. We're gonna have to hitch a lift to a gas station."

I reached to open my door, felt Ty's hand on my leg. When I turned to him he nodded at the river, which was still off to the left, less than a mile away.

"What's your hurry? We got all day."

If he'd squeezed my leg it would've been too much, if he'd leered or smirked or grabbed his crotch (or, God forbid, mine). But all he said was "We got all day" and then he held my gaze, not fearlessly, no, but not plaintively either, as if to say that just spending time with me was nice, and if anything else happened, well, that was just gravy.

We pushed the car off the road first. That was another thing I'd never done before. Pushed a car, I mean. It was interesting. Made me realize that this vehicle, which had ferried my dad and me across nearly a dozen states and racked up almost 200,000 miles, wasn't really all that big, all that special. Just a rusty box sitting on top of four wheels that were almost as inclined to respond to a two-boypower push as a 200-horsepower engine. As the Taurus inched into the ditch I thought it could just as easily stay there, and in a blip of time—a century or three—it'd rust away to nothing. But then, when it picked up speed and rolled deeper into the ditch and we couldn't stop it—hello, boys and girls, this is why you shouldn't drink—I thought it just might end up staying there after all. The ditch was steep as Kansas road-side drainage ditches go, with a deep narrow channel at its center, just like the river, and the Taurus' right front tire sank into this depression, which caused the left rear tire to rise up off the ground about six inches.

Ty and I stared at the seesawing car for a good long time.

Finally he handed me the bottle and I drank down the last of it. We were already drunk; the car was already stuck; it couldn't do any more damage.

"Who wants to—" I burped "—gimme an 'Oh crap'?"

"Oh crap," Ty said, although he made a minor substitution with his word choice.

I walked to the car, gave the free-floating back tire a spin, which obliged with a half revolution. "That *can't* be good for the alignment."

Ty shmirked, which is a shrug/smirk combo, although maybe I should say shmunked, since it was really a shrug/smirk/ wait-am-I-drunk-already? combo, then walked to the front passenger door and leaned into the cabin. A moment later his head was back.

So was the gun.

"You bring them phones?"

Somewhere in my head I knew that if guns were a bad idea, then guns and drinking were a really, really, really bad idea. *Somewhere* I knew that. I just didn't know how to get to that place at that particular moment. Did I take a left at the cerebral cortex and then head on down to the medulla oblongata? Or, you know, should I meander through the corpus collosum until I came to the temporal lobe, and from there make my way to the good old cerebellum? I had no clue. As it was, I could barely get the key in the trunk lock, and almost ripped the bag of phones in half as I lifted it out.

Ty looked in the bag and smiled approvingly. "The thing about target practice," he said, stuffing the gun barrel-first in his waistband and setting off towards the river, "the thing is, you want something that'll explode. Cans or plastic bottles just don't give the same thrill. Glass bottles're good, but my dad takes them back

221

for the deposit. These phones however—" he turned and looked at me with a wicked grin "—these phones're gonna be *awesome*."

I nodded my head as if Mr. Schaefer, the world history teacher, had just pointed out a heretofore unconsidered connection between global trade and factors leading to the rise of the American Civil War. Gun + phone = explosions = fun! The fact that there were two equals signs in my equation should give you an idea how clearly I was thinking. I was going to shoot up a bag of twice-stolen cell phones in a stranger's field a good twenty or thirty miles from home, leaving my dad's already decrepit old car catterwonky in a ditch with the rear axle audibly bending out of shape. I'm pretty sure if you go to your mom's cookbook or epicurious.com and look up "Disaster, Recipes for," you'll find that set of ingredients pretty close to the top of the list.

There was a fence on the far side of the road, an open pasture a few hundreds yards wide beyond it, then the huddled, half-leaved trees that marked the edge of the riverbed. It seemed so close that when I reached for the fence's single strand I felt like I was going to lift up the river itself and pull it the last few inches towards me.

"After you-ooo-ooo-ooo-owwwwwwwwwwwwuhhhh hhhhhhhhgyawd*DAMN*!"

Ty's fit made his response to "Car! Car!" seem like a quiet titter at a fancy restaurant. He laughed so hard I thought he was going to crack a rib or crap his pants. When he was finally able to speak, he picked himself up off the ground and reached a hand down to help me stand, which is the first time I realized I'd fallen on my butt. I'd dropped the bag of cell phones and they lay scattered about me like the last of my commonsense.

"Nice fro dude!" he sputtered, and haloed his head with his hands.

I touched my hair tenderly. It crackled alarmingly, as though electricity still coursed through it.

"Jesus," I said. "Aren't they supposed to put a *sign* up? Or something?"

Ty, busily scooping up phones, nodded towards a metal placard flapping about six feet down the fence.

WARNING!

1,000 VOLTS

"Like that one?"

"Ty! You could've warned me! I might've been killed!"

"Relax, missy, it's only a thousand volts close to the circuit box. This far out, it's probly not even five hundred." He tossed the last phone in the bag, where it landed with a loud cracking sound.

"Hey, be careful. You're gonna break that."

"Um, news flash, Bradford. We're gonna shoot them?"

"Oh right." I grinned sheepishly. "I'm not as think you drunk I am," I said, and reached to lift up the fence.

"Daniel!" Ty's voice was half concerned, half amused. He pointed to the sign again. "Electric?"

I shmunkurped, which is a shrug/smirk/Man-am-I-drunk combo, capped by a good long burp. Ty pushed down the top strand of the fence with the sole of his shoe, and I stepped over it very, very, very carefully. I only fell once.

As we began our final march to the river, he said quietly, "Keep your eyes peeled."

I looked around for a farmer or a cop or the congregation of the Westboro Baptist Church. "Huh? Why?"

"Electric fences are expensive. Wouldn't put one up unless there was something to keep in."

"Like?"

"Dunno. Bulls probly."

"A pasture full of bulls?"

"Getting ready to be steered." His fingers illustrated: snip-snip.

I glanced around. It was a big pasture, and I couldn't see where the fence stopped. The river was still a ways away, and I picked up my pace.

"Maybe we should run."

Ty shook his head. "The vibration of our footsteps. It'd bring 'em to us faster than a heifer swishing her tail to spread her pheromones around."

He slowed still further, and I slowed with him.

"You know the word 'pheromones'?"

"*Sshh*."

He slowed even more, placing his foot gingerly on the ground as though it were the thinnest crust over a pit of molten lava. I slowed as well, which was strangely more difficult than walking fast. At one point I was halfway through a step and forgot that my front foot was still in the air when I tried to lift my back one to follow. Oddly enough, I could not do this.

"*Sshh!*" Ty hissed when I tumbled to the ground.

Slower, slower, slower. Eventually we were taking slo-mo Saturday morning–cartoon steps, one foot hovering off the ground for five, ten, twenty seconds before landing on the ground, and my rum-addled brain *finally* figured out he was jerking my chain.

"You buttwipe!"

I lunged for him, but he dodged, and then we ran all the way to the river (adrenaline seemed to counteract the effects of the alcolol—I mean alcohol—and I was able to do this without falling). The dry grass of the pasture gave way to low brush—

itch ivy of course, and ragweed and nettles and, you know, plants—and then we were in the trees. We beat our way through a good fifty feet of fairly dense undergrowth, then suddenly burst through the other side. The river was narrower here, faster, deeper. A single stream ran through the line of trees with only half a dozen feet of muddy bank on either side. Ty stopped dead in his tracks to keep from running into the water, and I ran right into him. He fell forwards and I grabbed him, kept him from landing in the mud. I pulled him upright and against me and my arms fell naturally around his ribs. He was breathing heavily. Not gasping or anything, just taking in long deep drafts of air and letting them back out again. His body was warm, and I could feel the dampness beneath the hem of his too-small shirt.

He dropped the bag of cell phones and adjusted something in his pants. I stiffened (I mean my *arms* stiffened, pervert) and only when I felt its handle press against my hipbone did I remember: the gun. I shifted slightly to the left so it was no longer touching me.

Even though they'd lost most of their leaves, the trees were still so thick that only a thin ribbon of cloudless sky hung over the water, the latter reflecting the former perfectly. Shadows of crows swam in the shallow water like fish, and the whole impression was of some private rift in the Kansas landscape, which was usually one of endless vistas, the constant feeling of being exposed and vulnerable. I pulled Ty a little closer. Our curves lined up, fitted into each other. The handle of the gun nudged my hip again but I ignored it. I put my chin on his shoulder, pressed my cheek against his ear. Unlike the rest of his body, it was cold, and I rubbed my cheek against it until it was warm. It took a long time, but we had all day.

A crow cawed. Ty giggled.

The center of the river undulated with its dark fast current, but where it lapped the bank a grayish scum had accumulated, studded with twigs and leaves and bits of trash. The layer of flotsam was almost two feet wide and so thick and stagnant it looked like it would hold you up if you stepped on it, but every once in a while an air bubble popped through from underneath, though whether it was a fish or just the riverbed farting out some gas was a mystery to me.

Ty reached for his pants again. I heard his zipper this time.

I stiffened. Arms and legs this time, abs and chest. I couldn't take a breath.

A moment later, I heard a sound that all boys instinctively recognize: the piddle of liberated urine splashing against defenseless earth.

I jumped back. "Are you taking a *whiz*?"

Ty giggled again, his shoulders and back shaking slightly. A few amber drops splashed off to either side of his legs.

When he was finished he tucked himself away with exaggerated gestures, as though he were stuffing an elephant's trunk in his Fruit of the Looms (or FTL as his waistband said, which is also the acronym for Faster Than Light, but, um, yeah, off the subject). Then he pulled out the gun, grabbed the bag of phones, and set off upstream. After a moment's hesitation, I followed. A part of me was glad for the distraction of the gun, since without it I wasn't sure what else we might do. But another part of me (I'll let you guess which part) wanted to grab the gun and throw it in the river so that there wouldn't *be* any more distractions. (Actually that part of me couldn't grab the gun, because it didn't have any fingers, but I think you know what I'm trying to say.)

Up ahead the corpse of a cottonwood lay across the river's

breadth, and this, apparently, was Ty's destination. "Wait here," he said, and handed me the gun. He kept the phones with him, however, and, carefully—more nimbly than I could've done it, that's for sure—he used the fallen tree to cross the river.

I touched the gun barrel, which was still warm from where it'd been tucked into Ty's pants, then shoved it in mine. Immediately I felt a sharp pain. There being no bang, however, and no blood, I was pretty sure I'd just rammed myself, and not actually shot off my privates. I shifted the gun to the right slightly, and it promptly fell down the leg of my pants. I suspected that the whole gun-in-waistband thing probly worked better with briefs than it did with boxers, or at least with a belt. I shook my right leg till the gun fell out of my pants and then just held it.

On the other side of the river, Ty had broken off a good-sized branch of the fallen cottonwood and was driving the sharp end into the soft bank. When it was more or less firmly in place, he found another branch, long and on the thin side, placed one end on the top of the post he'd just set up, then rested the other on the fallen cottonwood, so that it formed a surprisingly level bar. I was pretty sure I couldn't've done that in a million years, with or without the complicating factor of a liter of rum-and-Pepsi in my system. I thought about asking him what he was doing, but I also thought about sleeping, since the alcohol had made me drowsy. I decided to compromise, found a branch that was seat height and sat on it. The gun was still in my hands. I found that if you turned it upside down it made a sort of V shape, and I rested my chin on the trigger guard.

"Don't shoot your face off," Ty called, his voice so unexpected that I, well, nearly shot my face off. I decided the best place for the gun, at least for right now, was on the ground.

By that point I'd figured out what Ty was doing: he was

using the horizontal branch as a shelf for the phones, which he stood up one by one down its length. No doubt you have at some point tried to stand a cell phone up like a salt shaker or a beer bottle and found it hard to do so, most phones being rather narrow at the base, and curved, and generally not given to standing upright. It is therefore understandable if you wonder how Ty was able to do just that with no fewer than sixteen cell phones, and on a rounded branch to boot. I myself took it as a sign that there really was a God, and he was looking down on us with approval. On the other hand, the moment Ty stepped on the cottonwood tree to cross back to my side of the river, nine of the phones immediately splatted to the muddy riverbank, so who knows.

"Screw it," Ty said, and made his way back over the water. "Now then," he said when he reached me. "First of all"—he grabbed me and kissed me—"and secondly"—he bent over and picked up the gun, proffered it to me handle first. In a professorial voice, he said, "It is time that Daniel Bradford learned how to shoot." Well, maybe it wasn't professorial. Let's say teacherly. Student teacherly even.

I looked at the gun. "Daniel Bradford thinks he would like to practice kissing a little more, please."

"All in good time, Peng-you, all in good time." He placed the gun in my hand, then stepped behind me. I turned to follow him but he shook his head and pointed me back towards my target. "Aim, please."

I lifted the pistol with both hands. Before I could aim, however, Ty said,

"First of all, you are not *Charlie's Angels*. You are a man. You shoot a pistol with one hand."

"You've seen *Charlie's Angels*?"

"Just the posters. Now. Listen. Are you looking at the gun?"

"Yes."

"Why would you do a stupid thing like that? It's already in your hand. Look at your *target*, Bradford. And don't say, 'Oh. Duh.'"

I shut my mouth, refocused on the cell phones. It occurred to me that I couldn't actually point the gun at "the cell phones." I had to, you know, pick one. They all seemed so lonely and vulnerable all the way over on the other side of the river, but I finally settled on a pink one towards the center of the branch.

"Okay," Ty said. "So if you think about the gun as a gun, you're never gonna hit anything. But if you think about it as a substitute for your index finger, you'll hit your target every time." He paused. "You picked the pink one, didn't you?"

"I did."

"You are *such* a homosexual."

He stepped close to me. Pressed his stomach against my back the way I'd done to him a moment ago. But instead of circling his arms around my waist or my chest he squeezed both of his hands in a tight circle around my right arm and ran it all the way down to my wrist. A wave of tense energy ran ahead of his fingers, bursting so palpably from my hand that I was surprised the gun didn't go off.

"Relax," Ty said quietly into my ear. "You're *firing* the bullet, not throwing it."

He was stiff against my body, and I *hope* you don't think I mean his arms and legs.

His hands were on my wrist now, lightly, steadying my aim. "Mrs. Miller took 'em all from kids in her class, yeah?"

"That's what she said," I said just as quietly, more of my attention focused on what was behind me than what was in front.

"She just teaches the advanced classes, right? Stuck up

229

pricks." Ty's voice was just a whisper now. "Steady, Daniel. Get 'em in your sights."

I tried to still my arm, but even with Ty's hands supporting me I couldn't hold it level. My whole body was shaking. I tried to tell myself it was the alcohol, but it wasn't the alcohol.

"Who do you think she took the pink one from?" Ty whispered, and I was about to say I had no idea when he hissed, "Ian Abernathy?"

And there it was. The thing about Ty that scared the crap out of me. The sudden shift from playing to real life. The hatred in his voice was so sharp I was surprised it didn't puncture my eardrum. It was just so specific. I mean, it was a pink phone—it was obviously a girl's. Why not say Ruthie's name, or any of the 250 other girls at BHS? But no. He'd gone straight for Ian, who'd never once picked on Ty, but who picked on me all the time, and got us both detention. It wasn't just random hatred, I mean. It was *jealousy*.

Suddenly I was completely sober. I know you've heard that expression before, and I know you also probably know it's impossible, at least from a biological standpoint. But it was true. The wobbling stopped, the blurry parts at the edge of my field of vision snapped into focus, and I no longer had any desire to sing "Ninety-Nine Bottles of Beer on the Wall." The pink phone on the other side of the river swelled in size till it was as big as the proverbial side of a barn. I couldn't miss it if I tried. But just before I squeezed the trigger the barn door opened and there was Ian's face, staring at me with that pleading, helpless look he'd given me yesterday in Ruthie's car. *Just say it*, that look said. *Say it so I don't have to.*

Ty didn't speak. Just breathed in my air.

I pulled the trigger.

Click.

I pulled the trigger again.

Click.

Click. Click. Click.

The—

gun—

wasn't—

loaded.

It seemed like there was an earthquake then, but it was just Ty. He was laughing so hard his whole body was shaking, and a moment later, when the sound of my imaginary gunshots faded from my ears, I heard it too. Shrieking peals of laughter so loud and uncontrolled they dropped Ty to his knees.

"Oh—my—*God!*" He grabbed his stomach as though someone had kicked him in the guts, but he still couldn't stop laughing. "The—look—on—your—*face!*" He extended an arm, cocked a finger. "Blam!" he said, and fell forwards on his hands and knees in the mud, laughter and snot coming out of him in equal amounts. After what seemed like forever he managed to sit back on his heels. "Jesus, Daniel. You didn't think I'd bring a loaded gun on a *joyride*, did you?"

I dropped the gun on the ground, reached for Ty's shirt instead. Grabbed a fistful and hauled him to his feet. He was still laughing, was barely able to stand up. And there it was. That other side of Ty. The side that trusted me so much he didn't even realize I was about to punch him in the face. So I didn't punch him in the face. I kissed him instead. Kissed him with some screwed-up mixture of anger and desire that made me wish I could eat him instead. Chew him up into little pieces so he could never

231

pull a trick like that again, but also take him inside me, so he could never get away.

God, it was a good kiss.

A long time later he stepped back from me. All the humor was gone, and the anger, and everything else. The gun, the river, the cold sliver of Kansas sky: all gone. There was just the two of us—and a lot of itch ivy.

It says something about us, that even through a couple of liters of rum-n-cola and the acute hormonal press of our sixteen-year-old bodies, neither of us was willing to lie down in it. We set off upstream, had to stop and take a couple of kissing breaks, but soon enough we came across another fallen cottonwood. You might've thought lightning had split it down the middle, leaving those charred blackened edges on the trunk, but once again I knew it was the hand of God. He'd laid out this nuptial bed for his two favorite sons. The tree had lain exposed for so long that the heartwood was soft and crumbly, kneaded like pie dough between our fingers. It would have been nice to pretend we were the first people to use it as a bed, but there were a half dozen cans and bottles scattered around, and a copy of *Entertainment Weekly* from June 2006.

"Hey! *The Devil Wears Prada* got a B."

May God strike me dead if that wasn't the last thing I said before I lost my virginity—for real, I mean, and not some half-assed groping in the janitors' closet at school.

Afterwards Ty lay on his back and I lay on top of him. He stared up at the sky, one of his arms curled around me, under my jacket but over my T-shirt. I thought he was watching the clouds or maybe the crows, contemplating their celestial movements while I contemplated his face to see if it looked any different. But then:

"This is as far as I've ever been from home," he said, and by the time I thought of something to say to that, we'd both fallen asleep.

When we woke up we did it again. It had been early when we left and it wasn't very late now, and we didn't rush. There are any number of reasons why I'm not going to tell you what we did exactly, let alone *describe* it. I will tell you that there were a lot of giggles and a couple of "Ouch"es, one "Um, no, not yet," and, later on, a "Now."

"Now."

Now.

It was only after we were finished that we got fully undressed, because we had to shake the wood crumbs and dust and bugs out of our clothing, not to mention all those other little bits and blobs and blemishes we didn't examine too closely, this being nature after all, and nature being full of things that, like Ty, go to the bathroom outside. The cold gave us goosebumps, and there are certain parts of the body that look particularly funny when they're covered in goosebumps. I pointed at his and laughed, and he said, "At least mine don't have green streaks on it," and laughed even harder, and everything was the same as it had ever been between us, only now we'd done what we'd been wanting to do for a long time.

"Since the day I told you about Holly," Ty said, in answer to a question I hadn't asked.

"Since the day I saw you," I said, though the truth of the matter is it felt like I'd been waiting my entire life, or at least since I moved to Kansas.

. . .

233

It took us about twenty minutes to flag down a pickup truck. The driver never told us his name, but he bought us five gallons of gas and towed us out of the ditch as well, which turned out to be a lot easier than it looked. Never asked what we'd been doing or why we looked like we'd just stumbled out of a lumbermill, just tipped his hat and shook his head, and though it would've been portentous to imagine the word he muttered as he drove away was "Faggots," I'm pretty sure it was actually "Meatloaf," which I'm guessing is what his wife made for the noon meal.

Ty held my hand in the back of the pickup truck on the way to the gas station, and in the car on the way home he held my leg. I thought about how before his fingers had fumbled at my flesh nervously, but now they just sat on my thigh midway between hip and knee. Sex: it calms you down.

"You want to pick up Mickey D's?" I said.

"Who's that?"

I glanced over, saw that he wasn't kidding.

"Lunch," I said. "You want something to eat?"

"Nah. I should get home before my dad does."

He kissed me short and hard when I stopped the car in front of his gate, then jumped out of the car and disappeared up his driveway. I waited a moment, and I don't know, maybe he heard the car still running by the gate, or maybe he just heard my heart doing its trapeze act inside my chest, cuz a moment later he was back and I was cranking down the window and we kissed one more time.

"I miss you already," I said, cuz when you get right down to it I'm a cheeseball, and then I stomped on the gas, and, slowly, the Taurus lumbered away.

No good deed goes unpunished

The best thing about that day was the fact that Ty's dad never found out he left. Mr. Petit didn't like his children wandering around like stray dogs. One time when Ty came home with a long scratch on his arm that he said came from a barbed-wire fence, Ty's dad said the nearest barbed-wire fence was two and a half miles away, and chained his son to the doghouse overnight—which would've been warmer, Ty said, if his dad hadn't shot the dog three years earlier for killing a rabbit and not eating it, which Ty's dad regarded as a sign that the dog had gone bad. Not the killing part. Killing was perfectly natural. But a normal dog—or person for that matter—ate what he killed. I didn't want to imagine what he'd've done if he'd found a bitemark on Ty's butt.

Oh, and what the *hell* am I saying? The best thing about that day was the sex. Hands down. Numero uno. No question. If you've had sex, I don't have to tell you what I mean by this, and if you haven't had sex, well, let me just say it lives up to the hype. But even so, the *really* good parts are the things you never thought about—the things that don't make it into pictures or movies or Wikipedia. Because it's not just about flesh. Bodies fitting together like puzzle pieces. There's an alchemy that happens during sex that causes $1+1$ to add up to so much more than 2, even as those halves meld in an almost magical way to form a single unit that's more complete than either of them alone. I don't know, maybe it's just endorphins, but I've run an entire marathon and it didn't make me feel that good (actually it pretty much made me feel like cutting my legs off, but whatever). And so anyway, yeah: sex. *Awesome*. But almost as great was the fact that Ty's dad never even knew he left the house, which meant we were able to get together the very next day—by which I mean we were able to have sex again the very next day, because it turns out that one of the things about sex is that once you've done it you want to do it again and again. But at some point while we were at it the second time Mr. Petit discovered the missing pistol, which we'd forgotten by the riverbed. I didn't see Ty for a whole week after he went home Sunday afternoon. Not after school, not in school either. The only reason I knew he was still alive was because he called me the third night. "I'm still alive," was all he said before he hung up. When he came back to school he was limping, his bottom lip was split and scabbed and there were purple crescent bruises under both eyes. His fingers trembled as he handed his father's note to Mrs. Helicopter in the front office.

"She didn't even read it," he told me at lunch. "Just told me to get to class."

The nidus and the nodus
(no really, look 'em up)

My mom was home for eight days after her cancer treatment failed. Because she was on morphine we were required to have a nurse in the house, although, once she'd shown us how to adjust the drip, she (the nurse, not my mom) spent most of her time in the dining room, drinking coffee and reading magazines and every once in a while responding to a text message, her phone muted so that the only sound was the mechanical clicking of the keys. My mom'd had a flood of visitors at the hospital, but now she sent everyone away except for her own mother and my dad and me. She said her goodbyes individually. To be honest I don't remember most of what she told me. A lifetime of motherly advice packed into a few minutes, but what stands out is how tightly she clutched my hand—not like she was trying to pull herself up, but like she was trying to save *me* from falling. She squeezed my hand. She told me to be good. She told me to be happy. Told me never to put off till tomorrow what I could do today. Never to deny myself anything as long as it didn't come at someone else's expense. She squeezed so tightly. My mom and my dad were both atheists and the prospect of death didn't change that. But my mom did say death had nothing do with her love for me: a mother's love is just a fact in the world, she said, like the ground or the sky. It didn't matter if she was alive or not, her love would always be there and I should always remember that. *Always*. Tell you the truth, it can be hard sometimes. Especially in winter, when the leaves have fallen and the vines that cover our house look like a raggedy old net and the trees look like so many prison bars. But it's just then, just when I'm looking out the window feeling trapped by . . . by Kansas, I guess you'd say, it's just then that I realize I'm squeezing one hand with the other, and I remember the feeling of her hand on mine. How tightly she squeezed. How hard she fought to keep me from falling into the abyss. A mother's love. A fact in the world, even if she herself was gone.

I'm bringing this up now because I originally started this chapter by saying that the week Ty disappeared was the longest of my life. But really, it was the second longest. The entire time he was gone, though, I couldn't help but think he'd never come back, just like I'd believed my mom was never going to get out of the hospital. But it was worse than that. Because my mom *did* get out. She came home. But once she was home, a part of me wished she'd never left the hospital, because the only reason she returned was to say goodbye. To die. And I know the two situations are completely different, but after Ty showed up again I found myself swamped by those same feelings. The feeling that I only had him for a limited time. That I had to maximize every single second. Had to hold on with all my might, before he slipped away again. Slipped away for good.

I guess what I'm trying to say is that the past has a way of catching up with you. I mean, duh, right? Paging Dr. Freud! But sometimes the past is more present than other times. In the last six weeks of the semester—the last six weeks before the State

Essay Contest—the ghosts of my pre-Kansas existence seemed to dance before my eyes, and sometimes it was hard to tell who I was looking at. No, that's not quite it. I always knew who I was looking at, but sometimes I forgot who was doing the looking. Who *I* was: sixteen-year-old Sprout Bradford, well-coifed gay teen on the make, as opposed to eleven- or twelve-year-old Daniel B., praying fervently to a god he didn't believe in to save his mom. To bring her back. It didn't help matters that Ty was the first person since my mom to call me by my given name. We'd be in the middle of things when one whispered "Daniel" would knock me out of orbit, and I'd fall back into that awful year and a half after my mom's diagnosis. The whispers. The smells. The endless hours in the waiting room.

"Endless," I call them. But of course they ended.

I dunno. Maybe it happened because, once the whole physical thing with Ty worked itself out, my mind was free to look elsewhere. Or maybe it was just because, well, we needed a place to get physical. To have sex. I only had the car on Saturdays, remember, which meant we had to find a rendezvous closer to home the other six days of the week. Someplace secluded, but offering certain, shall we say, horizontal amenities. Ty's property was out, as was the Regiers'—frosty fields and the threat of being disemboweled by ostriches don't exactly set a romantic mood, and plus Ty said his dad had taken to wandering the Regiers' land with a rifle, ostensibly to hunt deer or pheasant or turkey (or ostriches), but Ty was pretty sure he was really just looking for evidence of what his son'd been getting up to the last couple of months. That left our place. The trailer was no good. My dad went to Mrs. Miller's pretty much every night, but he was usually still home when school let out, and then too he sometimes popped in because he'd "forgotten" something or other—a pretty lame excuse, but he was my dad, so what could I do? The only alternative was the forest, and, though there were any number of trees that would've worked in a pinch, there was one place that made more sense than any other, and it was high time I showed it to Ty.

And, I suppose, to you.

"I call it the nidus."

"Okay." Ty peered at the shadowy outlines barely visible through several layers of moldy plastic.

"Nidus means nest."

"Sure." He was running his fingers over the plastic now, trying to find a seam.

"Because, you know, it's kind of like a nest."

"Yeah, I got that."

"And also cuz I'm a geek."

Ty turned just long enough to give me a little kiss. He used only the right side of his mouth, to avoid pressing on the scab on the left. "Yeah, I got that too." He found the flap then, pulled it open; a long low whistle plumed from his mouth in a foggy cone. "Jesus, Daniel."

So, uh, you remember the things that hadn't fit in the trailer? The sofa, the dining room table, etc., etc.? I think I told you my dad left them in the front yard, like it was our second home or something, albeit one without walls or floor or roof. He even slept there on warm nights—said he was going to spend some time in "the summer house, har har." (His hars, not mine. Really.) Anyway, maybe his joke inspired me, or maybe I just got tired of looking at all his crap, but a month or so after we moved in I decided to drag everything into the forest: sofa, table, three mismatched chairs, the bottom half of the china cabinet (the top never made it off Long Island), the long dresser that'd been in my bedroom, the tall dresser that'd been in my parents', a big Navy trunk that'd belonged to my father's father, a tall IKEA-style computer desk with attached shelves, and then an endless assortment of pretty much random stuff: books, dishes, lamps, clothes, board games, pictures, and, well, a lot of junk. My dad'd draped plastic dropcloths over everything to protect it from the rain, and I took these into the forest too. Tied some clothesline between a trio of tree trunks and laid the plastic over it to make this kind of bulbous opalescent tent that was practically as big as our trailer. Truth be told, it looked more like a soap bubble than a nest, a giant pearl, a crystal ball, but "nidus" had been Word of the Day on Nov. 17, 2004, and, like I told Ty, I'm a geek. And Nov. 17 had been my mom's birthday.

He limped into the little enclosure warily. The plastic walls were as thin as, well, plastic, but the nidus still had a self-contained, almost otherworldly air about it. Moisture had collected between the layers of dropcloth, frozen now into glittering, paper-thin strips of ice that refracted the light into little rainbow raindrops. A healthy coating of mold and mildew added a greenish tint, and four years of fallen leaves mulching on the roof contributed their own dark shadows. The cumulative effect was of stepping into a cave on the bottom of the ocean, one that just happened to be furnished with the flotsam and jetsam of a suburban home. The outlines of everything in the room were softened by darkness and decay, but once your eyes had grown accustomed to the dim light, you realized it wasn't darkness that had altered the furniture, or even exposure to the elements, but a more purposeful consciousness. I'm talking about me, of course, but as I walked into that room with Ty—the first

241

time I'd ever entered it with another human being—I had a hard time believing I was responsible for the hallucinatory vision that swam before my eyes.

For his part, Ty seemed to have a hard time believing it wasn't a hallucination, period. Tapping the seat with his toe, as if to make sure it would take his weight, he sat down on the sofa, wincing slightly as his bruised butt made contact. He brushed at a twig that poked from between two cushions, then realized it was actually the stem of a young tree growing up through the sofa's innards. Realized a second later that another one grew from the opposite end. Realized that in fact there were trees and vines growing through or coiling around most of the other pieces of furniture in the room. Realized, finally, that they hadn't just grown there. That they'd been planted. That I'd planted them, in the same way my dad had planted all those vines around our house. I could see him fighting this chain of logic—could tell the exact moment he reached the part about my dad and the vines—but all he did was look at me. His tongue worried the scab on his lip and the fading bruises under his eyes made him look tired, so tired, but he didn't say anything.

I nodded.

He turned to face forward. The TV had been set in front of the sofa on a pair of milkcrates. ("Broadway Dairy, Bay Shore, NY," one of them read; the other was from Idaho, where, as far as I know, no one in my family has ever gone.) The thin brown husk of bindweed spiraled around the TV's powercord and up the purely symbolic rabbit ears I'd made from a couple of coathangers. The rabbit ears were symbolic because, one, we'd had satellite, and two, the TV had neither screen nor tube. Instead a single fat book sat inside the empty shell, its moisture-soaked pages swollen like a spoiled can of food.

"So, uh." Ty paused to clear his throat. "Get good reception out here?"

"Little fuzzy," I admitted. "Lot of times no picture at all."

Ty nodded. He turned to the left, looked at the computer on the desk. The chair was half pulled away, as though the user'd dashed to the bathroom for a pee break in the middle of an all-night IM. Flower petals and beetle shells had been glued to the keys on the keyboard, which was connected to the terminal by a length of vine, and a suspiciously symmetrical bird's nest sat in the shell of the empty monitor. On closer inspection, you saw that the nest was made of sparkly plastic swizzle sticks, No. 2 pencils, and something that looked like the inner filament of old-fashioned cassette tapes.

"Spend a lot of time surfing the web, do you?"

I shrugged. "Not so much, really. You ask me, the internet's not all it's cracked up to be."

Ty nodded again, continued looking around the nidus. On the ground, moldy books had been buried spine up in a circle around the perimeter of the room, as if to form a ring of protection. On the ceiling, garland made from intricately knotted lengths of strips of old clothes hung from the ropes that held up the sheets of plastic. A half dozen framed pictures had been mounted to shorter and taller stakes around the room, and another dozen or so hung from the roof on lengths of twine or vine. Leaves had been glued over faces, bird bones and twigs affixed along limbs, backgrounds painted out with green sap or red pokeberry juice or the nacreous fluid that comes out of milkweed stems. Strange ceramic collages made from bits and pieces of broken dishes dotted every available flat surface: simple things, like a teapot's spout mounted on the base of an inverted mixing bowl, or a half dozen coffee cup handles ringing a dinner plate; and then more elaborate constructions, such as a turtlelike creature, made from dozens of one- and two-inch shards with the necks of four Amstel bottles serving as legs, and several other four-legged creatures that could be identified no more specifically than as quadrupeds. There was only one attempt at a human face: a cracked white oval of dinner plate fragments studded with the circular red base of a candy dish for the mouth, a Wedgwood chariot for one eye, a ceramic Garfield head for the other, and a spiky mane of hair made from shards of Heineken bottles that looked less like grass than the teeth of a shark with serious plaque buildup.

When he'd finally taken it all in, or as much as he could process, he turned back to me.

"It's a little, um, *Through the Looking-Glass*."

I picked up one of the pottery collages. It could've been a fish, a sunflower, a '57 Chevy. "I always thought Humpty Dumpty myself. You know, all the king's horses, all the king's men?"

"Couldn't put Sprout's life together again?"

"Sprout's . . . past." I shrugged. "Sprout's mom."

Ty opened his scabbed mouth, then closed it. Opened it again. Closed it again. I found myself worrying that the scab was going to rip and start bleeding, but all that came out of him was a long sigh. Grimacing slightly, he heaved himself up and took a couple of limping steps in my direction, and then held out his fists to me, knuckles up, palms down.

On Long Island we'd had a neighbor, an old man named Mr. Villanueva, who used to walk the sidewalks with one pocket full of candy, the other of quarters, and whenever he ran into a kid he would hold out his hands like this, and as Ty did now, he always said,

"Pick one."

Every kid on the block had profited from Mr. V.'s generosity a dozen times, until a family named Smith moved in down the street when I was eight. Mrs. Smith said it was creepy for an old man to give candy to strange children (never mind that he'd known most of us since we were born) and, by the end of her first summer in the hood he'd retreated to his porch, sucking on his candies himself, and jingling a pocketful of change.

"Before my arms fall off," Ty prompted.

I roused myself. "Um, what are my choices?"

"One of them"—he shook his right hand as he spoke—"holds an ironic comment about your atrocious lack of crafting skills, and is designed to downplay all the implications of this weird-ass little hut you've got going on—"

"Nidus."

"—while the other"—he shook his left—"contains a serious inquiry into the state of your mental health, and is meant to show that I'm not, you know, completely insensitive, even if I do think this place is a little, well, freaky."

"I call it the nidus."

"Yeah, I'm not gonna say that, cuz I'm not a tool." He put his hands behind his back, made movements as though he were passing the two questions back and forth so I wouldn't know which hand either was in, then put his fists back in front of him. "The choice"—dramatic pause—"is yours."

I stared at his hands for a moment, noticed for the first time that his knuckles were chafed and bruised. Realized with a start that he'd fought back this time. That he'd hit his dad. For some reason this shocked me more than the idea that his dad had hit him, and I looked away guiltily. And there it was. The nidus: TV, computer, altered pictures, ceramic collages, all the rest of it. My own version of bruised knuckles. Or, who knows, maybe just my own version of bruises.

I turned back to Ty. I put each of my hands on one of his, but instead of tapping one or the other I used them to pull him close to me.

"I choose this one," I said, and planted my lips over his, and when I felt his battered hands open and reach around my back to press me against him I imagined his questions falling to the ground and breaking into little pieces, just like all those dishes I'd diligently packed when we moved from Long Island, the broken fragments of which now looked down on us with skeptical but mercifully silent expressions.

Right in the middle of things Ty got up from the sofa and limped over to the china cabinet, where the ceramic version of me stared at us with its round red polyp of a mouth and two crazy eyes.

"It's not the eyes actually," he said as he placed it face down on the shelf. "It's the mouth. Looks *way* too much like a poo-hole." And then, bending his knees and clasping his hands as though he were getting ready to dive off a cliff, he jumped back on top of me.

Okay, so maybe I'd done a bit more than drag the leftover furniture out into the woods and cover it with some plastic. Maybe I'd carefully cleared and leveled a plot of land between a few trees, leaving behind a few saplings and shrubs and vines to use later. Maybe I'd arranged and rearranged the furniture a few hundred times until the feng shui was exactly right. Maybe I'd trained the plants I'd left behind to grow into and around the furniture to make it seem like the various pieces had been there for decades rather than a few years, and maybe I'd spent hours on end turning dozens of family pictures into crazy collages with bird bones and feathers, leaves and flower petals, twigs, pebbles, seeds, until all those naively optimistic faces mounted atop lissome bodies had been transformed into animated Day of the Dead caricatures. And maybe I'd relied on a bit more than my dad's drunkenness to keep me stocked with all the broken crockery I needed to make my collages. Maybe I'd broken a few dishes myself.

Maybe you figured this out already.

I swear, though, it was a long time before I realized I was actually making something. At first I was just getting our stuff out of the yard so I wouldn't have to look at it anymore, or face the questioning, condescending looks of anyone who ventured up our driveway and saw half a house's worth of furniture sitting on the lawn. The plastic was just a way of protecting everything, so that if my dad came to his senses one day and we moved into a real house, we wouldn't have to start over. And if I left the occasional plant behind when I cleared the land, it wasn't with any intention of using them, it was just because something about that particular plant had caught my imagination. One of the first things you learn in botany is that a tree spreads its branches so its leaves can absorb as much sunshine as possible, but also so it can keep the sunshine from reaching the ground beneath it, which is a good way of keeping new trees from growing up and crowding the originals out. So for a plant to manage to take root beneath the shade canopy was a fairly determined feat, and it was hard for me to just up and nix that with one good tug. And when I was dragging the stuff under the plastic it made more sense to have it six feet off the ground so I could move around beneath it, and then some things just naturally seemed to go here, some there, a chair flanking the sofa, say, or pushed up to the desk. But it wasn't until a cold wet day during our first fall that I came to think of the room as anything other than a make-do attic. My dad was drunk out of his mind, and when he gets that way he starts talking to people who aren't there—my mom, usually, or his parents, with whom he had such a bad relationship that he refuses to speak to them, or some totally random person. "I am not drunk, ossifer. I am three sheets to the wind. I am sheet-faced. As opposed to you, who has a face—like—*shhh! You'll—wake—up—Daniel!*" Usually when he gets like this he goes for a walk or a drive—it's a good bet a stump'll show up later, or some vines'll get planted around the house. But that day he was glued to a chair, so, since he wouldn't leave, I had to.

It was raining when I went out. That wasn't a big deal during the summer. I knew half a dozen places in the forest that were as dry as an attic. But the leafless trees weren't up to the task of sheltering me, and somehow my mind just came straight here. The first thing I noticed was that water had leaked through the plastic in a couple of places, and even seeped behind a couple of picture frames, staining the photographs. Well, one photograph in particular. The photograph of my mom on her wedding day. This wasn't, you know, an omen or something. I'd hung the picture off a bit of rope (not vine, but garden-variety store-bought rope) that I'd run through a little hole in the plastic to a branch of the tree above, and even at the time I worried moisture might get through.

I took the picture out of the frame, laid it on the desk. It was hard not to think of the tracks of water as tears. I tried sponging it dry with an old washcloth but that just made it worse. Half my mom's face was warped and swollen like the Elephant Man's, and, well, no one wants to see their mom looking like that. Why I used a leaf to cover it up—the youngest palest green shoot from a locust tree—is anyone's guess. But that left this strange faceless green oval sticking out of a wedding dress. So I covered the hands next, and then I added little bits of twig to connect head to hands, and then I went ahead and added torso, legs, feet. "Stick-figure" is what I was thinking, but of course what it looked like was a skeleton. And instead of being scared off by this, I was inspired. I began gathering bird bones, which is a lot easier than you might think, given the fact that a local fall pastime is shooting crows out of the sky, whose abandoned carcasses are promptly set upon by coyotes, skunks, and other crows, the gnawed bones picked clean by flies and ants and other insects.

And then, well, it was off to the races. Doctoring pictures, gluing together broken dishes into crazy new shapes, training trees and vines to grow into and around all the furniture in the room. I suppose it was one of those combos of cathexis and catharsis. (No, I'm not showing off, or taking refuge in my dictionary. One was Word of the Day, March 14, 2006, the other came out of Advanced English on Oct. 22, 2007. And anyway, you don't have to know the *name* of what you're doing to do it. Peristalsis is a vital part of your daily existence, and I bet you don't ever think about it.) And when it was done it was done. It'd be nice to say I stopped spending time in the nidus after I started writing, but the truth is my last big stint out here was after my dad broke the computer, and that happened a couple of months before my fifteenth birthday. Tell you the truth, I was surprised to find everything still standing. I'd half expected it to've all collapsed. But I guess the past is more durable than that, huh? Or, if not the past, the monuments we make to it. Just call me Ozymandias—

"Ozzy who?" Ty said. This was sometime after our third or seventh or nineteenth trip to the nidus, when I'd finally finished telling him the story (we didn't do a lot of talking when we were there). He shushed me before I could answer. "Never mind, show-off."

We lay coiled together on the sofa inside a four-foot-thick stack of old clothes and towels and sheets. Somewhere incredibly far away I could feel my left big toe, which was sticking out into the twenty-degree air, but the rest of my body could've been submerged in a tub of warm water.

"Whatever," I said now. "But still. Aren't you glad I made it?"

"I wish we never had to leave," Ty said. "But . . ." He extracted his arm from the pile of clothes, pantomimed looking at a watch. Or, who knows, maybe he was just looking at the bruise on his wrist. He extricated himself from the pile and stood up. All he had on was his socks and a stocking cap, and he immediately started shivering as he tried to find the rest of his clothes. Shirt and pants were pretty straightforward—no one in my family had ever gone in for black polyester slacks or off-white shortsleeved poly-cotton buttondowns—but finding his Fruit of the Looms was trickier, guys' underwear all looking pretty much the same.

"You know," he said, sniffing undies, trying to tell which pair smelled like sweat and which like mouse feces. "We *could* just put our clothes over there instead of mixing them in with everything on the couch."

Still snugly inside the pile, I said, "Yeah, but then we'd have to get undressed in the freezing cold air."

"Well, this way we just end up having to get dressed in the cold, and it takes like ten times as long."

I shrugged, but the gesture was lost inside the pile. "What can I tell you? Logic. Not sexy."

Ty looked down at me with soft eyes, still naked but no longer shivering, and I have to tell you, his gaze made me even warmer. Then:

"Where'd you get off to?"

Before I could ask what he meant, he knelt down and pushed my own cap off my head, ran his hand through my hair. He waggled his fingers at me. Green smudges winked like flecks of moss.

"There you are."

I took his hand and licked the stains off, then, braving the cold, stood up and looked for anything that even hinted at green on his skin, and licked, nibbled, chewed and otherwise rubbed it off. I'd've painted his whole body green if I could have, just to let the world know he was mine, but I was afraid his dad would see. The bruises scattered over his body—blue-black smudges that wouldn't rub off no matter how hard or gently I kneaded—reminded me what the consequences would be of leaving my own mark on Ty's flesh.

He had his shirt on now, and the expanse of skin between it and his socks was whiter than either. The last time I'd seen skin as green-white as Ty's butt was on my mother's face after a round of chemo.

Yeah, I know. Totally inappropriate. What can I say? The unconscious doesn't give a crap about propriety.

He stopped dressing, took two steps towards the TV. "Oh wow," Ty said now. "Is that the famous dictionary?"

He wiped a spiderweb from the glassless cube, reached inside to pull it out, blew dust—well, dirt really—from the open spread in front of him.

"*Homily* to *honesty*," he read. "Any reason why—oh. *Homosexual. Of, pertaining to, or characterized by sexual attraction between persons of the same* . . ." His voice trailed off. "Let's just turn the page on that whole question, okay?" He turned about a hundred pages actually, backwards, forwards, backwards again, until he reached the inside front cover, which nearly came off in his hand. There was a long moment of silence while he stared at the inscription, and then he read it aloud, as though I might not know what was written there.

Presented to *Irene Morgan*
upon her graduation from *Brentwood* H. S.
in the year Nineteen Hundred and *81.*

There was a little puff of dust as the cover fell closed. "It was your mom's?"

"She always said it was her favorite book."

His eyes fell on the circle of books planted around the perimeter of the nidus. "What was she, an English teacher or something?"

I walked over to him with his underwear, exchanged it for the dictionary, put it back inside the TV. "Come on," I said, "we need to get you home."

It's tempting to call the nidus our home away from home, but really, it was pretty much a shagpad. November had given way to December by then, which meant fall was pretty much over. We had our first frost on the 2nd, and a stretch of days afterwards when the thermometer never went above 20°. And despite what Ty said about never wanting to leave, the truth of the matter is that when every minute you spend away from the house increases the likelihood that your dad is gonna beat you with a belt or a wooden paddle, throw a cup at you, a boot, a brick, a bible, might lock you in the basement or a closet or a dog collar, or, hell, just get it over with already, grab that baseball bat and bring it down *BAM!* on your skull, you really don't think about much besides buttoning buttons, zipping zippers, pulling on shoes and gloves and stocking caps, and getting your ass home to be kicked before it freezes off. And, as well, once the hump'd finally been crossed, Ty's inhibitions fell away faster than the leaves on the trees. We snatched kisses in the bathroom before school started, behind the cedar break at the northern end of the football field, under the bleachers during lunch, and then I had a brainwave (or maybe just a stroke) and I told him to cut out of history and I cut out of civics and we met in the study carrel in the library that I had occasional access to as a student working on a semester-long project—i.e., the State Essay Contest, which was just weeks away. It helped that the librarian thought she and I shared some kind of magical bond (her name was Mrs. Greene, and even though she scolded me for the fingerprints I left all over her books she was so proud of me for reading something besides *Harry Potter* that she was willing to over-look it). The carol was 4'×4' and half the floor space was taken up by a desk, which meant we had to do it standing up, but it was still better than feeling a blast of frigid air on your private parts, which could cause them to wilt like summer squash caught in an early frost. But at the same time, the carol was in the library, which meant we couldn't talk, let alone, you know, moan, curse, cry out, or sing hallelujah. In fact, I only remember one sentence from all our meetings there. Ty had caught me looking at the marks on his body, trying to decide which had come from me, which from his dad.

"We could run away," he said, pulling his shirt over his chest. "We could disappear."

His voice sounded unconvinced, and I wondered if that's what he really wanted to do. But I also knew it wouldn't work, because it's what my dad and me had tried to do, one of us consciously, the other dragged along for the ride, only to discover that your past comes with you no matter where you go. Still, on Saturdays, when I had the car, we'd drive around for hours, testing the limits of our leash. We circled Hutch first, inside the city limits, then outside, and then we pushed out to the edge of Reno County, and then we crossed the county line, McPherson County, Harvey, Sedgwick, Kingman, Pratt, Stafford, Rice, and then back to McPherson. The number of names made it sound as though we'd traveled a huge distance, but the truth is we were never more than twenty or thirty miles from the center of town. Only one time did we spike up north, towards Salina and I-70, and then, almost like it'd been choreographed, we spiraled up the long on-ramp to the interstate and spiraled right back off the same exit. As we left the interstate we passed a sign that read

HUTCHINSON 65

which was the same sign my dad and I had passed four and a half years ago, when we moved here, and after that our spiral tightened even further, our plans contracting like our route and like the ever-shortening winter days, until eventually—who knows, maybe inevitably—we ended up in the park.

Carey Park.

Before my dad trashed the computer, I'd gone online to do

a little investigation. All protestations to Ruthie aside, I had to admit I *was* kind of curious about what did or didn't go on there. Needless to say, Hutchinson doesn't have much of an internet presence, and gay Hutchinson is pretty much off the radar. There was that movie *Mysterious Skin* that came out a few years ago, which was based on a book by a writer who actually grew up here, and which seemed to confirm the general suspicions about what went on in the park—but then, the story also featured a guy who thought he was kidnapped by UFOs, so who knows what was real and what was made up? Other than that it was pretty much bits and pieces . . . but all the bits and pieces seemed to say that if you wanted a little gay action in Hutch, Carey Park was your best bet.

None of which explained what I was doing here with Ty.

It was Saturday morning, around 11. Ty and I sat in the Taurus, a good two feet between us. The windshield reflected thin gray clouds streaking across an ice-blue sky. A cold front had moved in from wherever it is cold fronts move in from ("Hey there, Kansas. Just in from Salt Lake. How's it going?") and the temperature hovered around zero, with forty-mile-an-hour gusts pushing it down to something like twenty-five below. All the groping and writhing and thrusting in the world wouldn't warm us up enough to combat that, and so we huddled in the car instead.

"So, uh, what're we doing here?" Ty said.

If you've never seen a Kansas municipal park, I can tell you that they all look pretty much the same. A few cottonwoods (in this case leafless), a few elm trees (ditto), an artificial pond slightly smaller than a Hollywood swimming pool (frozen, duh), and a patchy brown lawn flatter than Terri Schiavo's EEG. From where we sat we could see a cast-iron horse, beetle, and duck, all of which were exactly the same size, and mounted on rusty metal coils. All three were gaily painted save for their backs, where the butts of countless toddlers had rubbed the paint away and burnished the metal to a brilliant shine.

Did I mention that there was one other car in the parking lot too? There was one other car in the parking lot.

"You ever ride one of those?" I said.

"I don't think my dad would approve."

"See, the thing about those rides is, they're scaled for three- and four-year-olds, but they weigh about five hundred pounds, so no three- or four-year-old could possibly get them to move."

Ty didn't say anything for a minute. Then: "Think your balls'd stick to them? If you sat on 'em naked?"

"We're juniors, Ty! Juniors! We've still got a year and a half left at this crappy school! A year and a half left in this crappy town!"

Ty's silence lasted even longer this time. Then, quietly: "Well, let's just go then."

"Go *where*? Go *how*?"

"Anywhere. Anyhow."

See, that was the difference between me and Ty. He just wanted to run away. But I had to have a destination. I had to know where we were going.

Oh, and there was a man in the car.

"It's like thirty below," I said, staring at the man across fifty frozen feet of barren parking lot. "Where are we gonna sleep? What are we gonna eat?"

"We'll go south." Ty's voice was stronger now. "Texas. Galveston or Corpus Christi or Laredo. All the way south. We'll sell your dad's car for a couple hundred bucks and sleep outside and wash dishes for food. We'll learn Spanish from the guys in the kitchen and hitchhike down the Gulf coast of Mexico, end up in the Yucatan peninsula climbing to the top of some Mayan temple."

"How do you know so many border towns?" I said, still staring at the man, who was staring back at us. "And how do you know there are Mayan temples in the Yucatan? And how do you know the Yucatan is a *peninsula*, for God's sake?"

"Don't, Daniel. Don't make one of your random comments to change the subject and don't treat me like an idiot. We can do this. You and me. Together. We can do whatever we want."

"What is he *doing* in that car? Does he think we'll just walk over to him? Ask him if he needs a teenage boy to do some yardwork or if he'll buy us beer or something?"

"Who are you—that guy? In the Buick?"

"Don't you know what he's doing here, Ty?"

"Why the hell would I know anything about that guy, except for the fact that he's dumb enough to drive a Buick?"

"He's here for *us*, Ty. *You—and—me. That's* what he's doing here."

"What are you talking—oh."

"Yeah: *oh.*"

Ty stared over at the guy in the Buick. He was far enough away and his windows were dirty enough that we couldn't see much more than an outline. His face could've been made out of bits and pieces of old dinner plates for all we knew, his scalp could've been covered with hundreds of shards of green glass bottles in lieu of hair, but we could see still tell exactly what he was.

"Is that what happens to you? When you're gay?"

See, kids, this is why grammar is important. Did Ty's *you* really mean *one*, as in any gay person, or did it really mean *me*, as in the only gay person in the car? Did Ty's *you* mean that if I dropped the car in gear and pointed us towards Texas that he'd stick with me, through Galveston and Corpus Christi and Laredo and all the way down the Gulf coast of Mexico? Or did Ty's *you* mean that he'd wake up one day, realize what he was doing with me had more to do with his dead brother and his evil S.O.B. of a father and his general sense of being lost and alone in a world that didn't care if he lived or died, and that *he'd* be the one to ditch *me*, leaving me stuck in the Mexican equivalent of Carey Park with Spanish skills that, well, weren't quite as good as Ian Abernathy's?

"We—" I stopped, split the pronoun; two letters became four. "*I* won't turn out like that," I said, "because *I* have *you*."

Ty continued to look at the guy.

"Let's just go home, Daniel," he said finally. "He's giving me the creeps."

The sense of a ticking clock grew louder during the last couple of weeks of the semester, and I wasn't the only one who heard it. Ty started calling me in the middle of the night, but, because the phone was right outside his dad's bedroom (I hope you don't think Mr. Petit ever went cordless) all he could do was breathe heavily into my ear. If my dad was home that's all I could do too, because every room in our house was right outside my dad's room, and if my dad was at Mrs. Miller's, then, well, I'm not going to tell you what I said. And *no*, it's not what you're thinking (that is, if you're thinking what I think you're thinking). It's just that there was such a plaintive quality to Ty's sighs, such an overwhelming mixture of need and fear and, yes, lust, that I found myself saying things I never should've said. Offering him things I could never give him. Making him promises I had no way of keeping. And the more outrageous my promises, the more his breathing seemed to calm down. I would hear his sighs and I would try to picture him curled up on the floor with the phone pressed to his ear, but it was always Holly I saw, not Ty. Holly with his silent mouth and blank eyes, his stick figures and his dirty feet. Holly at the bottom of that shallow pond, sleeping on his side, like a baby.

And then one night he showed up. The moon was full, or almost, and Ty said the forest was like a black and white Tinkertoy planet, all lines and shadows, nothing flat except for the glittering frosty ground. A wild smile framed his chattering teeth and his cheeks were tinted pink like an orphan in a Dickens novel who's just about to die of tuberculosis. He hadn't put a coat on because he was afraid the zipper might wake his dad but he didn't care, it was exhilarating, he said—"Yes," he said, "I know the word 'exhilarating' "—and a part of him had wanted to stay out there all night, wanted to clamber over the moon-dark shadows of the trees until he melted into them and disappeared. But another part of him—the stronger part, he said—had wanted to see me even more, and so here he was.

That was the only time we ever had sex in a bed. Afterward he looked out my window through the lattice of vines for a long time. I thought he was contemplating his walk home until he said, "Your dad's the stump man? I always thought he was apocryphal. And yes," he added with a sigh, "I know the word 'apocryphal.' "

After that, all that was left was the janitors' closet.

Don't think this was some huge coincidence or something. The janitors' closet was pretty much notorious at school. I mean, one time Ian turned the knob, only to find the room already occupied. Fortunately the guy was a jock, and he and Ian touched fists like, Yo, bro, wassup? "Just here for a smoke," Ian said, flashing his pack, which looked like a wadded-up washcloth after two years in his pocket. "Guess we'll take it outside." There was even a rumor that one of the custodians had gone up to a pregnant senior and said, "I hope you plan on naming him Lenny," and tapped the nametag on his chest to make sure she knew what he was talking about. How the teachers never figured it out is anybody's guess, and how Ty did is equally mysterious, since he was even more out of the loop than the faculty.

"That floor has more jock jizz on it than the locker room. This is as close as I'll ever get to lettering."

The closet was just smells at first: bleach and Lysol and that magically repulsive substance the custodians sprinkle on teenage vomit. There was a single lightbulb, some thirty- or forty-watt thing that hung down off a frayed cord, and when you pulled the chain the room seemed to get darker rather than lighter. Drying string mopheads hung from hooks like scalps mounted on a lodgehouse wall, plastic gloves were folded over an iron pipe like a line of severed blue hands. We got into a push-pull match to see who would be in charge. A pole slid to the floor, a half-empty plastic bottle tipped over and rolled around with a hollow, sploshing sound. I felt Ty's hands on my butt. "It's my turn," was the last thing Ty said to me before the door opened.

"It's my turn" was the last thing Ty said to me.

"Sprout!" came the familiar, conspiratorial whisper. "I knew you'd come—"

Ian Abernathy broke off, stood there blinking as if he was the one who'd just been in the dark, not us.

"Ty? What are you . . . ?" He trailed off again. "Sprout? What is *he* doing? *Here?*"

Oh, but it was worse than that. So much worse.

"Ian! What the heck are you *doing*?"

Ruthie Wilcox poked her head around the corner of the door. I saw that she'd dyed her hair black, frizzed it up into an Amy Winehouse beehive, and immediately felt guilty for noticing.

"Well well well. The truth *finally* comes out."

The fact that we were actually *in* a closet seemed lost on Ruthie. Or, who knows, maybe not. She kicked a bottle of borax and said,

"Time to come clean, Sprout. What's the deal with you two? Are you in love or what?"

I should have looked at Ty, right? Not at Ruthie, with her smug, smiling (and, to be fair, not at all condemning) face. Not at Ian either, who looked even more guilty than if it'd been someone opening the door on him. I should've reached for Ty's hand the way he reached for mine, but the truth is I didn't even feel his fingers. Didn't hear him scream "Yes!" until after I'd said,

"Um, *duh*. We're just fucking."

Did I just write that? So much for this book ending up in a high school library. Which is kind of ironic when you think about it, since that was one of our favorite places to have sex.

The lightbulb in the closet wasn't strong enough to reveal who blushed most deeply between me and Ian and Ruthie. But I'm pretty sure it was me. Only Ty didn't blush. His face turned so white it looked blue. Without a word, he pushed past me and ran from the closet. All three of us watched him run down the hall, and first Ian and then Ruthie turned to me to see if I was going to go after him.

I didn't.

The sound of Ty's shoes squeaking on freshly waxed terrazzo grew fainter and fainter; a door crashed open, and then the squeaks were gone.

Not to be outdone, Ruthie put her hand on her stomach and sighed dramatically.

"So? Eee tell you the news? I'm preggers."

This is the last part!

"Did you disappear,
or were you just misplaced?"
—Sleater-Kinney

He's still gone

It's times like this when all the things you learned in school, all the science and history and civics and above all the language, seem completely useless. I suppose I could use a word like *inadequate* or *insufficient*, but when you're taking the time to say how you feel, when you're putting it all on the line, exposing yourself, you want to make sure you get it exactly right. I'm not going to fake it, or water it down. This is too important. This is love, and love lost, and I'll tell you straight up: no words are equal to the task.

And don't misunderstand me. *This* isn't how I feel. These words. This is just me saying that I don't know the words to say how I feel. That's, well, that's another blank page, like the previous chapter. Feel free to draw a picture on it, or write something yourself. Maybe about me, if you think you understand me, or about yourself, if you think that's easier. Maybe you want to write an ending for Ian's story, or Ruthie's, cuz God knows they each deserve a book of their own at this point. But I have no idea what to put there. The only thing I want to put there is Ty, and Ty's gone.

I mean, is it worth saying that I miss him? Is it worth saying that I cried? That I went to all the places we went together, that crazy hole we dug, the pond where his brother drowned, the tree where we had our first kiss? The river where we first had sex, the nidus, Carey Park? That I even went to his dad's house? Walked right past that "Trespassers WILL Be Shot" sign and pounded on the door so hard that the

God Bless Our Home
And CURSE the Homes of Sinners!

sign fell off its hook and broke on the ground? The man who opened the door wasn't what I expected. On the one hand, I mean, he was: crewcut, white shirt buttoned to the collar, drab polyester pants. What I didn't expect was that he would have Ty's face. His chin, his cheekbones, his eyes. His defiant, frightened stare, which took me in from my Nikes to the Yankees cap I'd used to cover my hair and saw me for the sinner I was.

"Yes?"

"Is Ty—" I began, and he cut me off.

"No," he said, and closed the door.

Yes; no. Opposites, right? The far ends of a line that should contain everything between them, like New York and California. Yet here I was in Kansas, smack dab in the middle of the country, and it seemed like I could reach out with my right and left hands and grab either coast and wad the whole damn continent together like a single sheet of paper. Throw it away and start over. Or, better yet, leave everything blank.

And here we are again.

I don't know what to tell you. You want to know how it feels? Turn back to the beginning of this book and read all the way through, and when you get here go back to the beginning and do it again.

Then do it again.

And again.

Again.

When you think you finally understand—or when, like me, you just don't have the energy to go through it one more time—then, well, go ahead and turn the page.

Mrs. Miller said she'd pick me up at four in the morning to drive us to Topeka, but neither she nor my dad mentioned anything about him coming by too. But he was there on the loveseat at 3:30, cheeks smooth, hair parted and combed, pants sporting the same ironed crease Mrs. Miller's had. He nodded towards a Kwik Shop cup surrounded by a small mountain of sugar packets and creamers.

"I brought you coffee. I hope there's enough sugar and cream."

"I take it black," I said, which is completely not true. "You showered just for me?"

"Can't go to work with yesterday's armpits."

"You found a job?"

"Flegler's. The vacuum cleaner plant down by Yoder. But"—my dad waved me silent—"I didn't come here to talk about me."

I sipped at the black coffee, which tasted like a mechanic's driveway. "_Mmmm._" I sipped again. "You come to wish me good luck?"

"According to Janet you don't need luck. She says you're the best she's ever had. Best she's ever seen."

"Aw, golly gee, Dad—"

"I come to offer you some advice, so you don't blow it."

"I—" I shook my head. "Whatever. Speak."

"You're not mad at me for dating Janet. You're mad at me for getting over your mom."

"I thought you said this wasn't about you."

"It happens, Sprout. You get over people. Even when you don't want to."

Again I opened my mouth for a wisecrack, again I closed it. "And your advice?"

"You'll get over him."

I blinked. "You mean this is about Ty? Not the contest? You're worried about my love life?"

"Not your love life. Your life, period. Janet tells me you're about to flunk out of eleventh grade because you refuse to do any work."

"I think Janet—"

"Mrs. Miller."

"I think your girlfriend—"

"Fiancée."

I shook my head. "Are you trying to make my brain explode? Jesus Christ, Dad, you get a job, you get engaged." I sniffed the air. Dust, a little damp seeping in from outside, the coffee in my hand. That was it. "Are you *sober* too? Is it the *Rapture*?"

"No, Sprout, it's not the end of the world. And that's what you need to realize. It's just a breakup."

"It is not a *breakup*, Dad. He's *gone*. He's *disappeared*. Don't you get it? No one knows where he *is*."

"He's a teenager, Sprout. Teenagers run away. He'll be fine."

"It's been *three weeks*."

"It is not your problem."

"He is not an it. And whose problem is he? Who's looking out for him? Who's looking *for* him, period?"

It would've been easier if my dad'd gotten mad, or gotten desperate. It would've been easier if he'd been drunk. But he was calm and sober as a Unitarian minister.

"You can't save him, Sprout. He's not your mom. And even if you did save him, it wouldn't bring her back."

As if on cue, lights appeared in the window. There was the sound of cracking ice as Mrs. Miller's car shattered frozen puddles in the driveway. I took a deep breath. The conversation was over, but even so, I felt like going out with a bang.

I pulled the front door open and a blast of frigid air swarmed past me into the room.

"You feel that, Dad? That's *winter*. And he's out there somewhere. You're telling me not to worry about him. Telling me to think about myself, my future. But who's thinking about his future? Who gave him something to look forward to? To work for? To *live* for?" I put my coat on. "His brother killed himself because he couldn't see a future. And you want me to worry about winning some contest? Getting my grades in gear so I can get into a good college, get a scholarship, let you off the hook for drinking up my future? I've let you off the hook for the past four years. You should be ashamed of yourself."

And then I grabbed my stuff and headed outside.

The heater was blasting and the inside of Mrs. Miller's car smelled as dry as sawdust, and after a moment, when she didn't put the car in reverse, I clicked my seatbelt, but she still just stared out the window. The shadowy forest, nothing more than vertical bars of black and gray; the hoary stumps, lined up like wild-haired moai staring out from the past; little bits of window glinting like winking eyes through the net of vines covering the

271

trailer. Once upon a time the only meaning these things had for Mrs. Miller was what I gave her, but now she had her own history, her own associations, with my house, and I couldn't help but wonder what she was thinking about as she stared out at it. Was she thinking about me, I mean, or about my dad?

The car was so hot I could feel my eyes tearing up, so I turned the heater down a couple of notches. Mrs. M. started at the sudden silence, turned as if she'd just noticed I was in the car. For once I didn't think she was being dramatic. She really did seem surprised.

"Your dad—" She stopped when she saw the dictionary. "Your dad says good luck." She placed her hand on the battered book in my lap as tenderly as if she were touching a barely healed wound. "You know you can't bring this in, right?"

I tapped the dashboard clock, which read 4:01. "It's almost four hours to Topeka. We'd better get a move on."

She took Highway 61 up to Salina, picked up I-70 heading east. I had to turn around to see the sign

HUTCHINSON 65

that I'd passed twice now, once with my dad and once with Ty, but it seemed to have less significance this time around, not more. The sun rose directly in front of us and the world became tricolor: black smears of shadow and white sheets of snow and swathes of golden field. The ruler-straight lines of cedar windbreaks and the double-backed trails of cottonwoods following streambeds reminded me of the trees in my forest, on the one hand, and, on the other, of the river where Ty and I had first had sex, but what I found myself wondering was: what path had he followed? Had he taken the direct route represented by the cedars so he could get away as quickly as possible, or had he chosen the cottonwoods' meandering path, as if he wanted someone to catch him before he got too far away? And why, whenever I contemplated this question, did my mind always flash on that Buick in Carey Park? Why did I feel as though I'd all but pushed him in the trunk and slammed it closed and watched it drive away?

Mrs. Miller didn't talk during the entire trip. Didn't even ask perfunctory questions like "Are you hungry?" or "Do you need to use the restroom?" but when we got to Topeka, she pulled me aside before sending me into the gymnasium where the contest was being administered.

"I did a little research," she said. "Your mom was working full-time when she died. You were entitled to social security benefits that your dad never applied for. You can still get them— all of them, retroactively. It comes to about $30,000. It'll pay for school if you stay in-state, and if you go for something private it'll at least get you on your way."

I stared at her in confusion. "Why are you telling me this now?"

Mrs. Miller nodded at the gym. At the five hundred students seated at long rows of folding tables and the judges walking between, the kids clutching their sharpened pencils, the monitors clutching cups of coffee, the big clock hanging above everything, its red digital letters set to

1:00:00

She looked back at me. "I can't help but feel that I had something to do with what happened. That all the mixed messages I was sending you about when it is or isn't okay to say you're gay somehow made you think your sexuality was something you should hide to protect yourself. The truth is, that's how it gets power over you. Not when you're open about it, but when you have to spend all your energy keeping it secret."

It took me a moment to realize what she was really saying.

"You mean Ty, don't you? You think I couldn't say I loved Ty because I was too scared to show him—or Ruthie, or Ian—who I really am?"

"You weren't scared, Sprout. You were protecting yourself. But sometimes when we think we're protecting ourselves, we're really hurting ourselves. And sometimes the people around us too."

A voice from the gym called out: "One minute warning. Places, please."

Mrs. Miller put her hand on my shoulder, turned me towards the open door.

"I want you to forget what I told you when we first started. Everything I told you. What's good writing. What's bad. What you should say. What you shouldn't. Write what you want to write. Say what you have to say. Screw them," she said, nodding at the panel of judges seated at the far end of the room. "Screw me. It's your life, not ours." She gave me a little push, as though I were a four-year-old ballerina too scared to venture on stage. "Go on, Sprout. Take off that cap and let the world see just how green your hair really is."

"My cap?"

Mrs. Miller pointed to the top of my head.

"Oh. Right. My *cap*." And I took it off, and Mrs. Miller looked like she was going to faint.

"Don't worry," I told her. "I'm Sprout, not Samson. My strength doesn't reside in my hair."

I took a seat at the first empty place I came to. There was an envelope in front of me, and a small stack of blue composition notebooks, and I was instructed not to open either until time was called. I lined up my pencils. One of them had a green smudge on it, but this didn't make me think of my hair. It made me think of Ty's skin, and I had to resist the urge to lick it.

A fat man in a gray suit got up and droned for a few minutes—eyes front, write on one side of the page only, if you need your pencil sharpened hold up your hand and someone will come do it for you—and then, with a mischievous smile, he pulled out a starter's pistol and fired it into the air. The gym was filled with the sound of ripping paper as 499 students tore into 499 envelopes to find out what the topic was, but I just stared at the gun still raised above the gray man's head. A puff of smoke wafted from its barrel like a lazy genie reluctantly summoned from its bottle. I felt Ty's arms curled around mine, his fingers steadying my aim, his body pressed up against mine from his lips down to his toes. His voice in my ear.

Are you looking at the gun?

Yes.

Why would you do a stupid thing like that? Look at your target, Bradford.

Oh. Duh.

I reached for the envelope, opened it, pulled out a full-sized sheet of paper on which had been printed only:

"Actions are visible, though motives are secret."
—Samuel Johnson

and below it the instructions:

"Discuss, using examples from life and/or literature."

. . .

Secrets, huh? A little snort came out of my nose, seemed to land on my notebook in the form of a couple of sentences. I looked down and read the words as if someone else had written them.

> I have a secret. And everyone knows it but me.

I lifted up my pencil, then stopped, looked again at what I'd just written.

> I have a secret. And everyone knows it but me.

The more I looked at it, the less sense it made. How could I have a secret that only other people knew. So I crossed out *but me* and put a period at the end of the sentence, added another. Now it read:

> I have a secret. And everyone knows it. But no one talks about it.

That's better, I thought, and pushed onward.

> I have a secret. And everyone knows it. But no one talks about it, at least not out in the open. That makes it a very modern secret, like knowing your favorite celebrity has some weird eccentricity or other, or professional athletes do it for the money, or politicians don't actually have your best interests at heart.

I stopped again. Looked at what I'd written. Realized suddenly that it was all a lie. No, not a lie. Just a deflection. A way of avoiding that original statement. Before I knew it I was scribbling out the whole paragraph so hard I snapped the lead on my pencil. I reached for another and with a shaking hand rewrote the first version.

I have a secret. And everyone knows it but me.

I set my pencil down and stared at these two sentences for a long time. I mean, there it was. Right in front of me. Some peculiar facet of my being on display to everyone but me, like the small of my back, or the crown of my head—my freshly shaved head, covered with an eighth of an inch of pale brown peach fuzz. But that wasn't it. My hair—long or short, green or brown—wasn't my secret. Neither was the nidus, the trailer, my dad's alcoholism, my mom's death, or the fact that I liked to have sex with boys. There was something else. I knew it, even if I didn't know what it was. There was some part of myself I didn't know, something about my character I didn't understand. Something that might've been the thing to make me fail Ty at the crucial moment, but then again something that might be the one thing that he could hold on to. That could bring him back. And if I was going to discover that thing then I was going to have to chase it down and corral it like a wild horse. And so I picked up my pencil and started writing furiously. But this time I wasn't writing to run away from something. I was running after something, and I wasn't going to stop till I caught it.